Some Whisper, Some Shout

by

K. K. Weil

Truth Be Told Series

Some Whisper, Some Shout

COPYRIGHT © 2017 by K. K. Weil

Cover Art by *Debbie Taylor*

The Wild Rose Press, Inc.
PO Box 708
Adams Basin, NY 14410-0708
Visit us at www.thewildrosepress.com

Publishing History
First Crimson Rose Edition, 2017
Print ISBN 978-1-5092-1582-9
Digital ISBN 978-1-5092-1583-6

Truth Be Told Series
Published in the United States of America

"Your sax and your bag. Where are they?"
This was the first time I'd seen him without them.

"Oh, they're outside," he pointed. "In my car."

Before we reached the door and Reed unlocked it, I could have sworn I saw a tall, dark shadow glide past it. When Reed opened the door for me, no one was there.

"Did you see that?" I asked.

"No, what?"

"I think someone was outside."

He turned his head in both directions. "I don't see anyone. Must have been your imagination."

I flinched at his words, but he couldn't know how they'd bother me. I shook away the thought.

He motioned his hand in front of us. Parked two feet away was his navy SUV. "I have to move it soon. Alternate side," he answered, as if in response to my silent question about why there were no other cars on the block.

Except for one...a black two-door sedan.

A door slammed. The tinted windows prevented me from seeing inside, but my heart raced as it pulled out of its spot and flew down the road. I turned to Reed to see if he thought it was strange that someone would be here after midnight when no stores were open and there were no homes around, then speed away like a bat out of hell. He just took my hand and walked me back to my car, noticing nothing strange.

I tried to be subtle as I scratched my neck and over my chest. I tried not to let him hear my quick, clipped breathing.

I did not imagine someone watching me in that store. I did not fabricate a car pulling away like they were caught spying on me.

Praise for K. K. Weil

SHATTERPROOF:
Voted one of Bookboyfriendaddict.com's
Top Picks of 2015

"Due to the sensational talent of author K. K. Weil, you can actually feel the pain he endures as he struggles to face and overcome his fears and demons. The depth of the emotion conveyed within this book is mind-boggling. My heartstrings received quite a workout. A Rewarding Read!"

~Stephanie Lasley, from The Kindle Book Review
~*~

"The story felt raw and real. I would highly suggest *SHATTERPROOF* to readers looking for an intense NA contemporary romance with real life issues."

~A Novel Glimpse

Dedication

To the original Mamie

Acknowledgements

Once again, great thanks to my editor, Cindy Davis. I learn more from you each time we work together. I always know my characters are in good hands with you.

Thank you to Debbie Taylor for another beautiful cover. With each book, I'm excited to see what you will come up with, and the results are always more beautiful than I could have hoped for.

Thanks to the wonderful Wild Rose Press, especially Rhonda Penders, RJ Morris, Lori Graham, and Lisa Dawn for your hard work and support for all of your authors. Always so happy to be a Rose.

Many thanks to my dear friend Karen, who advised me on the legal matters in this book, so I could make sure to get it right.

A world of gratitude to my grandmother, who inspired the character of Mamie (though in fiction we have to exaggerate for the sake of entertainment). The influences of strong women should never be overlooked.

And finally, unending thanks to the real organizations that help the homeless. The work you do is invaluable.

Part 1

Jolie

Chapter One
Device: Surround Yourself with Reliable People

I hated the attention. The press. The interviews. The barrage of cameras making me cringe with every click. Still, I flashed the most sincere smile I could muster.

Some people were born to be in the spotlight. As I accepted this year's Award for Excellence in Philanthropy, my sweaty palms confirmed that I was not one of those people. The tight squeeze on my forearm reminded me that the woman standing to my right, however, was the embodiment of one.

My grandmother's coal gray eyes shimmered and she stood straighter than I'd seen her in years. This was a huge honor for us both. Though just a local award in our Jersey Shore town, this certificate, presented by the mayor, acknowledged we were doing what we set out to do—make a difference. Even if it was a small one.

Mamie fielded all the interview questions, beaming more with each response. She ran a hand over her silver hair, flirting a little with Brett, the young reporter conducting the interview. Brett played back, as was par for the course. Everywhere Mamie went, people fell in love with her.

It turned uncomfortable when she inevitably nudged me with her elbow and winked, her sign that she thought he was cute and I should make a move.

"Reliable?" I whispered, displaying teeth for the camera.

Mamie groaned. She didn't like hearing about my devices any more than I liked needing to use them. But those coping mechanisms were the only way I could be sure I was with people who'd help me stay grounded; the only way to make sure I wasn't slipping; that the disease with its claws in my family wouldn't take me as well. I couldn't let go of my devices, because if I did, I might not realize I was spiraling away until I was already gone.

"Sure, but more importantly, he's got a great ass."

Brett blushed. He heard Mamie's comment.

Mamie didn't care. She was a confident spitfire, afraid of nothing, probably a result of her French upbringing.

I cared, though. I was no Mamie. If I was a breeze, she was a hurricane whose gales surpassed mine in every way—force, magnitude and volume. She might have been impervious to embarrassment, but I wasn't. I closed my eyes, dug my sandals into the sand and inhaled.

Growing up in a beach town ruined me for every other environment. The sounds and saltwater smell of the ocean washed a calm over me. Whether it was cool and tranquil or gray and angry, I found better advice from its crashing waves than I did from my closest friends. They wouldn't understand, anyway. The only person who totally got it was my brother, Tristan. But that was before. Before the ocean held mixed emotions for me.

The small ceremony was about to come to an end. My grandmother gave our creperie a shameless plug. It was a good thing she was in charge of marketing. If it had been my responsibility, no one would've known we existed.

Down by the water, with our backs to the boardwalk and our shop in the backdrop of the pictures, the air grew moister and breezier by the second. My black, chin-length hair expanded around my face and I tried in vain to wind it up and tie it in a knot. It fell almost immediately. It was much too short. The gentle spray of the ocean would make it wider. It would have been nice to get through the interview looking somewhat tame.

As I pushed my hair back out of my eyes, the tide came in faster than any of us realized.

"Brett!" I leaned forward to save the poor reporter, but I was too late. Water splashed over his loafers and the ankles of his dress pants.

"Shit. That wasn't the best place to stand." He laughed as he did a little skip-move to slosh out of the water and I resented my grandmother a little for being able to spot a good-looking guy faster than I could.

Brett shook off the water, dancing around like he was doing a jig, while holding his heavy equipment. It was futile and he looked ridiculous.

"Why don't you come to the store and we can get you a towel or something?" I tightened my cheeks to keep from laughing in his face.

"Nah." He kicked water from his foot. "I'll be fine."

I would have let it go, because if the guy wanted to drive home with puddles in his shoes, that was his business, but my grandmother smelled a set-up opportunity.

"Nonsense," she said. "You'll soak up your car and then it will smell like fish for Lord knows how long. You're coming with us." She snaked her arm through his and, after thanking the mayor and everyone else involved in the awards ceremony one last time, led him toward the boardwalk.

Each of Brett's steps made a squishing sound. He crooked a wide-eyed grin at me, over his shoulder. I wasn't sure if it was a cry for help or a look of amusement. Either way, I shrugged. I couldn't help him. Though I felt for the guy, with waterlogged socks and pants, he was on his own with Mamie.

"C'mon in." I unlocked the door to Stuff Your Crepes. "I'm sure we have something that can dry you off."

A slight puddle formed at Brett's feet. "I'll stay here." He stood close to the doorway. "I don't want to make a mess."

"Hush," my grandmother said. "Sit." She drew him farther inside, pulled over a chair from one of the tables, and pushed his shoulders so he sat. She removed first his shoes, then his socks, and poor Brett's jaw hung low as he sat stone still, speechless. He was so uncomfortable with this exhibit of half-nurturing, half-molestation that I had to intervene.

"Mamie, I think the man can take off his own shoes." I threw him an empathetic pout.

"Able to and willing to are two different things, Jolie. Now"—she directed her attention back to him—"I'm going to find a way to dry these off while my lovely granddaughter whips you up one of our delicious crepes."

She disappeared to the back room in an anything-but-subtle fashion leaving me alone with the man she most recently assigned the role of my future husband. This had happened so many times, I barely noticed it. Only enough to pity the men she targeted.

"You should be thankful she stopped at your socks. Your pants are soaked, too."

He gasped, pretending to be frightened, but his eyes were warm, easygoing. They all looked the same, the men I dated. My grandmother knew my type, and even though she didn't agree with my need for order, she wanted someone reliable for me as much as I did. It was the one thing missing from my life.

"Thank God for small miracles," Brett joked.

I walked behind the counter and heated up the flat, round stone we used for cooking the crepe batter. "What kind would you like?"

Brett followed me to the counter, careful not to leave wet footprints. "Um..." He inspected the boards behind me, filled with more choices than I could believe we were able to invent. "I'll have a Mr. Basic, please."

Hmm. A Mr. Basic. Named for exactly what it was: a plain crepe with fresh strawberry jam and powdered sugar. Basic and boring. I knew you weren't supposed to judge a book by its cover. Similarly, I shouldn't have judged a guy by his order, but I did. Every time. I was growing a little tired of Mr. Basics. Did dependable have to equate to dull?

My grandmother and I created countless, original combinations of crepes. Things you'd never imagine could be put together in a soft shell. And they worked. Some better than others, of course, but they were all delicious. I'd never put them on my wall otherwise.

Coming up with cute names for them was the best part. So what did it say about a guy when he looked at all those choices and picked the most ordinary one? I even purposely gave it an unappealing name to dissuade people from ordering it. Mamie insisted we had to offer the standard, simple ones, and I knew she was right, but it bothered me even making them.

"Okay, coming up." I spread some batter over the hot stone with the back of my ladle, careful to distribute it evenly. The scents of melted butter and the thin pancake filled the air immediately. "Want anything else in it?" *Throw in some coconut and surprise me.*

"No thanks, that's fine."

I hoped he didn't notice my sigh.

"So this is the famous jar?" He ran his pointer over the rim of the best item in my store. In my world, really.

"Yup, it is."

Brett jiggled the jar and the tokens inside made the clinking sound that brightened even my worst days.

My jar. My contribution. My meaning.

"It's a wonderful concept." Brett held his hand out for his crepe. "I mean, it's simple enough, a jar filled with boardwalk tokens. When a customer pays for an extra crepe, a token goes in the jar. If someone can't afford a meal, he can remove a token and pay with that instead of cash. Brilliant." He took a small bite. "Yum." He nodded. "Really good."

"Thanks." I appreciated both compliments, though I knew his recap served the purpose of letting me know he was paying attention during the interview. "My grandmother has been amazing about welcoming my suggestions ever since she asked me to be her partner.

The day I came up with our token program, she went out for a break and came back with the biggest glass jar she could find, tied up with ribbon."

I'd helped with her small business since I was able to walk. It was my second home, especially when I was in my teens and things at home were pretty out of control. Spending time here, learning and chatting, made life a lot more enjoyable, but I always knew I wanted to do more than just sell the crepes.

We chatted for a while, as Brett took longer to finish his food than necessary. Since he already knew what I did for a living, I asked him about being a reporter. He shared some of the sillier stories he'd reported: stories of lost pets and food eating competitions. He was cute in a self-deprecating sort of way, talking about how he'd like to do more hard-hitting reporting rather than the local stories he was currently stuck with, which were all fluff.

"Not that I mean this story isn't important." He shook his free hand out in front of him.

"Not to worry. I didn't think this one was up there with breaking news on foreign policy." I poured more batter on the stone so he wouldn't have to eat alone.

He chuckled again, indicating he might be fun to spend time with, if I could overlook his unimaginative taste in crepes. Was he equally unimaginative in other areas of his life, as well?

A short lull in conversation drew my eavesdropping grandmother out of the back. "Here you go, darling." She handed Brett his shoes and socks, which looked almost dry.

"Wow, how did you do that?" he asked.

"Never ask a woman her tricks, dear. I'm very

resourceful." She blew a kiss and I imagined competing with her for this man. I laughed at the idea.

"What?" she asked.

"Huh? Nothing." I stumbled on my words. Yeah, I wouldn't be revealing that thought out loud.

"Okay, well then." Her attention focused back on Brett. "How do we leave this? Would you like to give Jolie your number or should she give you hers?"

My cheeks heated. "Mamie!" I used the most outraged voice I could find, but she had made the whole number exchange thing much easier.

Brett cleared his throat, and looked from my grandmother to me. "I'd love to get yours, if that would be okay?"

"Sure," I said. "You can go now, Mamie. Your work here is done."

My grandmother waggled her eyebrows at me and conveniently disappeared again as I plugged my number into Brett's cell.

He gathered his equipment and glanced at my info in his phone. "So, Jolie Durand, I'll give you a call during the week and maybe we can get dinner or something?"

"Sounds nice."

Nice. And typical. Like his crepe.

No, I was determined to stop judging by covers. He was handsome, and he appreciated my jar. Nice could be good.

Chapter Two
Device: Keep to Your Schedule

Seaville was similar to some of its neighboring shore towns in New Jersey. On the boardwalk, and a couple blocks in, it was like a wonderland. During the warm months, it was filled with laughter, the constant dinging of winning arcade games and smells of fried dough and barbeque. Families flooded the area and kids ran amuck, pumped up from sugar.

A few blocks away, though, the scene changed. Deeper into the town, the hustle and bustle disappeared. The homes weren't maintained with meticulous care for high paying renters, like the condos on the ocean side. There was no sign of disposable money. Seaville was, at its heart, a blue-collar town, full of hard working people scraping by. The fairy tale of the boardwalk masked this, but all you had to do was take a five minute walk to find the real world, the day-to-day world, the one not veiled in cotton candy, ring toss and henna tattoos.

I took that walk every Thursday night. A creature of habit, I found comfort in routines, and I was a regular in my yoga class. Nothing centered me like an hour of downward dogs and half moons. I chose a gym on the other side of town, because it insured that I would take a specific path there, which included a very important pit stop: I walked through a small park to my first destination, a section on the north end of the park that most people familiar with the area intentionally avoided.

The cardboard box I carried along a desolate path, cloaked by tall weeping willows, was heavier than usual. Its weight energized me, but my arms shook a little. I tightened my muscles so they wouldn't give out before I could lay it down.

"Jolie!" said a man the others called Crooked Curt. He rose from his bench and approached me. "Let me help you with that." Without waiting for an answer, he took the box from my arms and placed it on the grass by the bench. He smiled wide, revealing his mouth full of missing and misplaced teeth.

"Thanks, Curt." I shook out my arms. How would I make it through class if I couldn't even carry a box for five minutes?

He pointed at me. "You don't thank us. We thank you."

"We thank each other." I nodded.

Some regulars from the area gathered as soon as they saw me coming. I opened the box, revealing a heap of wrapped, warm, assorted crepes. We had a good week, so I was able to pack more than usual.

"God, they smell like heaven," one of the women sighed.

"Help yourself." I extended my arm toward the crepes and backed away. I never hovered when they explored the contents. "There are a bunch of different kinds today, plus the usuals."

A few people who knew me dove into the box, searching for their favorites while others stayed back. A woman I'd never seen before, with a child pressed against her side, squatted by a bush, watching. Her appearance and the hunger in her eyes told me she was homeless too.

My approach toward her was cautious. "Hi. My name is Jolie. I make these crepes. You're both welcome to have some if you'd like."

She eyed me, then the box, now filled with rummaging hands, with skepticism. "Why?"

I shrugged. She wasn't the first person to ask this question. "Because I can." I swallowed the lump that always choked me when I talked about this, and walked away. Now the option was out there, but it had been my experience that some people weren't comfortable with it. The choice was hers.

"Jolie," Crooked Curt mumbled through a mouthful of chicken, cheese, and broccoli. "You outdid yourself today." He wiped his mouth with his sleeve. I forgot to bring napkins this time.

"I'm glad you're enjoying it," I answered, taking in the scene around me. The chambers of my heart fought each week. Two of them ballooned with gratitude that Mamie and I made enough profit to be able to do this regularly, while the other two cracked with the knowledge that people were constantly hungry. I was always trying to figure out how I could give more. Some of those people came to my store for the token exchange, others didn't. I wanted to feed all of them all the time, but we were a small shop with limited money. I could have gone to the local shelter and donated the food there, but these people weren't in the shelter, for whatever reasons they chose, which were none of my business. If no one helped them, what would happen to them?

Shadows shifted in my peripheral vision. The mother with the child crept toward the box and peeked inside. She removed two crepes and handed one to her daughter. She bit into it, closed her eyes, and released a lengthy exhale.

My chest pinched. It was time to leave.

"Jolie," called a man I'd seen before, but whose name I didn't know. "Stay. Eat with us."

"Yes."

"Do."

A few more voices agreed. Crooked Curt scooted over on his bench to make room for me. I'd never stayed before. I always dropped off my box and left. I was touched that they invited me and I didn't want to insult them by refusing.

I sat but waved off their attempt to offer me a crepe. I would not take back what I'd just given.

They talked about families, friends, and memories. They referred to people in each other's lives by name. It gave me a little solace to know that at least they had each other. Though there had been many attempts to "clean up" the park, this spot remained a location for the homeless. I never understood the concept of cleaning it up. That was basically shifting people from one place to the other. Fix the problem, not the location, was my philosophy.

I listened to them for so long I didn't realize the sun had set. I couldn't walk into yoga once it had already started. That was plain rude and disruptive. I'd missed my class.

I headed back to the store to relieve Mamie of closing the shop, our normal Thursday ritual. She may not have admitted to her age but I could tell her body felt it from time to time. I tried to get her to work fewer hours and stay off her feet, but she yelled at me for calling her old and swatted me with whatever she had handy.

I checked my cell out of habit as I walked back to the shop. A text had come in from Brett about an hour before.

A week earlier, he had taken me to an Italian restaurant a short drive from my store. Conversation was easy. Over a shared tiramisu, I admired his calm voice and kind expression. He told me about strategies he used to get his boss to see him as a real journalist. I talked about Stuff Your Crepes and my grandmother. Nothing too deep.

He walked me home from the restaurant and gave me a soft kiss at my door. No parting of the lips. No assumption that there would be tongue. The whole thing was sweet. Exactly the way a typical first date should go. A date with Mr. Basic.

I shook the thought from my head and read his text. He wanted to see me over the weekend. We'd tried to get together during the week, but between it being Memorial Day weekend and starting summer hours, I worked late every night. We made the majority of our money between Memorial Day and Labor Day, so it was important that I was there. But I had to try to find some time to see him. Mamie would have beaten me if she thought I was sacrificing what little social life I allowed myself because of the store.

A thought did nag at me, though. Would I have squeezed in a date during the week if I were more excited about the person I was meeting?

The shop was crowded when I got back, which was

not unusual for a beautiful early June night. It was even less unusual since that interview aired two weeks before. The publicity brought people in droves, which was fantastic, because the more business we got, the more we could give away. That alone was enough reason to give Brett another date.

The lines were long and Morgan, one of the girls who worked for us, was frazzled behind the counter alone. Working two stones at once, she'd spilled ingredients all over the floor around her. I stuck my phone in my pocket. I'd respond to Brett later.

"Where's Mamie?" I threw on an apron, washed my hands, and heated two more stones.

"I told her to go home. Her hip was bothering her a lot."

I frowned. Her hip pain was the only tangible indication that she was growing older.

"She's okay, Jolie," Morgan whispered. "I figured there was no reason for her to stay if she was uncomfortable. I thought I could handle it, but the people keep coming."

"Well, I'm here now." I took my first order, splitting her line in half.

It wasn't long before the familiar chink of a token falling into the jar, tapping the other tokens, made me break into an involuntary smile. To me, it was the sound of a slot machine hitting a jackpot. Actually, it was way better. It meant someone cared enough to buy a meal for a faceless stranger.

A surprising and wonderful discovery accompanied the presence of the jar: people were generous. They may not have known how to help on their own, but when provided with the opportunity, they pitched in with enthusiasm. In the last two weeks, my beautiful jar practically overflowed.

After a while, things slowed down. Closing time was forty-five minutes away and we could finally take a breath. It was a good thing I missed my class because there was no way Morgan could have kept up with that crowd alone. Sometimes the universe had a way of sticking you in the right place at the right time.

I cleaned up around my stations as Morgan finished wiping down her own. The door chimes went off, letting us know we had another customer.

"I've got it," I told Morgan.

"Okay," she said. "I'm going to put some of these toppings in the fridge." She carried two armfuls of trays into the back, and I gave my attention to the new customer.

I lifted my head to ask what he wanted but he lingered in the doorway for few seconds, which was actually a good thing, because, holy cow, I needed a minute.

I was pretty sure an underwear model had walked into my store.

I swallowed and look down at the stone, pouring a ladle-full of batter on it to gather myself. My hand shook and the batter dripped off the side. I cursed as I wiped it with a towel and tried not to burn myself. What was wrong with me? He was just a guy.

I raised my head, hoping the shock would lessen with my second glance. Nope. He was just as spectacular the second time around. I shook off a chill.

His approach was tentative, probably because I was visually accosting him. As he came closer, he stood straighter. He seemed to grow half a foot between the entrance and where I stood. The unsure expression he wore in the doorway melted away by the time he reached the counter.

"Hey." The single word felt intimate, like he'd said it to me a thousand times before. His glare through slate blue eyes hinted that he knew all about me, but that was impossible. This was not someone I would forget.

"Hi. What can I get you?" I fought my cheek muscles to remain controlled and attentive and not break out into a ridiculous full-out giggle.

He saw my struggle, dammit. He flashed the cockiest, most wicked smile I'd ever seen, with teeth so perfect I thought I might be blinded for a second. He ran a hand through his brown hair, which was a touch long and fell right back over his eyebrows.

"What's your favorite instrument?" He placed all ten fingertips on my counter and leaned his weight forward, causing the muscles in his arms to bulge. The polo he wore was a little too tight, maybe on purpose, and it looked like his triceps might split the material. The conservative collared shirt, with some kind of store logo, seemed like a contradiction to his impish expression—and to the bruise splattered across one side of his jaw.

I wasn't a person who found violence sexy, God knows, but somehow the discoloration on his almost painfully beautiful face made the ladle in my hand tremble.

I was otherwise motionless for a few beats. My head was a bit fuzzy, but his question made no sense. I must have heard him wrong.

"I'm sorry," I used my best customer service voice. "What did you say?"

"Your favorite instrument, you know?" He removed his fingers from the counter and motioned with his hands like he was playing a guitar, with one hand holding its neck and the other strumming the strings. His voice was smooth and rich like chocolate. And damn, the bastard could make his grin even cockier by tilting it to one side.

"Um…" I looked around aimlessly, as if I might find an array of instruments strung from my walls to give me a clue. I suddenly couldn't name a single instrument and each second that passed paralyzed my thoughts more. How hard was it to think of an instrument? Anything?

"Piano," I blurted as soon as the image appeared in my cloudy brain.

He nodded once and turned to walk away. His back muscles rippled through his polo as he stood straight again. "Oh." He spun to me and I cast my eyes to the side, afraid he caught me checking out his back. "A smokin' hottie."

My jaw dropped and my eyebrows rose sky high. Was he talking about me? Or worse, himself? "Huh?"

He tilted his head up and pointed his chin to the board behind me, above my head. "The number 7, please," he chuckled.

Oh. He meant the chicken, salsa, and jalapeno crepe. The Smokin' Hottie. Why did I have to give these products such cute names?

I tried to recover, as if I knew what he meant all along. After all, I was the one who named the damn crepes. I was the one who served them every day. I should have recognized when someone ordered one of them. "Right, of course," I fumbled. "The crepe. Sure, of course, right away, coming up." With each additional word, I dug myself a little deeper into a ditch of humiliation. I wanted to follow my words and jump in behind them.

I rung up his order with my head aimed at the register. Things could only get worse if I looked directly at the sun.

"For here or to go?"

"For here," he answered.

Crap. I almost wished he said it was to go. Almost.

"Would you like something to drink?" I begged my cheeks to cool down.

"No thanks, just the crepe."

I told him the total and I didn't even lift my head to collect his money. I just stuck out my hand. Good God, it was like I'd never seen a hot guy before.

"Someone will bring it right over. Thank you for your business."

A minute later, I asked Morgan to bring the guy his food. She looked at me like I had two heads. One, because I dumped my customer on her, which we never did. More importantly, two, we didn't serve our customers. We were strictly a counter-service establishment. If someone had a big order or we were running behind, we'd take the customer's name and call it for pick up at the counter when it was ready. But table delivery? Never. I couldn't stand to have him wait in front of me, though, so I sent him away.

"Uh, sure, Jolie." Morgan grabbed his tray. She walked it over and set it down in front of him. His thank you to Morgan was polite, but his head, tipped to the side, aimed at me the whole time.

Over the next half hour, a few more stragglers

arrived. I kept busy and pretended not to notice the gorgeous guy on the other side of the room, who intently scribbled something on what I guessed was a piece of paper. Every so often, I caught him stealing a mirthful glance at me and I diverted my attention elsewhere.

Eventually, it was time to close. Morgan, somehow, hadn't noticed this creature and tidied up in the usual routine. Unaffected. He didn't seem to be leaving and I wondered if I would have to kick him out. My other option was to tell him we were closing, but I knew somewhere else we could go to be more comfortable and get to know each other. I laughed out loud at my idea.

"What?" Morgan asked.

"What? Nothing," I answered, annoyed at myself for always being so transparent.

"You're laughing at something."

"It's nothing," I repeated, but I had to know why she wasn't drooling, too. This wasn't a guy who wasn't your type. He was everybody's type. I turned my back to the counter and leaned against it so he wouldn't see me talking about him. "Hey, Morgan?" I whispered.

"Yeah?"

"How come you haven't said anything about that guy sitting over there?" I rolled my eyes and tipped my head in his direction, but it wasn't necessary. He was the only person left.

"What do you mean?" she asked.

"About how hot he is?" I whispered again, probably not as subtly as I was hoping.

She lifted one shoulder and fidgeted with her hair. "I don't know. He's eaten here before, so I guess I'm used to him."

"He's been here before?" No way.

"Yeah. Just a couple of times."

"I don't remember him."

She thought for a minute. "He's come in on Thursdays, when Mamie works. I guess that's why."

"Well, when he paid for his crepe, I couldn't even meet his eyes. I'm so embarrassed." I squirmed against the counter.

"Really?"

She seemed surprised. Why?

I scrunched my face and nodded.

"Well, I wouldn't be too worried. He keeps watching you so he wasn't too turned off."

I almost spun around to see if she was right, but I managed to stop myself, refusing to be that obvious. When the chimes jingled, though, I whipped around at the sound.

He had left.

He and his sky-blue polo were disappearing down the boardwalk. I was disappointed to an unreasonable degree.

I focused all my energy into cleaning my already-tidy work area and tried not to reveal how silly I was being to Morgan. What did I think would happen? He came in to buy a crepe. He ate it. And then, like he was supposed to, he left. He was just a customer. I'd never see him again. It was fine. Whatever.

I called bullshit on myself.

"Uh, Jo?" Morgan played with something on the stranger's table.

"Yeah?"

"I think you need to see this."

For a second, I didn't understand why Morgan wanted me to see the napkin he left behind. Was she showing me that the guy didn't clean up after himself?

Then I took a closer look.

Scribbled at the top, it read:

When I saw you behind the counter…

Underneath the words were tiny bars of notes. Lots of them. I took the napkin between my fingers and turned it over. More bars with notes. I couldn't believe how many he fit on one rectangular napkin.

At the end, it said:

For the piano

Now, my four heart chambers competed with each other for the fastest beat. "Do you think this is for me?" I asked Morgan.

She laughed. "It sure as hell isn't for me."

Of course it was for me. I told him I liked the piano and he watched me the whole time, even if I was too shy to return the favor. "It is for me."

"Duh. Can you read music?"

"Not a note," I answered, but I wasn't even sure if it mattered. The mystery of the notes might have been enough.

"Lock up and come with me," she said.

****

By the time we arrived at Morgan's apartment, her roommate was in bed, but Morgan assured me he'd be happy to help. "Chase," she tapped on his closed bedroom door. "You up?"

Nothing.

She knocked a little louder. "Chase?"

A mumble came from behind the door and, taking it as an invitation, she went in. "Hey, can you do

21

something for Jolie?" She disappeared into his room, closing the door.

Two minutes later, a tired Chase shuffled into the living room and threw himself on the couch. "Hey Jolie."

"Hey, Chase. Sorry to wake you. This could've waited until tomorrow."

He rubbed his eyes underneath glasses I'd never seen him wear before. "No problem. I was watching TV in bed."

Judging by his appearance, he was a terrible liar. His bloodshot eyes and disheveled hair said he had been sound asleep, but he would have done anything for Morgan. She might have been blind to that fact, but even though I'd met the guy just a handful of times, it was pretty obvious.

"So, I hear you have an admirer." He sank farther into the couch.

I enjoyed the idea. "I don't know about that, but someone left this." I handed him the napkin, which I'd folded into fourths and tucked in an empty pocket in my purse.

He looked it over for a couple of minutes, squinting and humming to himself as he read the notes. The hint of his interpretation of the song was a tease. I wanted to yank the rest of those notes out of his throat to hear whatever it was my gorgeous mystery man created.

Finally, Chase nodded. "From what I can figure, this is gonna sound pretty cool. You don't know the guy who wrote it?"

"Not a clue."

"Okay, well, bring it by my job after school

tomorrow and I'll play it for you. We don't exactly have a baby grand here." He waved his arm around their small living room. "The kids leave at two-thirty and I'll probably stick around until about four, so come anytime in between." He laid the napkin on the coffee table. I wanted to stick it back in my purse for safe keeping. It was lying there, unsecured, on the table. It could get lost.

I restrained. It was just a napkin, after all.

He rose from the couch and took a step toward his room. "Night, guys."

"Hey!" Morgan pouted. "What about my goodnight kiss?"

Chase sighed and slogged over to her. He planted a soft, chaste kiss on her lips with a frown. She wrapped her arms around his neck and squeezed. "Nighty night, Chasey," she sang.

"Goodnight, Morgan," he murmured.

Poor guy.

Chapter Three
Device: Maintain a Routine

Customers traipsed in and out of Stuff Your Crepes all day, but even the hustle of serving the lunch crowd wasn't enough of a distraction. The seashell clock over my head tormented me with its second hand moving at a snail's pace. Two-thirty would never come. I cursed myself for never learning to play an instrument or read music. Who knew that would be a skill I'd need in the future?

To make matters more irritating, my grandmother noticed my fidgeting and clock-watching. Naturally. "That dentist appointment must be pretty important to you." She gave me the same *I know what you're up to* squint she shot me when I was in high school and I told her I was sleeping over a friend's house when she knew damn well I was sneaking off to hang out with my boyfriend. We all had more important things to worry about than if I was having some good sexy time, but we lived together and she always wanted me to know I wasn't getting anything over on her. She had her eye on me.

That never changed.

"Yeah, this tooth's really bothering me." I cupped my jaw with my palm, but kept my back to her. It was too hard to lie directly into her glassy spheres of coal, but I wasn't ready to share my mystery music man yet.

"Uh-huh." Her snide tone had me lowering my head, just like when I was sixteen.

Tokens rustled and I whipped back around to find an older, salt and pepper man standing at the counter.

"Hi, what can I get you?" I asked.

He read the extensive, overhead menu. "Uh, can I please have a Quiche Exclaim?" His voice was hushed as he slinked the token along the counter toward me. He raised his eyebrows in question but kept his head low. A first timer, no doubt.

"Sure thing." I nodded to reassure him that he didn't need to say anything else. "Coming right up." I loaded the cooking crepe with egg, ham, cheeses, scallions and a little tabasco sauce for good measure. My version of a Quiche Lorraine. "For here or to go?" I folded the crepe onto itself.

"To go, please."

I wrapped the crepe in paper and handed it to the gentleman. "Here you go."

He thanked me as he took it, but made no move to go anywhere, unsure of the protocol.

"I hope you enjoy it and think of us again. Have a wonderful day." I took a step away from the counter to let him know we were finished.

He understood. "Thank you very much." He rubbed his forehead.

"It's my pleasure."

Mamie patted me on the back as she walked behind me to grab some supplies. She knew about the goose bumps that tickled my body whenever one of those chips got cashed in.

The next time I had a chance to look at the clock, it was two-fifteen. I scurried to wipe down my stone and untie my apron. Morgan walked in as I hung it on the wall of hooks to my right. She gave me an apprehensive look before greeting my grandmother. She must have been uncomfortable lying to Mamie, too.

If Morgan weren't covering my shift, I would have begged her to come with me. I'd never been to Chase's school before, and I had the worst sense of direction of anyone on the planet. I lived in fear of cloudy days because they screwed with the satellite reception on my GPS. If there were a fork in the road, nine out of ten times, I'd take the wrong path. Tristan used to take pity on me and drive me everywhere, but not before teasing me, calling me directionally challenged.

I would have given anything to have Tristan rib me and drive me to Chase's that day.

Miraculously, I made the forty-five minute drive without a single wrong turn. By the time I arrived at the high school where Chase taught, a few kids lingered, but most of the summer school students were gone. He met me at the front door, because he said his classroom was kind of hidden. Though he was unaware of my inability to follow directions, I was grateful.

"I played it through a couple of times, Jolie," he said as we walked. This was the first time I'd been alone with him, and I didn't know if we'd have a lot of awkward pauses, so I was relieved when he started discussing the music.

"And?" I asked.

"It's really good." Chase dragged his feet as he walked through the halls that smelled like every other high school: a decades-old, slightly mildewy brick building with a hint of cafeteria food in the background. He took his sweet time to get to his room. I considered moving behind him and shoving his back, just enough to get him to pick up the pace. But it wasn't his fault I'd been chomping at the bit to hear this since the day before. What was all the excitement about anyway? In all likelihood, I'd never see the guy again.

Still, I wanted to run to that piano.

After making our way through the labyrinth of a building, we arrived in a classroom filled with rows of folding chairs and music stands. In the back corner, up a step, was a set of drums. A black piano sat in the other corner.

"This is very cool, you know. Somebody writing music for you."

I chuckled. "I don't know if this is his own music, or if he'll even come by again. I don't know anything except he wrote this on a random napkin. He didn't say a single word to me before he left."

"Even so." He trudged toward the piano. "This is his way of telling you how he feels. That's pretty brave, if you ask me."

His morose expression made me forget about my song for a second. He sat on the piano bench and lifted the key cover. I extended my hand to give him the napkin, but didn't let go when he grabbed it, forcing him to meet my stare.

"Have *you* told *her*?" I asked. So much for awkward pauses. I volunteered to have an entire awkward conversation. I released the napkin.

"What do you mean?" He turned as white as the keys in front of him.

I tilted my head to the side and raised an eyebrow.

"How long have you known?" His back and shoulders went rigid.

"When did we meet?" I winked.

"Oh man," he groaned. He ran the hand with the napkin through his hair and I had to stop myself from reaching out to protect it. Absurd.

"So, have you said anything?" I asked, instead of revealing my ridiculous thought.

"I can't." He shook his head vigorously, appalled at the suggestion. "She doesn't see me like that."

"You don't know unless you ask." I tried to give him hope.

"Jolie, the woman kisses me on the lips every single night and feels nothing. I don't have to ask."

He was probably right. That was a brotherly kiss I witnessed, and Morgan always spoke about Chase platonically at work.

I sat next to him on the bench and hip-checked him. "Scoot, and let me hear my song." I changed the subject, sorry I brought it up.

"Okay. Ready?"

"*Hells*, yeah."

When Chase tickled the keys with his fingertips, the sound surprised me. I was expecting something slow and romantic, like a melodic love poem, with notes instead of words, but this song was fast and upbeat, with a lot of clipped notes. It was full of power and strength. It made me feel…alive.

When Chase came to the end of the second side, he turned the napkin over and started again. He played it three more times in its entirety before stopping.

"What do you think?" He closed the lid over the keys.

"I love it."

"The staccato notes really bring it to life. The more

times I play it, the more kinetic energy it has. That's why I repeated it for you. It sounds like someone so excited by something he can't catch his breath."

He hit the nail on the head. Leave it to a music teacher to interpret my song.

"Can I record you playing it?" I scrunched my nose. He was already doing me a favor. This was kind of pushing it.

"Record me?"

"It's the only way I can hear it when I'm not here. Would you mind?"

"Uh…sure, I guess." He uncovered the keys.

I pulled out my phone and aimed at his hands. He played the song over and over, and each time he did, my pulse rate increased. After five repetitions, he stopped.

"Is that good?"

"It's perfect. Thank you so much." I stood from the bench.

"He'll be back, Jolie."

"You think?" I asked. I hoped.

"If this is how he felt when he saw you the first time, he'll be back for a second look." He closed the piano and handed back my napkin. I started to walk away, but Chase grabbed my wrist.

"Please don't tell her." His grimace pled with me.

"I won't."

He was skeptical, naturally. Morgan was my friend and employee. I spent a lot of time with her. I barely knew Chase. I certainly wouldn't have wanted anyone interfering with my love life, even if they knew something I didn't. So I had no intention of interfering with theirs.

"I promise. On…" I held up the music. "On my napkin."

****

The color returned to his face. "Okay. Thanks."

"I mean it, Jolie. I don't want you walking through there by yourself this week. Are you watching this?" My grandmother turned up the volume on the television in her living room so I could hear it through the phone.

"No, Mamie, I'm at work, so I'm not watching TV. But yes, I heard about what happened." Though we had an overhead TV in the store, it was rarely on.

The night before, there was a slashing in the park I always walked through. Someone stabbed a homeless man. They weren't sure about the motivation yet, but my grandmother had called no less than forty times insisting I drive to yoga.

"I'm not going to that class this week, Mamie."

"What? Is everything okay?"

"Everything's fine. I just decided to try a class this morning instead."

She was silent on the other end, no doubt wondering what would cause me to alter my set-in-stone routine.

"It was a good class. Cross-fit. It kicked my butt." If I kept talking, maybe I'd distract her. In truth, I changed my class with the hopes that my stranger would be back on Thursday during my yoga class. He hadn't been back yet, and if he didn't come by then, chances were he wouldn't come at all. If I missed him, I'd be furious at myself.

"What aren't you telling me?"

"Nothing, Mamie. Really. I like this class. I might take it more often." If I got a visitor on Thursday.

Eye roll.

"And what about the delivery?"

It was my turn for silence.

"Jolie?"

"I'm going to be in and out. Super quick. I'll be fine."

"Jolie!"

"Mamie, I need to do this. Bad enough one of them was hurt. Some of them count on this. Besides, I need to see if it was someone I know."

Ever since I heard the news the night before, my stomach was in knots. What if it was Crooked Curt or one of the other guys? The victim's identity hadn't been released, and I couldn't shake my fear until I saw for myself. I'd be as fast as possible and then I'd come back to the store. I even asked Morgan to stall the Music Man's order if he came in while I was out.

If.

My grandmother sighed. "Can't you take someone with you then?"

"I'll try, okay?"

"All right. I'll be in a little later. Love you, *ma petite fille*." Her line clicked and she was gone.

****

Brett and I were finally able to pick a day to get together. We grabbed a late dinner, since it was my day to close. He picked me up at work and we went to a casual Italian place at the end of the boardwalk. He was able to escape with all articles of clothing intact this time, but not before Mamie questioned him about his job and some other equally unassuming topics.

Over appetizers, we talked a little about work and Brett's family, who lived in Virginia, but he moved to

31

NJ for this job. I told him a little bit about some of my customers, but skirted the issue when he asked about my family. It was just me and Mamie, I told him, which was only half a lie. He didn't pry.

"She sure is something," he said. "She's got so much spunk for someone in her, what, mid-seventies?"

I bugged out my eyes and covered my mouth with my hand in jest. "Don't ever let her hear you say that."

"What? Am I wrong? Is she in her sixties?"

"She's eighty-seven," I whispered, as if Mamie were next to me and might hear. "But if she heard you ask if she's in her seventies, she'd rip off both of your arms and beat you with them."

He chuckled, realizing that while he might think it was a compliment, Mamie would not.

When our entrees came, we were quiet for a few moments enjoying our food. It wasn't uncomfortable at all. In fact, it felt like I was having dinner with an old friend.

"That's a great tune," he said.

"What?" I asked, with a mouthful of pasta and vodka sauce.

"The song you're humming. It's very catchy." He stabbed his chicken, so he missed my mouth fall open and a piece of pasta tumble out. I dabbed it with a napkin before he noticed the sauce wetting my lip.

I'd listened to my stranger's song maybe a hundred times since Chase let me record him and it had been stuck in my head for days. I hadn't taken a day off since the stranger came in, hoping he'd come back, but nothing.

"Oh." I shook my head. "I don't even know what that is. Must've heard it somewhere."

We ate in silence, but for me, the mood had shifted.

Brett walked me to my car. "Are you sure you're okay driving?"

I had a glass of wine, but I was fine to drive. "Yes, but thanks for worrying." I considered asking if he wanted to go somewhere else, but we had two cars, so we'd either both have to drive or I'd have to drive somewhere and then drive him back. Logistically, it didn't seem worth the effort. "I had a nice time."

"Me too." He leaned in and kissed me against my car. This time, he went for more than a peck. With the mystery song still playing in my head, really kissing this guy wouldn't have felt right. I pulled away.

"I'll call you tomorrow," I said.

He nodded, hiding his disappointment. "Goodnight, Jolie."

Chapter Four
Device: No Drama

"You said you were bringing someone!" my grandmother bellowed as I hurried toward the door, arms buckling under the weight of the box. I needed a little more cross-fit training.

"I said I would try." I blew a kiss her way to try to pacify her, knowing it was a waste of facial muscles.

"Trying isn't doing!" She couldn't care less that she was chastising me over the heads of a store full of customers. "Bring anyone. Bring him." She pointed to some random guy sitting at a table sipping a smoothie. His utter confusion, with a straw dangling from his lips, would have made me laugh if I wasn't so embarrassed.

"Mamie!"

"Don't Mamie me, young lady. You're putting yourself in danger."

This display had to end immediately. Since I was a grown woman, and not actually the fourteen-year-old girl my grandmother sometimes made me feel reduced to, I told her I'd be right back, and ran out the door before I had to face any more.

Relief flooded my veins when I found Curt lying on a bench with a knit cap thrown over his face. I picked up my pace and plopped the box in front of him. He didn't move.

"Curt?" I patted his arm.

He jumped, lifted his head with a jolt, and removed his cap. "Why hello, lovely lady." He cleared his throat and tried to hide the alarm my touch caused. He may have lost another tooth since the week before; I couldn't be sure.

"I was so worried." I plucked open the flaps of the box.

"You heard? It's all anyone can talk about. You know there's crime here and all, but it's more petty stuff. Muggings, some drug stuff. It's not usually violent like that. Makes you wonder." He released a sigh as he laid his head back down and covered it with the hat. This was the most affected I'd ever seen him. My gut squeezed at his unfamiliar sadness.

"Was the person who was hurt…anyone you know?" I was afraid of the answer.

"Nope. No one from the Palace."

I'd heard them joke about their section of the park as the Palace before, but today there was no humor in Curt's voice.

"Well, thank God for that," I said.

"Yeah. God is good." His tone was flat as he adjusted the hat over his face, making my quick getaway easy.

"Okay, well, I'm glad you're all right. I'm gonna be off."

"Jolie." He sat up a little. "Thank you for the food."

"Of course. See you next week."

I was despondent on my way back to the store. Curt was always so cheerful when I was around, it made it easy to hide his reality a little bit. In fact, even if I was having a shitty day, ironically, visiting him brought me up somehow. Tonight was different. Tonight I got a moment's glimpse into his true life. It was ever so tiny, and even that was difficult to swallow. I found myself pulling at my eyelashes as I walked. A bad habit I'd spent many years trying to conquer.

But when the door chimes rang and I stepped into my small shop, every sad and nervous thought selfishly floated from my head, replaced by the fact that in front of me was a beautifully sculpted back, covered by a blue polo. His head turned at the sound of the chimes and his mouth formed the half grin that almost had me in a full drool the week before.

I forced myself to smile back this time as I passed him to walk behind the counter. Somehow, during the entire week of hoping he'd return, I didn't play out one potential conversation we'd have. I played out a lot of other things in my head, mostly having to do with the counter or the supply closet or the beach, but no words. How was that possible?

I snuck a peek at his table. He had a half-empty drink in front of him. No food. Damn, I was too late. How long was I gone?

"Someone's here to see you," Morgan whispered in my ear as I laced my apron. Her gloomy expression told me I was alone in being happy about his appearance.

"Maybe not. He's already eaten." I pulled my bottom lip back in as soon as it broke into a frown.

"Nope. He said he was just having a drink for now, which I'm sure is code for *until Jolie gets here.*"

"I don't know," I said, but before I spoke the last word, he was standing in my line, which was somehow already three people deep. I hurried through the other orders, trying not to let the customer in front of him see my tapping foot. She read every single item on the damn menu and I regretted offering more than two choices.

Finally, I got rid of her and there he was, standing in front of me. "Did you like your song?" He wrapped his palms around the edge of the counter and leaned in with a swag like he owned the place...or me.

Cocky bastard. He needed to be taken down a notch. I shrugged. "Sure, it was okay."

His face fell.

I stifled a laugh that threatened to burst from me.

"*Okay*?"

"Yeah, I mean, it was a little pop-music-ish, but it was okay." I wiped the spotless counter with a cloth.

He lifted his hand to his mouth, nibbled on his thumbnail and squinted, studying me. Then his grin returned with his finger still in his mouth, and I swear it took everything in me not to hop the counter.

"You're bullshitting me."

"Am I?" I lifted an eyebrow and shot him back a face chock full of coy.

"Well, either that or you have horrific taste in music."

Oh, this was fun. I dropped my jaw to the floor in a mock-appalled fashion. "I have fantastic taste in music, among other things," I said.

"Oh yeah? We'll see."

A customer cleared his throat, making me realize there was a line forming behind my guy. The noise caught his attention too, and he glanced up. "I'd like a..." He scanned the board. "Strip tease."

I turned to where he was looking. "That's a Triple Cheese," I guffawed.

"Oh is it? My mistake. I guess I'll have to settle for that. For now." He leaned farther over the counter and my suddenly dry mouth had no witty quip to return. I made his crepe at lightning speed before I completely embarrassed myself. I handed him his food, took his money and breathed.

"Enjoy," I said.

"I plan to," he shot back and took the same table as last time.

Music Man made no attempt to hide the fact that he was watching me serve other customers. I pretended to reach for ingredients as I stood on tiptoes and leaned around customers in line to get a view of his table. What was he writing? Another song? His address? Phone number? Favorite breakfast? I felt like ripping that napkin out of his hand. Maybe this time he'd give it to me at the counter. Or wait around until I closed and he could play it for me at his place.

Closing couldn't come fast enough.

I ran into the back to replenish the olives and check myself in the mirror, but I almost dropped the bin on the floor when I went back out front. Another customer was sitting at my Music Man's table. He was gone.

What the hell?

I flew to the table, leaving someone waiting in my line. "Be right back," I called over my shoulder. I searched the table that held the new person, resenting her for being there. Nothing. I inspected the floor around her. Spotless. Shit.

"Excuse me," I used my sweetest voice. "Was there anything at this table when you sat down?"

"No."

"Are you sure? Not an old napkin that maybe you

threw away?"

It was possible I'd grown a third eye, by her expression. "Uh, no. I just sat down. Nothing was here."

How could that be? I saw him writing. Why didn't he say goodbye and finish what he started?

"Okay, thanks." I walked back to my counter, but barely heard the next order. That napkin was somewhere. I just had to find it.

We closed the doors at ten and I grabbed the broom. I didn't want anyone else sweeping up. No matter how thorough my search of the garbage lying around, though, there was no napkin with anything written on it. Disappointment flooded me. I wanted to punch myself for allowing this quick, flirty interaction to get into my head.

Even though Mamie often walked the short distance from her house to work because it was good exercise, one of us always drove her home at the end of the day. As we sat in my car that night, she read my mood. My silence was probably *why* she was able to read my mood.

"What's wrong, love?"

"Nothing. I'm just tired." I gave the empty road on the two-minute drive my full attention.

"It seems like more."

"Nope. I'll be better after I sleep." I pulled up her driveway and waited for her to get out of the car. For the first time in a long time I had the urge to accompany her inside. I'd crawl into the full-sized bed of my childhood, while she lay next to me, stroked my hair, and sang a French lullaby until I fell asleep. That had always given me comfort. But I wouldn't revert to that over such a silly thing as guy problems. There were much worse things in the world.

Besides, she wasn't going anywhere. She sat in the passenger seat with a knowing expression. "Does your sour face have anything to do with this?" She dug in her purse and pulled out two napkins covered in beautiful musical notes.

"Where did you get those?" I tried to snap them out of her hand but the corner of one tore off in my fingers. Thankfully, none of his writing was there.

"Why didn't you tell me about him?" It was more of an accusation than a question. I always told her about the guys I dated. I probably shared more with her than any other twenty-six-year-old told her grandmother. Too much, maybe.

"I don't know. There wasn't anything to tell yet. Anyway, how did you know?"

"Morgan told me. Even if she hadn't, he didn't exactly hide the fact that he'd rather be having you as his tasty treat than that crepe."

My face heated from equal parts of embarrassment and anger. Why the hell did Morgan tell her? Didn't that defeat the whole *covering for me* thing?

"When he left while you were in the back, I figured I better grab this before someone else did. Then when you were searching so furiously for it, I held on to it for a bit as payback for hiding something from me." She poked my side with a bony finger, letting me know she was only slightly annoyed.

"Did you see him?" I couldn't hide my ridiculous enthusiasm.

"Let's put it this way, honey. I may have finished menopause a couple of decades ago, but my hot flashes came back tonight in full effect." She fanned herself with my song. She kissed me on the cheek and handed me the napkins. "Goodnight, dear. Don't stay up too late trying to teach yourself to read music online. Morgan's boyfriend will translate it for you tomorrow."

Sometimes, my grandmother was extremely annoying.

Part of me wanted to ream Morgan out for betraying my confidence but the other part, the bigger part, knew I needed a favor.

—*You told my grandmother???*—

I texted her the second I locked my apartment door. She answered immediately.

—*Sorry :* ☹—

No explanation followed.

—*Well, then I guess you owe me.*—I hoped the happy face I attached made my text sound less accusatory than I felt.

—*I guess I do…what do you want?*—

—*Ask Chase to play for me again?*—

Of course, Chase was happy to do anything for Morgan's boss/friend, so I made plans to go there again the next day. At least this time I didn't have to pretend to have a cavity.

****

This song was unlike the first one. Chase played it for me on the sax, as the napkin directed. It was sexy, soulful and filled with desire, like a remake of one of those old Marvin Gaye songs from the seventies. It had me all tingles and sweats, thinking of the words he scribbled on top of the napkin… *Your smile's effect on me*. Again, I recorded Chase, but I wished I could get my guy on video playing instead of Chase, who was very nice, but should have been playing this for Morgan, not me.

"Can you write me a song to give him back?" I asked when Chase finished playing. I needed to step this up a notch. Writing something back could be the way.

"Write a song?" He laughed. "Jolie, I don't write music. If I did, I probably wouldn't be making a starting teacher's salary, and playing other bands' cover songs on weekends with my buddies. And if I could write something that sounded like *this*? I'd be too busy fighting off women to play this for you."

He wasn't wrong. Morgan, who'd come with me this time, was in a trance the entire time Chase played the sax. It was no wonder. The song sounded like silky, liquid sex. I could almost feel her heart beating in my chest; her reaction to him was so vivid. He must have felt it too, because he kept playing it on repeat, which was all good to me.

"Oh yeah?" she teased him. "What women would you want to fight off?" Morgan tangled his hair between her fingers, standing over him.

Chase almost choked, but hid it well behind the saxophone case as he packed it up. "Oh, you know. All those cute sorority sisters you're always bringing around."

Morgan's face dropped. She yanked her hand from his hair. "Which one, specifically?" Her playful tone was gone, replaced by what I thought was unmistakable jealousy. A second's glance at Chase let me know he heard it, too, because, while almost microscopic, there was a smirk hiding inside his lips.

"Hmm," he pretended to think, using the

opportunity to his advantage. "That ginger with the greenish eyes is pretty. What's her name again?"

"Shari," she spat. "I'll let her know you think so." She grabbed her cell and purse off Chase's desk. "Do you have everything you need? You have to get to work, right?" she ordered me.

"Yeah." I couldn't hold a poker face as well as Chase. "I'm all set."

"What's funny?" she snapped.

"Nothing," I answered, but as she stormed out the door, I mouthed at Chase, "Brilliant."

He blushed.

I was fairly certain Morgan would get pulled over on the way back to Stuff Your Crepes, because the speedometer hovered around 75 and the speed limit on the road was 50. But no one stopped us and Morgan was free to take her rage out on the road, slick with rain, instead of directing it at the man we just left behind.

"You know," I dared. "If you care who he dates, why don't you tell him?"

"I don't care who he dates," she snapped back.

"Kinda seems like you might."

"No, Jolie. I don't."

I may have been her boss at work, but here I was her friend sitting shotgun in her car, so I shut up and minded my own business.

But she brought it up again after a few minutes of flying down the highway. "I don't think it's appropriate for him to be checking out friends I bring to my apartment. That's all. It's not my fault the sorority house was full before I could sign up. Sometimes I have to bring sisters around to plan events. Just because I answered his stupid online ad for the apartment last year doesn't mean he has the right to drool over them."

"Okay," I said, but I didn't remind her that when a spot opened up in the sorority house this fall, she'd turned it down.

"That's really all it is, Jolie. Seriously."

Protesteth much?

"Okay," I repeated, playing with the air vents. The AC wasn't on, but I needed something to do with my hands.

"God, Jolie, I think your grandmother is rubbing off on you. I said that's the reason, and it is, so why don't you believe me?"

"Morgan," I laughed. "I said okay. If you say you don't care, then you don't care."

She flushed. "Sorry," she mumbled.

"No worries."

She pumped the radio, so we weren't supposed to notice the quiet the rest of the way back.

The day's nasty weather dissuaded people from the beach, and when we returned to the shop, I found my grandmother sitting at a table with her feet propped on a chair. The lack of customers let her take as long as she wanted on her phone call.

I tied on an apron, but didn't bother to heat an additional stone. The rain was growing heavier. Morgan huffed around the store, cleaning furiously. It was her signature move when something annoyed her. Everything was already clean, but that was irrelevant. I'd stay out of her way.

"Business is good," my grandmother said. "Slow today because of rain, but good in general... Yeah, the interview worked wonders for us."

Her chatter was white noise. I was too busy replaying my new song in my memory—wondering what my Music Man saw about my smile that would make him respond that way—to hear her. It wasn't the first time someone commented on that, but coming from him, it was like night and day.

"No. No word. We haven't heard anything in months."

The music in my head stopped and I froze, because now I knew who Mamie was talking to, and what she was discussing.

"She's doing well. Working hard at the store. Seeing a nice boy." She didn't mention my secret guy. I had no fear that she would either. Mamie was Vegas. What was confided with her stayed with her.

She threw me a questioning glance. I shook my head. She frowned but didn't push. "No, she's at the gym...I'll tell her. Goodbye, Abby." She ended her call.

I walked into the back but the walls didn't shield me from her voice. "It's been a long time, Jolie."

"I know," I called.

"You haven't taken one of her calls in months."

"I know." I dragged back into the front. There was no point hiding when she was going to yell to me.

Morgan ignored us and continued her cleaning rampage. She knew I almost never accepted calls from my mother, but she didn't know why. She was considerate enough not to pry.

My grandmother walked over to me, to keep our conversation private. "You have to let go of the anger, Jolie. It will eat you alive."

"I've told you, Mamie, I'm not angry. I'm just done with her."

She shook her head. "She's your mother, dear. You don't have that option."

"She's the one who opted to throw her hands in the air and move to the other side of the country so she didn't have to deal with things. Not me."

She took my hands in hers. "Some people are blessed with infinite strength, Jolie. Others are given only so much. Your mother spent years using up her supply. Don't fault her for having nothing left."

"Please don't defend her. I don't want to hear it. If you want to talk to her and give her quarterly reports or whatever, that's your business. How I handle her is mine."

My grandmother gave me another frown but she didn't corner the market in stubborn behavior. I would not continue this conversation. We'd been over it too many times. She went into the back on some pretend errand.

The rest of the day was slow with few customers, making it too easy for me to obsess over my grandmother's conversation with my mother. I may have said her relationship with Abby was her business, but in reality, the fact that she kept the lines of communication open with her irritated the hell out of me. I wished she'd stop giving her updates. Actions should have consequences. She shouldn't have been privy to any information about this family. She'd made her choice.

Brett was a welcome sight when he picked me up a little early for our date. Dinner and a movie. He was very handsome in his brown button-down and dark jeans and we talked a bit as I cleaned up after a couple of stragglers who'd just finished eating.

"Add any new ones this week?" he asked, referring to my ever-changing menu.

"Nah, not feeling very creative right now," I said. In fact, I'd been lacking inspiration for a new crepe for a while.

Things were so easy with Brett. Exactly what I needed to distract me from my uneasy relationship with my mother. He stood at the counter and I chuckled at a joke he made while I wiped down my station.

When the chimes clinked, I sighed. We had almost no customers all day but now that I wanted to leave, people kept dripping in.

"I can help you," Mamie said from my left. "She just closed up."

I turned to thank her, but the words stuck in my throat. Her customer was my Music Man, and he didn't look happy. He stared at me for a second, before catching himself. He asked her for a small iced tea, yanked a couple of napkins from the pile and stormed to his table. I was speechless, and when Brett asked me some follow up question, I had no idea how to answer.

We were ready to leave, but I had to figure out a way to stall for a few minutes to see if this guy was leaving me something. Running out before things got more awkward, or before Brett noticed the way Music Man kept shooting daggers at him was probably a better idea. Unfortunately, my feet had become cemented to the ground.

The decision was made for me, though, because not two minutes after he sat, Music Man shoved back his chair, threw open the door, and marched out. My sweet chimes never sounded so angry.

"Let me wipe down that table and then we can go."

I rushed off to inspect my latest tune. My stomach dropped when there wasn't a single note written on the napkin on the table. There were words, but with Brett behind me, draping my sweater over my shoulders, I couldn't read them.

"It's chilly out from the rain," he said. Such a gentleman.

"Thanks." I shoved the napkin in the pocket of my jeans. I'd have to read it later.

I tried to put the napkin out of my head during dinner. After all, if you're dating more than one guy, it's bad etiquette to think of one while you're out with another. And I was obviously not dating this other guy, so it should have been easy. Still, my hip felt heavy with the weight of the napkin and I might have toppled to the side if I didn't read it soon.

"I have to run to the bathroom," I told Brett, before our appetizers arrived. It would have been more believable if I'd had more than one sip of my water.

"Sure," he said.

I walked off, feeling like a middle schooler sneaking out her bedroom window.

As soon as the bathroom door closed behind me, I uncrumpled the note.

I was going to write a song about my reaction to that guy standing over you, but I think I might be wasting my time. Maybe I'm wrong. Maybe there's not something brewing between you. If it's not what I think, meet me at the entrance to the beach closest to Stuff Your Crepes at 11 tonight. But if I'm right, let me know now, by not showing, and I won't come by or bother you anymore.

I was supposed to be in the middle of a movie at

eleven o'clock, but if I didn't show, that was it. I wouldn't see Music Man again.

He must have guessed I had plans. His note pretty much implied that. Yet, this was kind of a threat. Either I showed up or he was done. I didn't even know his name and he was giving me an ultimatum? What the hell kind of nerve did he have? And he wanted me to meet him on the beach at eleven? Did he think I was some kind of booty call? I had a good-looking, stable guy waiting at a table for me, and a player who kept disappearing, breaking my silent rule, who was probably anything but stable, asking me to meet him alone in the darkness of the beach. This choice was cake.

Chapter Five
Device: Keep It Simple

It started raining again, so not only did I do the dumbest thing and blow off the nicest guy, but now I was waiting at the entrance to the beach with water drizzling down the back of my shirt. Maybe one day I'd listen to a piece of Mamie's advice, like *keep an umbrella in your trunk, Jolie*. I pushed my short hair behind my ears. It was slick and wet and didn't want to stay in place. It fell right back in my face, dripping in my eyes. I considered leaving.

Why had I even shown up? I had been dead set against it in the bathroom. This guy was all wrong for me, the complete opposite of everything I looked for in a companion of any kind. I went back to the table to finish my date with Brett, sure I'd make the right decision, but as soon as he reached for my hand in the movie theater, my throat clogged with regret. I feigned an attack of diarrhea and rushed out. What an easy and disgusting way to guarantee an exit without being questioned.

I had to find out what was waiting for me on the other side of those notes, even if I was sorry later.

The raindrops stopped hitting me all at once. The large umbrella that shielded me from them was attached to a figure even more muscular than his polo revealed. His arm holding the umbrella brushed against my shoulder. It was like a rock.

"Didn't anyone ever tell you to carry an umbrella when it's raining?"

Holy hell, his voice sent shivers down my back that had nothing to do with the rain.

"Well, if someone would give a person a respectable amount of notice before asking her to meet him, she could be more prepared."

"I had to think fast."

"I did have plans, you know." I tried to sound annoyed, but how could I be annoyed with him inches away?

"Obviously they were less important than being here." His snide tone and self-important comment made me want to punch him in the chest, but they also drew me to him in ways any self-respecting feminist would hate.

"A little full of yourself, huh?" I backed away from him and his umbrella.

"I'm just kidding, Jolie." He took a step forward to cover me again. "Please, come with me."

"You know my name?"

"Your grandmother isn't exactly soft-spoken." He laughed easily. I couldn't argue with that.

"Do I get to know yours?" I kept the fact that I nicknamed him Music Man to myself.

"It's Reed. Now, will you come with me?" He extended the elbow of the arm holding the umbrella.

"Where to?" I didn't really care. I knew I was going with him. Otherwise, I wouldn't have fabricated a stomachache to get me out of the movie, but I had to at least act like I was being smart.

"The beach, of course."

"In the rain?"

"Trust me." He extended his elbow farther. I linked my arm through his. I did trust him. Why, I had no idea. A couple of amazing songs and a first name. That's all I knew about him. Normally, I had to have a person's rank and serial number before I decided if they fit with what I wanted. It was important for me to know what I was getting into. But there was something good and sincere behind his flirtatious eyes, so I abandoned my cautious behavior and let him lead me into the desolation.

As he walked us toward the boardwalk, I almost laughed out loud. Was this guy serious? He was taking me under the boardwalk? I mean, sure, anybody who grew up around the shore has spent plenty of time fooling around under there. But that was high school, dude. Maybe college if you were really drunk. My days of getting busy under the boardwalk were long over. I tried to pull my arm from his.

"Uh, Reed, I think you have the wrong idea about me." A few beautiful songs were not a direct map into my pants.

"I don't think I do, Jolie." He tightened his elbow, so my arm was not released from his. He walked us a few more feet and somewhere behind him, a light flickered. "I said trust me. You won't be disappointed."

I was intrigued enough to agree. I followed him again, until I could make out the light. It came from a lantern, inside a tent, under the boardwalk. Reed let me go, and extended his hand to invite me inside.

I leaned over to take a peek. A plush blue blanket covered the floor of the tent. A plate of cheese and a loaf of French bread sat next to the lantern and a bottle of wine with two glasses waited for us. An instrument in its case lined the back of the tent.

"Nice." I nodded, downplaying the impressive sight. This took some time.

"I figured you already ate, so we'd go light." He motioned toward the cheese.

I climbed in and tucked my legs under me. There wasn't much room, with the way he spread everything out. Reed sat across from me, crossing his long legs in front. He tore off a piece of the bread and smeared brie on it with a knife. He handed it to me.

"So." He poured me a glass of wine.

"So." I took a slow bite of my cheese. I'd never been out with someone whose name I didn't even know. This was unchartered territory.

We spent a few moments taking in each other. His blue eyes gleamed. This was the first time I'd seen him out of his work clothes. In his tight black T-shirt and sweat shorts, the shadows bounced off his muscles. The lantern light flattered him. Then again, I assumed most light flattered him. I wondered if the lamp on my nightstand would, too. I chuckled at the thought.

"What?" he asked.

"Huh? Nothing." I took a sip of wine to hide my blush. He lifted his glass at the same time and took a gulp.

"Ugh! This is terrible," he groaned. My reaction was slightly more subdued.

I laughed. It was terrible. It must have been the worst wine I'd ever had—and I drank wine out of a box in college.

"Sorry. I don't know anything about Bordeaux." He lifted the bottle to examine it. "They should label this *Shit*."

I laughed again. "Why did you get it?"

He shoved a piece of cheese in his mouth to mask the taste. "It went with the theme." He swiped his hand over the spread.

The brie, the bread, the wine. "It's all French?"

"Like you, right?"

My hand paused mid-air as I lifted my glass again. "How did you know?"

"Well again"—he winced when he took another sip—"your grandmother. Plus the whole crepe thing, and you call her Mamie."

"How very perceptive of you. You should be a private investigator or something."

"Nah, I only pay attention to things that interest me."

I took a drink and chased it with the cheese, which made it more palatable.

"This wine doesn't even deserve glasses. We should drink it right from the bottle," he joked.

"I'm fine with that." I put the bottle to my mouth and dared to take a slug. Each swallow burned a little less. "Anyway, I'm French on my father's side. His grandparents were immigrants and Mamie was born nine months after they got here. They kept a French household and they visited France a lot, which is why Mamie knows about the food and customs. She taught me all of it." I took one more gulp before handing Reed the bottle. My head was already a little fuzzy, since I didn't drink often. I didn't like anything that caused my behavior to shift too drastically.

"You seem very close to her," he said after a slug.

"How can you tell?"

"I don't know." He leaned back on his elbows and his shirt pulled tighter. "The way you talk to each other. Or maybe how you pass looks back and forth like you're speaking with silence. It's sweet."

"You got that all from one glass of iced tea?"

"Like I said"—he licked some brie off his thumb—"I pay attention to what interests me."

I fought a blush. "Well, she's my Mamie." She was also my mom, my dad, my sibling, my best friend. I didn't know what I'd do without her.

"She's your Mamie," he repeated, like he heard the other words I didn't speak. "Do you have any other family?"

"Some," I answered, but I'd already disclosed more about my family than normal. "Are you an expert camper or something?"

"Absolutely not. I borrow this from my cousin sometimes. I just thought it would be different, and maybe earn me a couple of points."

"It did," I said. "I was more impressed than I think I let on."

"Good. Then it was worth jabbing myself in the toe when I was trying to stake it into the ground. Apparently it's a lot harder to stake a tent into sand than grass."

We passed the wine between us as we talked. Reed worked in a music store not far from my shop. He was taught by his dad, and could play most common instruments to some degree. His favorite was the saxophone.

"There's a soul in a sax that I don't think you hear in most other instruments," he said.

I had a definite buzz now and I could almost see

notes coming from his lips when he spoke.

"I brought mine to play something for you, in case you wanted to hear. Do you?"

I nodded too vigorously. "Of course."

He grabbed the case from the back of the tent, unzipped it and pulled out the instrument. The brass shined like it had recently been polished, but it was marred by a number of scratches and a small ding on the bell: a term I'd learned online after Reed left me my second song. He caught me inspecting it.

"My dad gave me this when I turned thirteen. He thought I had a knack for it. This baby's been through a lot with me. She may be beaten up, but she plays as well as the day I got her." He ran his hand down its length like it was a treasure. To him, I'd bet it was. "This is what I decided not to leave for you on the napkin. I wasn't sure I wanted to give it away, if you weren't going to show."

He played a slow, beautiful tune filled with sorrow. Its notes reached into my chest and yanked hard. I wanted him to play it forever, but I also wanted him to stop because it broke my heart.

When he finished, he rested his saxophone in his lap and waited for me to respond.

"That was incredible. I've never heard anything like it before. It was so sad."

"So was I. I could tell you two hadn't been together long, because that guy was too tentative, but I thought that by playing around for these couple of weeks, I might have missed my opportunity. I'm glad I didn't."

"Why?"

"Why what?"

"Why are you glad? Why would it have made you

sad if I weren't available? You don't even know me." It sounded like I was fishing for compliments, but it was the wine talking. Why would he care so much about me when we hadn't spoken for more than two minutes?

He looked down at the cheese, losing his cocky air for a second. Then he found himself as he regained his confidence. "A bunch of reasons. Your smile, for one."

"What are the others?"

Half of his mouth lifted. "Nah. Later for those. Let's focus on that one for now. It may sound unoriginal, but when I see you smile, it's like all the world's problems get shoved away, and there's just you, brightening everyone in your radius. It even seems to erase your own usual seriousness."

"My usual?" From two chance meetings in my store, he could peg my *usual*?

"Maybe I am perceptive after all." He shrugged.

The plate of cheese became blurry as my eyes filled. "My father used to say the force of my smile kept the earth rotating."

The tent grew quiet for a second, aside from the light tap of raindrops dripping on the roof through planks of the boardwalk. Even the ocean seemed to still itself with apology at my comment.

"I'm sorry." Reed's voice was as gentle as the rain.

"For what?" I asked.

"For the *used to*."

I blinked a few times to clear my eyes and sat in realization of what I just said. I mentioned my father. Out loud. To a stranger. Damn cheap wine and tolerance of a fifteen-year-old girl.

"No worries," I brushed it off. "Can you play something else?"

"Sure." He took my cue to let it go. "What would you like to hear?"

"How about the second song you wrote?"

"I'm not sure I remember it exactly."

I dug into my purse and handed him the napkin. The other one was hiding in there, too, but I didn't need to mention the way I carried them around with me like winning lottery tickets.

He examined it for a second. "Ah, that's right."

He played a song that, from his fingers, sounded even more sensual than when Chase played it. To be fair to Chase, it might have been my reaction to the musician that was different and not the delivery.

My insides thumped with the beats as he wet the mouthpiece with his tongue every so often. He closed his eyes as he played, allowing me to stare at every bit of him for as long as I wanted. Music never had this effect on me before, like the strongest aphrodisiac known to man—er…woman.

Much too soon, but also after an eternity, my song ended. Reed kept his eyes shut for a moment, as if he was coming down from his own music high. When he opened them, the lust from his song had traveled into them. For the first time, he looked at me with desire and not a playful flirtation.

"What do you think?" he asked, cracking some of the energy between us. "Was it too pop-musicish for you?"

My heart pounded and I was embarrassed that I'd mocked his first song. He knew I was teasing him, but in that moment I wondered how I could ever have made light of his music.

"I think…I think…" Words wouldn't come

because I was a little too buzzed and couldn't form a thought, except that I wanted to kiss him. I never made a first move on a guy before but if he didn't do something fast, it might have been a night of some firsts.

He leaned forward. I thought he was going to kiss me but instead he reached for the bottle. He shook it a little. "How about that? It's empty. Must've improved as we drank."

Some of the fire left his eyes, but I was still all crackles inside. When he reached to the side to place his saxophone back in its case, I inconspicuously scooted closer to him. He turned back and gave a small chuckle. "It's cozier over here, huh?"

Maybe I wasn't as slick as I thought. I tried to come up with a witty comeback to reduce my humiliation. I faltered.

He leaned in, letting me know I wouldn't have to answer, or make the first move, after all. He reached up and ran a thumb across my bottom lip. "Smile for me."

Like a pavlovian reflex, my mouth broke out wide.

"Making the earth rotate is an understatement." Then his mouth was over mine. It took a split second for our lips to part and our tongues to dance perfectly to his song still playing in my head. One of his hands threaded through my hair. He laid the other on the small of my back and I visualized his fingers, the way they had depressed the keys on his sax and how strong they were against me. I was in heaven.

This was so much better than dinner and a movie.

After a while, our kisses lost some of their control. Reed's hand found its way underneath the bottom of my blouse. It travel up my back and his fingers, rough from years of playing, sparked every inch of skin he touched. He reached my bra strap and it was no surprise his nimble fingers had it unhooked before my heart beat twice again his chest.

I wanted to keep going, but if I had sex with him in that tent, I'd regret it on my way home in an hour. He'd never see me as anything more than a girl he screwed under the boardwalk on our first date.

And then, there was my device, which I wasn't ready to share with him yet.

"Reed," I breathed into his mouth.

He didn't take his mouth off of mine when he responded. "Say no more." He slid his hand from under my shirt and placed it on my back. He lowered me onto the blanket, laid on his side and kissed me until I dreamt of melodies dancing out of the bell of a sax.

Strips of light woke me. Opening my eyes, I was completely disoriented for a second. I took in the empty wine bottle, the tent, the saxophone, all in a split second.

I was alone in the tent. Where the hell was he? I clutched my head. Holy hangover. My lack of drinking apparently came along with not being able to handle the morning after either. My stomach churned.

When I sat up, my bra sagged off my chest. Other than that, my clothes were unaltered. I clasped it shut and unzipped the tent door. He wouldn't have left me here, would he?

The beach was lit with pinks and oranges of the rising sun. Years before, on the days my dad was agitated, I spent many a morning out there with Tristan admiring the beautiful sunrises from the lifeguard chair.

A jogger strode through the water in the distance,

but there was no sign of Reed, until the uneven pitter patter of water against wood grabbed my attention. A few yards away, back at the beach entrance, he was rinsing himself under the outdoor shower. He was dressed in nothing but maroon boxer briefs, which were soaked and clinging to him. My imagination came up quite lacking when picturing his body.

He pushed his hair back with both hands and wiped the excess water from his face before leaning over to turn off the faucet. When he pulled a towel from a bag I didn't notice the night before, he found me staring at him.

"See what you missed out on?" He shook out his hair with his towel but made sure not to cover any of his body with it. He was infuriating, standing there dripping on purpose.

"Shut up"—I tried to keep my eyes on his face—"and get dressed. You're liable to get arrested."

"Really? You think someone would ask me to put my clothes *on*?"

I rolled my eyes and grunted, but he was right. No one in their right mind would want that.

He wrapped the towel around his waist and laughed. *At* me, I'm sure. I made my way back inside, wondering if I'd still be as resilient if he got dressed in the privacy of this tent, inches from me. But when he entered the tent, he was already dressed and dry, aside from his hair.

Damn.

"I was wondering if you were going to sleep all day." He approached me and gave me a soft kiss on the lips. I felt disgusting, having just woken up in yesterday's clothes, but here he was, clean and dressed and his breath was already minty. How did that happen?

"All day?" I joked, retreating a little to spare myself morning breath embarrassment. "It can't even be six a.m. yet. Even the sun isn't awake. Do you always get up in the middle of the night?"

"I figured we better take this down before people show up. Pitching a tent under the boardwalk isn't exactly legal."

"Why do I think that doesn't matter to you?"

"Why? Do you think I'm a criminal or something?"

I laughed. "No, but you do seem a little mysterious. We talked for hours last night and all I know about you is that you're a wonderful musician."

"All in good time." He cleaned the tent, throwing everything in the bag that held his clothes. I tried to help him, but he moved his bag to the side, out of my reach. So I handled the rest of the stuff. I needed some guidance when we took tent apart. We worked quickly and my mood sank a little when we finished, because that meant my best first date ever was about to end and his speed implied that was exactly what he wanted. He zipped the bag for the tent and slung it over his arm. He lifted his duffel of clothes in one hand and his sax in the other. "Ready?"

"Yep." I wasn't ready to leave him yet. "Can I help you carry something?" I motioned to his bag of clothes and toiletries, but he pulled his arm back.

"Nah, I'm used to it."

We climbed the steps leading to the boardwalk. "Where's your car?" he asked.

"I'm fine. You can leave me here. Maybe I'll go to work early."

"Wearing yesterday's clothes? Your grandmother would have a field day."

He was right. "I'm parked over there." I pointed down the block. "How about you?"

"I'm a couple blocks away."

When we reached my car, I waited for an awkward goodbye. Other than hinting about learning more about him another time, Reed hadn't suggested we get together again. I thought the night was incredible, but it seemed he was looking for an easy hookup.

I unlocked my door with the remote and he reached past me to open it with his already full hand. I began to climb in disappointed at the way this was ending.

"Thanks for last night. It was very thoughtful." I prepared myself for a quick peck goodbye, the kind you get when a guy wants to brush you off without hurting your feelings. That would be the end of my Music Man. The thought bothered me more than it should have.

"It was nothing. Wait 'til you see what I come up with next." He moved into me, with his loaded hands hanging at his sides. He didn't need free hands to pull me into him, because as soon as his mouth planted on mine, I leaned in plenty for both of us. Immediately, I understood that I misinterpreted his speed. I didn't know what the reason was, but it wasn't about making a quick exit.

I breathed easier. "Bye." I put one leg in the car, but he raised his sax to stop me. He dropped his clothing bag and dug inside the instrument case.

"Here. Written while you were sleeping. It's short, but I didn't have much time." Notes, scribbled on last night's cheese wrapper, sat in my palm. "I'll play them for you tonight, if you're free."

"Tonight?" I asked, not because I was being difficult. I was just surprised.

"Jolie, I've never been one to run from risk, but I like to know my odds going in. What's the deal with you and that guy?"

"I'm not sure yet. We just started dating recently."

"Fair enough. Tonight, then?" He kissed my temple as if I already answered.

"Okay, I guess."

"You guess? The same way my song was okay?" He was serious now, waiting for an answer.

"Yes. Okay. I mean, *it* wasn't okay. I'm saying okay," I stumbled. "The song was amazing."

"From okay to amazing, huh?" he teased.

"Ugh, yes, fine, I'll go out with you tonight. Just go." I gave his chest a gentle shove with both of my palms, reminding me of the way he felt against my hands the night before when we kissed.

The night couldn't come fast enough.

Chapter Six
Device: Associate with People Who Are On Time

—I know you're angry and you don't want to talk to me and you have every reason to be, but it's important that I speak to you. I wasn't able to reach Mamie this morning. Please call me back.—

I pressed Delete on my cell before the word *back* ended. She could leave as many voice mails as she wanted. I wasn't answering a single one, even if she did sound nervous this time. She'd tried to reach me enough times, in enough ways, that I knew when I was being manipulated. It wouldn't work. I didn't even know why I listened to the messages. I should have automatically erased them when her number appeared. I must have been a glutton for punishment in some ways.

I did dial Mamie right away, though. I didn't like that my mother said she couldn't reach her. Mamie never screened her, even though she should have. In fact, if I was Mamie and my daughter-in-law took off the way Abby did, I'd never speak to her again. That was one of the many differences between my grandmother and me. Along with her huge personality came an enormous capacity for love. When she was angry with you, she'd rip you a new one, but seconds afterward, she'd squeeze the life out of you and tell you how she'd love you until the day you died. You, of course. She would outlive everyone.

I was the opposite. I wasn't a screamer. I never allowed myself to lose my temper. But I also didn't shower people with affection and I had a difficult time forgiving someone who wronged me. It simply wasn't worth the risk.

Mamie's cell went to voicemail, which concerned me a little. I called her house, but got a punchy recording telling me that if I were a gorgeous bachelor she'd call back right away. Otherwise, she might take her sweet time getting back to me. A few more failed attempts on her cell over the next few minutes left me more concerned.

The first blouse I yanked from a hanger was one I should have thrown away five years before. I didn't care. Mamie was probably in the shower or out getting the mail, but I'd swing by her house on my way to work, to be sure everything was okay.

My cell rang in my purse before I reached my car. My pulse slowed when her number appeared on the screen.

"Where have you been? I've been trying to reach you." It didn't escape me that the tables were turned. I sounded more like the grandmother, now.

"I can see that, my dear. Your number came up a few times here. And yes, I'm well aware of how to check my missed calls."

"Well, where are you?"

The other end was quiet for a second. "I just haven't come home yet, dear."

"Home yet? Home from where?" Where could she have gone so early?

A nervous chuckle came through the other end. Then she whispered. "You're not the only one who dates, you know."

What? Was my grandmother seriously telling me she had a sleepover last night? It was time to hang up. "Uh…okay. Well, do you want me to pick you up somewhere? I can come get you on my way to the shop."

Her answer was a rush of *no*s. "I'll find my own way home, Jolie. You go take care of that business of ours. But I might not be in today, if you don't mind. I have to, uh, well, I have some things left here that I need to take care of, if you understand what I'm saying."

Holy hell, I did not want to understand what she was saying. Yet, she was being very quick and evasive. My grandmother didn't make apologies for anything, including her dating life, so I didn't know why she'd be in such a hurry to get rid of me.

"Okay, Mamie, call me later so I know you got home all right. Okay?"

"Sure thing, baby girl. Love you." She was gone.

Without the urgency to make a pit stop, I had more time before heading out. Walking back inside, I gaped at my reflection in the full-length mirror in my bedroom. Not only was the blouse I threw on too tight in the chest but I missed a button and the whole shirt was crooked. I used to love this blouse. It cut me in all flattering places and made my waist look tiny. I'd stopped wearing it a number of years earlier when my boobs and hips discovered that I was no longer a teenager. They may have been late to the party, but they sure made up for it.

Unbuttoning the blouse, I allowed myself to imagine Reed watching me, with it pulling a little too much on the chest, and just enough cleavage that it bordered on inappropriate. Would he be dying to get a glimpse of what was under that second button, which was fastened so precariously he could blow on it to get it to pop open? I examined myself the way he might, taking his time to undo one button at a time, until I stood in front of the mirror in my open blouse and push up bra. I ran my hand over my stomach and closed my eyes.

A click from my cell brought me back to reality and for a second I was embarrassed about where my mind was about to go. I picked up my phone.

—I have another answer to your question.—

Seeing it was a text from Reed made me find myself in the mirror again and wonder if I could get away with that blouse.

*—What question is that?—*I texted back.

—Why you?—

My stomach rippled.

—Okay?—

—I love that you drank that horrible wine straight out of the bottle with me.—

Yuck.

—That's what you like about me? That I can binge drink like a wino?—

The speech bubbles drove me insane as I waited for him to finish typing.

—Nope. I like that you were comfortable with me and didn't stand on ceremony. No need to pretend. Just be real.—

I stared at the text for a second, not sure what kind of response to send. I wasn't exactly ready to be real with him yet. Real in my family came with a little too much reality.

He shot off another before I could answer.

—*Well, that and I couldn't stop staring at the way your lips surrounded that bottle. Exhilarating ;)*—

I laughed out loud at the way he went from open to suggestive in a split second. I was more comfortable with playful, anyway.

—*It was, was it? Well, maybe you should bring another bottle from the clearance rack tonight and we can try again.*—

The next text blasted right back.

—*Maybe tonight we don't need a bottle…*—

Shit. I gulped hard. I didn't know if he was serious or kidding. More importantly, I didn't know if I was serious or kidding, either. I had to stick to my devices…including the inconvenient ones, because if I didn't…

Maybe I could bend them a little.

—*Tonight seems very far away.*—

There. I was playing without promising. Nothing wrong with that.

—*Good things come to those who wait. I'll pick you up at 9.*—

The day swept by in a blur and it was three before I realized I never heard from Mamie. Her phone rang a single time before she picked up. "Hello there. How's business today?" She sounded out of breath but I wouldn't let my mind search for a reason.

"Why didn't you call when you got home?"

"I'm sorry, dear. It must have slipped my mind."

I didn't believe her. Nothing slipped her mind. Especially not checking in with me after knowing I had a date last night. She just didn't know I had two.

"What's going on with you today?"

"Nothing. I was up late and I'm tired today, I guess. Nothing to worry about, darling. I promise."

Hearing her tell me not to worry had the opposite effect, because her voice lacked expression and she sounded fatigued. Even if she had been with a man, it's not like she was out clubbing. Why was she so tired?

"I think I'm going to swing by to see you tonight, Mamie. After I close up."

"Now why would you do that, Jolie? I'm sure you have better things planned. Speaking of which, how was Brett last night? Or did you wind up spending the evening with your admirer?"

I almost lied, because who starts a night with one guy and then spends the night with another? But she'd see through my lie, and I was bursting to tell her anyway. I shared the details about the wine, the tent, my songs. When I told her I was seeing him again later, I expected a strong reaction one way or the other. I didn't expect her to like him, because he wasn't the usual pillar of stability I usually dated, but I knew she thought he was gorgeous, so that might have garnered some enthusiasm.

Yet, when I finished my story, she said nothing. "Mamie? Did you hear what I said?"

"Oh, yes Jolie. That's very nice dear." Her low voice was almost inaudible through the receiver.

"I'll be by after I close up. I don't want to hear another word about it."

She didn't fight me, and that concerned me more than anything. I picked at some loose skin around my finger.

****

—*How are you feeling?*—

Brett's text came through around dinnertime and before I could remember why he was asking, another appeared.

—*Is your stomach better?*—

This guy was too nice and if I'd met him sooner, things might have been different. But I thought of nothing but Reed the entire day and stringing Brett along would be unfair, so I called him.

"It's that guy who came into the store yesterday, right?"

"How did you know?" I didn't mention another guy, I just gave him a version of the *it's not you it's me* horrible line.

"I knew the second I saw him look at you, Jolie, but I didn't know if it was mutual."

"I'm sorry, Brett, but yeah, it's him."

He understood and wished me well. He behaved just as I expected, making me question whether picking a man who was as unpredictable as he was handsome was really wise.

Wise or not, I started watching the clock at eight-thirty. Sneaking to the back, I primped just enough to look fresh. I did end up wearing the favorite blouse, but stuck a camisole underneath, so I could open the buttons that pulled the most. I gave the ladies a good hoist, and waited for Reed to make his appearance.

When he didn't walk through the door at nine, an all-too familiar anxiety found its way into my chest. I found the pinkie I'd picked at earlier and worked the skin with my pointer and thumb. When I pulled a little too hard and tore a piece of skin that was still very much attached, I reminded myself that this was Reed, not my father, and certainly not my brother. If Reed didn't show it was no big deal. But by nine-fifteen, sensible thoughts disappeared and an itchy hive behind my ear took their place. I promised myself that if he didn't show in the next ten minutes, I wouldn't see him again. That was a device I couldn't break. I would not be with a guy I couldn't rely on. I refused to do that to myself.

Two minutes later, he strode in looking gorgeous and carefree, in another T-shirt and shorts. Of course he was carefree. He didn't know about my irrational fear of people disappearing, or any of the other red flags I watched for on a constant basis.

And he wouldn't.

He strutted across my store, pinning me into place with his stare. When he reached the counter, he leaned over, palmed the back of my head, and pulled me to him for a solid kiss on the mouth. As if I was his to claim. I couldn't decide if his presumptuous behavior pissed me off or melted me into a puddle.

Maybe a little of both.

"You're late." I pulled back. If I made like I was *pretending* to be pissed, maybe I could get my need for punctuality across without cluing him in on the crazy behind it.

"Am I?" He spun, looking for a clock. "Sorry. Had to finish this." He handed me a single yellow tulip, wrapped in a piece of paper, which was a bit crumpled. Unfolding it, I inspected the notes.

"Are you hiding your sax somewhere?" I lifted the tulip to my nose and inhaled, letting its scent bring me back to the present where there was a regular guy giving a regular girl a flower.

"Nope. I thought we could go by my job tonight, since you gave me all that grief about not knowing anything about me." He lowered my hand from in front of my face. "Better?"

"Your job?"

"The music store where I work. I can play for you there."

Ah. A piece to the puzzle that was this man.

"I'd love to see your store, but do you mind if we stop somewhere first?" A little dirt fell on the counter and, reflexively, I wiped it with a napkin. When another glob fell, I found its source. The stem of my tulip was jagged. Tiny bits of soil clung to its end.

I laughed. "Did you pick this?"

He blushed. "I wanted to do something clever with the song. I noticed the flowers on the way here. It seems I didn't clean it off very well." He wrinkled his nose and rubbed the muscles on his forearm.

"I like embarrassed on you. It looks good."

"You do, huh?" He reached for the tie of my apron and twirled it between his thumb and forefinger, immediately discarding all signs of discomfort. "How about your other guy? Does it look good on him, too?"

I shrugged. "Don't know. He's gone."

He tugged at the tie a little, bringing me toward him, though the counter still separated us. "Well that didn't take long. I must be quite the catch."

I definitely revealed that too soon. Way to put all the *balls* in his court. I shook my head. "Nah, I just like really cheap wine."

He chuckled and his shirt pulled on his pecs. "So where are we going?"

On the drive to Mamie's, Reed talked about his job

73

at Strings, a music store a short distance from the boardwalk. He hadn't worked there long, under a year.

"My boss has a bunch of people working for him, so our hours are limited." He played with the channels on my radio, searching for something he found acceptable. "I thought you said you have great taste in music." He scoffed at my saved stations.

"I've got satellite, too."

After he found an older rock song and tapped his fingers to the beat, he asked more about why we were going to see Mamie.

"I didn't like the way she sounded today. Something's off."

"Why? Was she quiet?"

His earnest expression gave no hint to whether he was serious or kidding.

"Actually, yes, how did you know?"

"Because I've never seen her reserved, so I figured that would be out of the ordinary."

I didn't understand how he was so spot-on after only seeing her a couple of times in my store. I mean, sure, it took less than one introduction to assess her, but the way he spoke about her, it felt like more than that. I squinted at him, trying to figure out what was going on in his head. He faced front, avoiding my pointed glare.

"Better get your eyes back on the road before you kill us, gorgeous." He smirked without turning his head.

I grunted and shoved his shoulder with my palm.

Mamie was wearing a nightgown when we arrived, which sent up another warning signal in my head. Yes, it was night, but she knew I was coming. "Well now, Jolie, if you told me you were bringing this fine man by I wouldn't be in my unmentionables." She swatted me with one hand while holding the door open with the other. "Come in."

I may have been overly concerned about watching for signals and I may have even been the word I couldn't stomach—paranoid—sometimes. But I recognized when two people knew each other. The way Reed stood in my grandmother's doorway wasn't the way a person stood when he was meeting a stranger. A look of familiarity crossed between them. Morgan told me Reed had been at Stuff Your Crepes before, but so had a million other people. Why would these two remember each other?

"Mamie, this is Reed. He was nice enough to volunteer to come with me and check out your sorry ass tonight."

Reed lifted my grandmother's hand and gave it a gentle kiss before walking into her living room.

"Well, he can check out any part of my ass he wants." She gave his hand a squeeze before allowing Reed to release it from his kiss. "The good Lord certainly blessed you five times over, didn't he?"

Reed's cheeks flushed for the second time that night. "Thank you, Ma'am."

This earned Reed a swat harder than the one I received, and a scowl that would send a lesser man running scared. "Ma'am is for old ladies and southern belles. I've never been south of the Mason-Dixon line, so I know I'm no southern belle. So that leaves old lady." Her eyes narrowed into tiny slits. "Do I look like an old lady to you, Reed?"

He shook his head. "No, ma…" He chuckled at his near miss. "No."

"Good." Her flirty grandma aura returned. "Then

call me Mamie."

Without asking if we'd like anything, she served us coffee thicker than dirt, and some homemade pastries. No matter how many times I tried it, I never acquired a taste for her coffee. I sipped it every so often and blanched at its bitter flavor, but Reed practically downed it in one gulp, pleasing Mamie to no end. He feasted on her pastries, commenting on how delicious each one tasted. Even if it wasn't his intention, he gained lots of brownie points with my grandmother.

While she stuffed Reed to the brim, she planted herself on the couch next to him and they chatted like I wasn't in the room. It was clear Mamie was enamored with Reed, as he devoured each of her stories with undivided attention. She held his hand in one of hers and tapped it with the other when she wanted to make a point she thought was crucial. The way he was so sweet with her didn't just earn points with Mamie. He racked them up with me, too. Big-time. I couldn't wait to leave and spend some time alone with him.

Unlike with Brett, Mamie didn't ask about his job, but she did shoot him a pretty pointed question about his sex life. Reed handled it well, only swallowing his tongue halfway before laughing it off like she was joking. She wasn't. She waited expectantly for an answer.

He deflected the question like a professional. "I'm sure a woman as beautiful as you has a torrid story or two to share." Reed flashed her one of his most mesmerizing smirks.

"Oh hush," she countered, pretending he was out of line, but the pale pink blush across her milky cheeks told Reed she was flattered. Then she told us about a boy she dated before she met my grandfather and how they used to make out on the park bench for hours, but she wouldn't let him go any farther than second base. Hearing my grandmother talk about running the bases was more than I was interested in, so I strolled into the kitchen to get myself something tolerable to drink.

When I emerged with a can of soda, Mamie had her hand on Reed's cheek. Her mouth retreated from his ear.

Reed's furrowed brows and pensive, downcast stare made me pause in the doorway. The interaction reminded me of the way she used to speak to my father when he needed someone to soothe him. And then to my brother. My face heated and my pulse raced.

"What are we talking about?" It came out sharp, like I was accusing them of something.

My voice startled Mamie and she pulled her hand away from Reed's face. When Reed's eyes met mine, they were filled with guilt. What could Mamie have said to make him guilty?

"Nothing, dear. Just giving Mr. Stud here some pointers on how to please you." She winked. Reed released a soft cough.

Shriveling up to die at that moment sounded like a good option, but instead I dropped my head, rolled my eyes, and covered them with my hand. "My God, Mamie." But I knew that wasn't what they were talking about, because Reed didn't look mortified. He looked like he got caught with his hand in the cookie jar.

"I'm afraid I've stolen your entire evening, kids." She moved on as if she didn't just mention pleasuring me to my brand new, ridiculously hot Music Man. "You should be on your way to enjoy what's left of the night."

I picked up my bag, but Mamie grabbed my arm and pulled me aside. "We need to speak tomorrow."

"Okay?" We spoke every day. Why was she saying this?

"I talked to your mother today. There are some things we need to discuss."

I jerked my arm from her harder than I meant to and took two steps toward the door. "I'm leaving now, Mamie."

"It's about Tristan."

I froze with my back to her. A steel rod bolted into my spine and my mouth went dry. "What about him?" I stared at the stained glass window on her door. Every time my brother's name was mentioned, I prepared myself for the worst. For the one piece of information I couldn't handle.

I prepared myself to hear that he was dead.

"He called her yesterday. We'll talk about it tomorrow."

The rigidity left me and all at once I felt like mush. It happened every time. Fear, then overbearing relief. I just knew one day the relief wouldn't come.

"Fine," I snapped and grasped the doorknob. Now I didn't want to leave. I wanted to stay and hear the news. We hadn't heard from him in so long. But I also wanted to run. Run and not hear about him. It was easier to pretend that he was somewhere safe and happy that way. I had to get away from her.

I yanked the door open and flew out, letting Reed trail behind. I needed to be outside, I needed to breathe. I managed to get a few steps away from her house before I hunched over, bracing myself with my hands on my knees and gasping shallow breaths. It seemed that Tristan's name alone could knock the wind out of me.

Reed's hand was on my back as soon as I leaned over. "Are you okay?"

Instead of answering, I attacked a counter-defense. "You can't be late," I snapped through clipped breaths, still trying to find enough air. "If you say you're coming at a certain time, you have to be there on time."

"I was only a few minutes late, Jolie." His words were defensive, but his tone soothing as his hand traced circles over my back.

"You have to be there on time!" I demanded, embarrassed as soon as the words left my mouth. I was chastising this guy for being a few minutes late on a second date. This was not normal. I never revealed my weaknesses this way. What was it that made me show him the things I worked so hard to keep hidden?

He stopped rubbing my back, a sign that he'd leave. Who would want to deal with drama this early on? I braced myself for him to leave me there. Instead, he dropped his pack on the floor and knelt in front of me while I panted. He took my cheeks between his palms and lifted my face to his.

"Okay." His voice was a strong whisper. "I'll be on time from now on. I promise. Just breathe, okay?" He touched his lips to mine, so that my heavy, coarse breaths went directly into him. I closed my eyes and concentrated on inhaling. The connection slowed my breathing and allowed me to find more air than any brown paper bag ever could. He held me in place and didn't allow me to take my mouth away from his until my breathing was deep and steady. Then he released my face and we stood.

I couldn't look at him. I just had all the makings of a panic attack, right in front of this guy who probably only wanted to have some fun. I stared at the concrete by my feet. "I can drive you home now," I said, more to the ground than to Reed.

"Home? Why?"

"Well…" What could I say? Wasn't it obvious? "I don't think this was really part of the plan."

He took the ends of my hair, right below my chin, and ran them between his fingers. "My plan was to spend time with you. I'd love for you to tell me what that was all about. If you don't want to yet, that's fine, but if you'll let me, I still want to be with you."

Any trace of arrogance was gone. Now Reed was just a beautiful, concerned guy.

"You still want to go to your store?"

He pushed my hair away from my face. "I think maybe we should get you home so you can rest. We can do the store another time."

I nodded. He flung his pack over his shoulder and took my hand. As we walked to my car, I shot a glance over my shoulder to find Mamie watching from the window.

We drove to my apartment in silence. I knew he was waiting for me to tell him why I got so upset, but I had to work through it in my head first. A mere second of hearing Tristan's name set me off, but it often took days for me to come back.

Reed made himself comfortable on my couch as I ransacked my kitchen searching for anything to serve. I didn't have any alcohol, which would have been useful at the moment. I wasn't much of a snacker either. When

I set two water bottles and a bag of trail mix on the table, he reached for me.

"Come here." He took my arm and pulled me toward him. Then he eased my shoulders down so I was sitting in his lap, straddling him. "Tell me."

"Tell you what?" It was such an obvious stall tactic I would have laughed if I weren't so sad and embarrassed.

"Jolie." He watched me and waited for me to speak with that same expression he wore the first time he spoke—as if he already understood me. It made no sense. It was impossible, but it made me want to open up to him in ways I never did with anyone else.

"You must think I'm..."

"Crazy?" He chuckled.

That word. That word that I despised, that struck my last nerve. "No, not crazy." I stood from his lap, but he was too fast. He held my hips in place until I sat back down on him of my own accord.

"Okay, not crazy," he said once I was back where he wanted me. "How about stunningly beautiful?" He kissed my lips tenderly.

"I'll take that one."

"So do you want to tell me now?"

"I thought you said I didn't have to," I said, but, oddly, part of me hoped he'd push.

"You don't." He brought his face away from mine and waited for me to lead the conversation. He wouldn't shy away from the topic. If I didn't want to talk about it, I'd have to change the subject. For the first time, I wanted to discuss Tristan with someone other than Mamie.

"My brother is sick." I couldn't look Reed in the

face. Instead, I found a small chocolate stain on his shirt that he must have gotten from one of Mamie's pastries, and traced over it with my pointer. "He's got"—I hadn't spoken the word in so long I didn't know if it would still fall from my lips—"schizophrenia."

Reed sighed against my finger. "I'm so sorry, Jolie."

"He was diagnosed at nineteen as soon as he started exhibiting symptoms. We knew what to watch for because, well, because my father had it too."

He took my hand and brought my fingers to his lips, holding them there. I fought to keep the tears from my eyes. I'd already broken down once tonight. I didn't plan on doing it again.

"He tried a couple of different medications, but we'd watched my father struggle through the tics and dosage adjustments too many times. Tristan didn't want to put us through that. A couple months after my father died, he took off. We hardly ever heard from him. Most of the time, I don't know if he's alive or dead."

It was no use. The tears refused to be hidden. They welled in my eyes and spilled out before I could stop them.

Reed kissed my cheeks where they fell and rolled his lips in, as if he was willing the weight of my tears onto himself. There was so much more to the story, but that was enough for one night. Enough to explain why I reacted to Tristan's name the way I did.

"Is that why you do those things? For the homeless?"

He knew that, too? I had to remind myself that we were on TV. He was talking about my token jar.

I nodded with our faces inches apart. "I know for a

fact that Tristan has lived on the streets from time to time. He might be right now, I have no idea. I guess it's just my way of hoping it gets paid forward, you know? I suppose I do this for the worried families as much as the homeless people themselves.

Reed leaned in the tiny bit it took for our mouths to touch and kissed me again. My tears were still salty on his lips and when they parted, our kisses were slow and tender. Vulnerable even. Though I was the one who divulged part of myself, it felt like Reed was the one opening up. It was a connection I'd never experienced before in a kiss.

"You're incredible, Jolie," he told me with his forehead against mine. "I think you should call your grandmother now."

"What?" I pulled my head off of his. I was not expecting that.

"You need to find out where your brother is." His voice had regained the silkiness from when we first met.

"I'm sure Mamie's asleep. She was exhausted today."

"I'm sure she's not. Did you see the way she tracked our every move when we were outside of her house?"

Chapter Seven
Device: Five Dates

Mamie didn't know where Tristan was, and my mother didn't either. All my mother knew was that Tristan called her, frantic. He'd seen something on television that set him off and he was positive someone was after him. My mother tried to calm him, the way she always did with my father. She reminded him that that was why he wasn't supposed to watch a lot of TV or go online much. Crime shows and horror stories had a way of triggering his anxiety, especially if he wasn't taking his meds, which by the sound of the conversation, he wasn't. Over the phone it was much harder to soothe him, especially when he was distraught and not speaking coherently.

She did get enough out of him to know he was okay for the time being. He talked about a friend he was staying with, so hopefully he was safe. We lived in constant fear that he would hurt himself, though. When my mother pressed him for information about where he was, he said something about the line being tapped and hung up.

Mamie told me everything slowly, wanting to break it gently, but I was okay. This little bit of information was better than nothing. I was relieved he wasn't harmed. Even though it pained me to know he was agitated and in a bad state, he was alive.

"Thank you for making me call her," I said to Reed after I hung up. "You were right, I needed to know what he said."

"I find the unknown is usually worse than reality." He took the phone and put it aside, halting me by laying his hands on my shoulders. I hadn't realized I'd been pacing.

He was wrong. That wasn't true. "Not when you know what the reality might be," I countered.

He nodded. "You're right. I'm sorry. I shouldn't talk about what I don't know." He twirled the ends of my hair again. It was cute and sexy at the same time. I could get used to it.

"Don't be sorry. You've helped me more tonight that you could know, Reed. How do you do that?"

"Do what?" He released my hair and trailed one finger down my jaw, stopping at my chin and working its way up again. Then he ran his entire hand along my neck. I tilted my head to the side and closed my eyes.

"Make me so comfortable telling you things. As if you already know me."

His hand stopped abruptly, causing me to open my eyes and lift my head.

"What?" I asked.

"I guess it's just one of my many gifts." His eyes gleamed, but what he didn't realize was I saw his expression a second before he cloaked it. It was the same one he gave Mamie earlier.

I didn't have much time to analyze it though, because within seconds, his mouth pressed into mine, he was leaning me back into the wall and I had no doubt that getting me to confide in him wasn't his only gift.

His kisses started slow but strong and probably would have stayed that way for a while if mine hadn't grown hungrier. Remembering how he looked standing under that shower on the boardwalk had me moving too quickly. My hands roamed his body, and even over his clothes, his muscles rippled, making me want more. He let me lead for a while, but when my hands found their way into the back pockets of his shorts and squeezed, he groaned in my mouth and pressed his hips into me.

His hands explored the curves of my body in return, less gently than last time. I wanted to feel his strength. The strength masked by compassion when I couldn't breathe, but I knew was under the surface. Now, every inch of him felt amazing against me. Powerful. I wanted him.

But.

His mouth teased my jaw and neck, weakening my resolve with every second that passed. When he took my earlobe between his teeth and sucked, I barely got the words out.

"Five date rule." Again, my breaths were clipped, but for a completely different reason.

"What?" He released his grip.

"I have a five date rule." My tone was shaky. Maybe I was questioning myself.

"For sex," he purred into my ear, more to explain to himself than to question me.

"Yes," I sighed, trying not to focus on what his tongue was doing to my skin.

I used the word rule instead of device because it sounded more acceptable and less like psychological mumbo-jumbo. The devices were, in fact, suggested to me by the psychologist I saw after my father's death.

Her intention, however, was not for me to dictate my life by them; it was to help me deal with my loss. She wouldn't be happy to know I abused them.

Five dates was a lot. I knew that. I didn't know anyone who really waited that long. But the way I figured it, five dates was, on average, just over a month. Anything less than a month and you couldn't really tell if a guy was going to be dependable or not. Even at five dates, guys are still putting their best selves forward.

As I answered, I recalculated in my mind. Normally, a first date was only a few hours long. Ours was all night, so maybe that could count as two. Plus, technically, each of the times he came by the store was to see me, and he left me notes, so I could have counted those. Maybe we'd already reached our date quota after all. Every nerve ending in my body told me we had. I drew him closer, but at the same time he pulled his hips back, allowing air between me and the wall.

"Okay," he whispered, to my surprise. His mouth was so assertive, I thought maybe he'd try to be a little more persuasive. I was disappointed, but I didn't want to seem like I was giving mixed messages, so I let him retreat.

His body did but his mouth didn't. He continued working my neck like he was savoring every bit of a meal. He spent time biting and tasting each spot, only moving so he didn't mark me. I tilted my head against the wall. He moved to the front of my throat, tongue and teeth exploring my skin. When he trailed down to my sternum, his tongue shot electricity through my veins.

"Okay?" I questioned, because he showed no sign of finishing his tasting menu and at that point, the more courses the better.

"Yes," he breathed into my throat. "That doesn't mean I have to stop doing this, though, does it?" He bit on my neck, harder than before and I felt it everywhere. I almost said screw the rule and stripped him down right there, but I was already bending my other rules with him. I had to have something to hold onto, even if everything inside me screamed to let go.

I suppose I didn't have any idea what I wanted in that moment. My thoughts were all mixed up, like jumbled letters in a word puzzle. You know all the pieces are there, you just can't figure out what order they should be in.

"No," I answered. It sounded like a plea.

He had me pressed into the wall again, with our bodies flush against each other. It would have been incredible if it weren't such torture.

"You're killing me," I sighed into the air before I realized what I was going to say. As I wrapped a leg around him, I had the sweeping thought that being murdered might be preferable to the line I'd drawn, which he was frustratingly respecting.

"Just following your rules, Jolie."

"My rules," I sighed as he took a bit of my skin, to the side of my shoulder, in his teeth. It sent a thousand watt volt right through me. I wished to God I didn't have a need for so many rules.

Then he gave me one last kiss, as light and soft as a downy pillow, untangled himself from my grasp and backed off.

"Goodbye, Jolie." The air between us was suddenly cool from the loss of contact.

I was all tingles and shivers. They must have been

fogging up my brain. Did he say goodbye?

"Goodbye? What are you doing?" I was dumbfounded.

He shot me that cocky grin that made me want to slap him and mount him at the same time. He knew exactly what he just did to me. I must have looked like a pile of goo, sagging toward the floor.

"Insuring that I get to date five." He grabbed his backpack and walked out my door.

Chapter Eight
Device: Avoid Arguments

I decided to take a few days off from Reed. Though it was the last thing I wanted to do, I figured it was for the best. So even though he requested a third date the day after our second, I postponed, joking that he was trying to rush through the dates to get to number five. I hoped I was wrong.

Either way, I was having a hard time staying grounded, which made me a little leery of seeing him again. When I was around him, I felt like I was flying, which for someone like me, could be as terrifying as it was exhilarating. A little distance was a good thing.

I kept busy. There was no shortage of work at the shop, and Morgan had started seeing someone, which filled the hours with girly conversations. She talked about her new guy a little more than necessary. It seemed pretty coincidental that, all of a sudden she was so into someone she just met right after Chase mentioned being attracted to her friend. I kept my yap shut. I wasn't clambering down that road with her again.

I looked forward to her arrival so I could hear her daily report. When she walked in disheveled, though, it was clear her new crush wouldn't be the topic of conversation.

"Holy cow, Jolie. The streets are mobbed and

crawling with cops. Did you see?"

I'd been inside all day, with my limited view of the boardwalk. I hadn't noticed a thing. "No. What is it?"

"Another stabbing in the park. Homeless guy again. People are spilling over into the streets, blocks away from where it happened, trying to figure out what's going on." She smoothed her blonde, wavy hair and tied it back. "I practically had to push past them to get to the boardwalk."

A lump the size of a softball wedged in my throat. "Did they say who it was?"

"I don't know," she said as she washed her hands. "All I know is people are upset. It's scary, really. It's broad daylight."

Broad daylight. Another homeless person stabbed. What was happening? I clicked on the local news channel, but they were reporting the record high temperatures. Who cared about the weather? A person was hurt. Where were their priorities?

Frustrated, I shut the TV. I fought with the strings of my apron for a second before they came loose. I tossed the apron aside.

"I'll be right back."

"Where are you going?" Morgan asked, replenishing the mushroom bin.

"I want to find out who it was."

"Jolie," she warned and I faced her. "You won't get anywhere near the park. There are people everywhere."

"Even if there weren't, you'd have to crawl over my rotted, stiff corpse to get there." Mamie's voice cut through the small restaurant. I'm sure my customers loved the visual of an old lady's dead body while they were trying to eat. Very appetizing.

"I just…" I knew it was futile to argue this. It was my corpse she'd be handing over if I tried to go. "Never mind. Hello, Mamie." I walked to my grandmother and planted a kiss on her cheek in peace offering. She'd won. I wasn't going to the park. Not at that moment anyway, but soon I'd have to make sure it wasn't one of the guys I knew.

Mamie grunted at my kiss as she gave me her cheek. "Of all the stupid things. You think you're just going to walk onto a crime scene?"

"I'm not going, Mamie."

"Damn right, you're not, but you would have if I didn't walk in."

I allowed her to chastise me a little more, because she was right.

"It's gorgeous out today," I changed the subject. "Lunch should be crazy."

"Nice transition." Mamie scowled. Her customer was a child who asked for "mounds and mounds of whipped cream" on her Strawberry Shortcrepe, and Mamie scraped the last of the strawberries from the plastic tub. "Morgan," she called to the back. "Would you be a dear and get me a refill of…" She paused and stared at the tub for a moment. "Never mind, I'll get it myself." She turned to the girl. "I'm going to refill this and get you some extra whipped cream. I'll be right back, darling."

She came out with a full tub of strawberries, a vat of whipped cream and Morgan at her heels.

"I would have gotten it for you, Mamie. I was just putting some supplies away."

"I'm perfectly capable of doing things for myself.

92

Being a senior is not the same as being an invalid." Mamie spooned a heaping dollop of whipped cream on top of the crepe and handed it to the girl.

Morgan didn't argue.

Instead, she frowned when the chimes went off and the door opened.

Reed wore his polo work shirt and khakis, with his signature backpack over his shoulder. He carried that everywhere he went, making me curious about what was in there that was so important.

"Hey, babe," he called from the back of my line, which was three people deep.

Babe? We were at babe already? He was way too presumptuous. Why did I like it so much?

I blushed behind the counter. "Hey, Reed."

Mamie asked to help the next customer, but not surprisingly, Reed waited for me. He waved a customer behind him over to Mamie's line. When it was his turn, he leaned over the counter and kissed me. "I'm starving. What's good today?"

"Well, excuse me, sir," I teased in my fakest customer service voice with my hands planted on my hips. "Are you implying that I might offer items that are not tasty every day?"

He leaned in, placed his lips against my ear and lowered his voice an octave. "Oh no, babe, I'm sure everything you're offering is very tasty, but I'm talking about what's on the menu."

Flames lit my cheeks and I couldn't even look at him, so I kept my head fixed at the counter and giggled. "What do you want? I mean, what crepe do you want?" I shook my head at my own lack of game. He watched me squirm, enjoying my discomfort yet again.

Morgan cleared her throat behind me. "Jolie, you have a line building up."

What was her problem? There was only one person behind Reed, and hello, this was my store, not hers. Why was she managing me in that tone?

Reed shot her a glance that was irritated, but cautious at the same time. He knew I was the boss, so he didn't really need to hold back, but I was grateful he did. He read over the board.

Then he found it.

"New item?"

My cheeks grew warm. Yes, I was taking a break from him, but that didn't mean I wasn't thinking of him while we were apart. The latest addition to my menu was embarrassing proof of just how much I couldn't get him out of my mind.

"I'll have a *Sax on the Beach*." He smirked.

I simultaneously regretted and delighted in my decision to put that one up, my crepe filled with oranges, peaches, cranberries—everything in the drink of almost the same name. Its description read "a symphony of flavors", bringing the sax part into it. It was by far my cheesiest word play yet, but I couldn't resist.

I wasn't sure how I felt about Reed knowing he already gave me enough inspiration to put him on my wall.

"Drink?" I wouldn't address it. Avoidance. Best tactic of all.

He shook his head.

I handed him the crepe and he gave me his money, tickling the inside of my hand with his thumb as we made the exchange. It was weird to charge him. He was kind of my...babe or whatever...but it also felt weird not to with Morgan hovering over me like my mother. Her brows twisted when he played with my hand with the money in it. She was judging me for flirting at work. I didn't like it.

Reed ignored her sharp stare. "I'm not writing you a song today because I still haven't played you the other one. Pick a day so I can. Soon." He was pressing me for a next date. I was happy to be pressed.

By the time I got out of work, everything had died down around the park. Crooked Curt wasn't on his bench when I got there. Another man I recognized sat there instead.

"Hi, Jolie. What brings you to the Palace tonight?"

"Hey." I didn't know his name, so *hey* would have to suffice. "I wanted to see if everyone was okay. Where is Curt?"

The man scratched at his wiry black beard. "Dunno. I haven't seen him for most of the day. Was his friend who got stabbed. Right in the middle of the park. In his shoulder. Curt's taking it pretty hard. Was talking about how the park's not safe anymore and we have to figure out who's doing this so we can get back to leading our lives. Then he took off. Haven't seen him since."

My palms got clammy. Curt couldn't disappear. "What friend was it?"

"I didn't know the guy, but I'd seen him around. A buddy from the Palace."

My heart sank. This was hitting too close to home. It could be one of the people I knew. Even if it wasn't, it was terrible, but if it was...

I wanted to do something.

"How can we find out if he's okay? Should I try to call the hospital?" I doubted they'd give that information out. It wasn't like I could pretend to be family. I didn't even know the guy's name.

"Ronnie's okay." Curt's voice cut through the evening air. I turned around, and before I realized what I was going to do, I grabbed him into a tight hug.

"I'm so glad you're safe."

The hug he returned was stiff before he backed away, adjusting his worn, musty jacket that was much too warm for the sticky summer evening. My hug had taken him by surprise as much as it did me. He was uncomfortable.

"Yeah, I'm safe, but Ronnie's arm is going to be out of commission for a while. I just came from the hospital. Told them I was the closest thing to a brother he's got, so they let me in. Not like anyone else was going to see him." Curt's voice was jagged and disgusted. I'd never heard that from him before. "Not bad enough his hands got the shakes, now he has to have this, too."

Now I knew who had been stabbed. I'd noticed a man with shaking hands many times when I came to drop off the food. He was one of the ones who'd asked me to stay the night I met Reed. I assumed he had Parkinson's or something like it.

"I'm so sorry, Curt."

"Yeah, me too, Jolie. It sucks. Hey, why are you here anyway?"

"I wanted to see how everyone was. How you were."

He shook his head and played with his cap. "You shouldn't be here. It's not safe. Next time, don't come by yourself, okay?"

I hated that he was right. As much as I had ignored the shadiness of the park before, this was a new dimension. If someone was slashing people, I shouldn't be in the park alone. Especially at night.

"Okay," I said. "I'll be by Thursday with a box, and I'll bring somebody with me."

"Thanks," he sighed. He lay down on his bench and covered his face with his hat. He was ready to be left alone and unfortunately, terribly, this bench was as much privacy as this man could hope to have. I wanted to lean down and kiss him goodbye. I wanted to stay with him, bring him home with me, do anything I could to keep him safe. I felt the need to be close to him, I was so grateful he wasn't the person who was hurt. But his body language was clear, and I wouldn't invade his space. I'd already made him uncomfortable once.

I scurried out of the park, checking the darkness behind me as I walked.

The news over the next few days did nothing to relieve my worry for those people who weren't my friends, but for whom I cared as if they were. There were rumors of areas of the park being closed off until they could figure out who was doing this. If that happened, I wouldn't know where to find Crooked Curt or any of them. Where would they even go? What would happen to them?

Aside from giving the criminal the nickname Seaville Slasher, which sickened me, no progress had been made on the case. The police were no closer to figuring out who was committing these crimes than they were the night Ronnie was stabbed. The act happened from behind, and even though it was the late morning, either no one saw anything or no one came forward. I found it hard to believe there wasn't a soul around. Sometimes people think the homeless are invisible. So even if something happened to them right in front of their eyes they wouldn't see it.

Or maybe that was just me being cynical.

I wasn't the only one affected by the news. Despite the record New Jersey heat, the boardwalk was eerily quiet. It wasn't deserted, but there were certainly far fewer people around than usual, considering the time of year and the weather. I heard that neighboring beaches were bustling, just not ours. People were nervous.

As a result, the weight of my Thursday box was nothing compared to what it had been in weeks past and even my token jar was looking a little sparse. I threw in some extras when there were no customers around. It was the first time I had to pad the jar since I started the exchange.

I peeked in the box one last time before closing it. I tried to shift the contents around so it wouldn't be obvious that it was half empty when I got to the park. But nothing would disguise a vacuous box when people remained hungry. I sighed as I folded the flaps.

"Wait, Jolie, you forgot these." Mamie sidled over with her arms loaded. She squeezed half a dozen more crepes in the box before I shut it.

"Where did you get those?" I asked her.

"Just a little extra." She winked at me.

"That's going to cut into our budget." When Mamie accepted my idea, we had agreed that we would give away as much as we could, but we wouldn't hurt the business doing it. I would have loved to do more, but I couldn't take advantage of Mamie's generosity.

"Not by much, and it won't be all the time. They'll get this whole slasher thing figured out soon and then everything will be back to normal."

I planted a kiss on her soft cheek and gave her a gentle squeeze. It may only have been six extra crepes, but six more people would have a hot meal that night.

"You're waiting for Morgan's boyfriend to come before you leave, though, right?"

"He's not my boyfriend," Morgan called from the supply room. "And I'd appreciate it if you didn't say that when Chase arrives. He's my roommate. Nothing else."

"Can't for the life of me figure out why," Mamie shot back. Morgan didn't snap at her the way she did me. No one snapped at Mamie.

"Yes, Chase and Morgan are coming to the park with me before they go to dinner."

Morgan came out of the back with her hair down, wisps flowing around her shoulders, and fresh makeup around her eyes. She smelled of violets. A new perfume, for sure.

"You look nice," I said. "Not like you worked an eight hour shift."

"What? I just washed up," Morgan spat.

"You look very pretty for your date," Mamie said.

"It's not a date. We're two friends having dinner." Morgan played with the contents of her purse, finding nothing.

"Then why did you change out of your T-shirt? Do *you* wear tube tops to eat dinner with your roommates, Jolie?" Mamie asked, getting me involved.

I decided to play along. "Well, you're the only roommate I've ever had, Mamie, but I think when we had dinner, sweats were the customary attire."

"Would you two stop?" Morgan barked, at me but not Mamie. "I wasn't going to wear some ratty old shirt to a nice restaurant. Chase has been busy all week, and we haven't had any time to spend together. So he suggested we go to Crimini's. That's it. Can we not make a big fucking deal out of it?"

The way Morgan got so defensive whenever we teased her about Chase was amusing. Until she turned the tables on me.

"Anyway, at least he's taking me somewhere I need to get dressed. Not hiding me away. You're seeing Reed again, tomorrow, Jolie? Where are you going this time? A playground?" Her voice was cold and reeked of sarcasm.

"What does that mean?" Now I was the one on the defensive.

"Well, he hasn't exactly brought you out in public or bought you anything yet, has he? Hell, he hasn't even picked you up and taken you anywhere. Wonder why that is."

"Morgan," Mamie snapped before she'd even finished her last accusatory sentence. "I need more cheddar cheese. Go get me some from the back." There was no please either spoken or implied. That was a direct order to get rid of Morgan.

I wasn't ready to be done with this yet. "We've only been out twice. Where exactly should he have taken me—London?" I felt my face heating, and since we still had customers this wasn't model behavior.

"I'm just saying before you mock a relationship between my friend and me and acting like you know what I should be doing, throw stones at your own glass house. You have no idea who this guy even is." Morgan turned on her heel and stormed into the back, maybe to retrieve the cheddar cheese, maybe to get away from me.

My chest thumped and my neck heated. I wanted to follow her into the back and yell at her. I knew she didn't like Reed. I could tell from the way she practically growled at him when he came by the other day. But she didn't know him. Why would she not like him? Was it because he came off as cocky? Why would she care about that? What the hell did she expect him to be doing for me at this point?

I was about to go back there and confront her, but Mamie's hip knocked into mine as she pushed past me. She spent a few minutes in the back. I couldn't make out what she was saying to Morgan, but when Morgan emerged from the back, she had cooled down considerably.

"I'm sorry, Jolie," she muttered under her breath like a child who'd been scolded. "I shouldn't have said that, especially out here." She tilted her head toward the customers.

"Do you want to tell me what you meant?" She was either insinuating that Reed was hiding something, or was cheap. I wanted to know which.

"I didn't mean anything. Let's just go drop off the box."

At the mention of the box, I got an uneasy twitch in the pit of my stomach. I'd asked Reed if he could go with me so I wouldn't have to travel through the park alone. He said he couldn't, but didn't give a reason. I didn't give it much thought when he said it, but now Morgan's comment had me wondering if he'd been evasive on purpose.

Shaking the thought away, and a little annoyed that Morgan put it there in the first place, I secured the box. "Fine. As soon as Chase gets here, let's go."

Within minutes, Chase walked into the shop, looking even more ready for this non-date than Morgan. He wore black slacks and a charcoal button-down, open at the collar. His hands were hanging in his pockets, a calculated, casual yet sexy stance. This was a guy definitely trying to impress a girl. And impressive he was. Morgan was nuts if she couldn't see it.

As much as he was trying to play the relaxed, suave guy, nothing could hide the expression in his eyes when he saw Morgan all made up for him.

The two of them stood like complete idiots for at least five seconds, Morgan behind the counter and Chase in the doorway, staring at each other. It was so pathetic; something had to be said.

"Okay, if you guys can stop gaping at each other, we have some mouths to feed."

Morgan's head's jerked in my direction. She gave me an unhappy glare, but her eyes shifted to Mamie over my shoulder and she said nothing.

"Yeah, let me grab your box, Jolie." Chase lifted the crepes and we made our way to the park.

While everyone ate, I tried to get some information about the park closing the area and whether the people had any idea where they would go if it did. Everyone was focused on the crepes, and either none of them had plans or they didn't want to discuss them. Eyes were downcast all around me. I followed their lead and said a quick good night.

Morgan and Chase walked me back to my car. For

two people who lived together and were usually very chatty, they were disarmingly quiet.

"I hear Crimini's is very nice," I threw out, so something would fill the air.

"It is," Chase agreed. "I've been there before. The food is delicious. And the ambiance..." Morgan looked up at him and he didn't finish the sentence.

I'd heard about the restaurant before. Expensive. Candlelight. Piano player. It was supposed to be elegant and very romantic. I wondered if Morgan knew that. Either he would win her over or they'd go home to one awkward apartment.

I thanked them for walking me and got in my car, wondering what was in store on my next date with Reed.

Chapter Nine
Device: Five Dates!

Mamie called out sick. Sick! She never called out sick, and this was the second time she had done so in as many weeks. Something was up with her. I had no idea what it was but if she told me that story again about having a sleepover and being too tired to come to work, I would drive to her house at that very second and see exactly what she was hiding.

I told her I was stopping by again after work. She refused. "Reed is taking you out tonight. You will not spend another date in your grandmother's house listening to old stories. Now you go out with that boy and let him do naughty things to you before I decide to let him do them to me instead."

I cringed through the phone. "God, Mamie. Must you?"

"A woman should never stop dreaming, Jolie. That's when she stops being a woman. Now go get your head in the gutter where it belongs, and stop worrying about me taking one lousy sick day."

Unfortunately, my head had been nowhere but the gutter since the night before. Knowing Chase was romancing Morgan with that restaurant had me imagining all sorts of things Reed would do to try to turn Date 3 into Date 5. Keeping my head in the gutter was what caused me to wear the black lacy boy shorts that allowed just enough cheek to peek out, and the matching demi bra that I was practically falling out of—articles of clothing I definitely should not have been wearing if I was planning to hold onto my Date 5 rule. Just knowing I was wearing these for him was getting me excited, and he wasn't due to come for hours. What I should have done was not shave anywhere for days and borrow a pair of undies from Mamie. Then again, maybe I didn't want to find out what she had in her panty drawer.

Morgan had the day off, so it was one of our less talkative workers and me all day. Greg was also a college kid, but he wanted to do his job, get paid and leave, which was fine, except I really needed some distraction or girl talk. I could have used Morgan to talk me down, since she didn't like Reed anyway. Greg served his crepes in silence, leaving me to my thoughts, which were neither chaste nor helpful.

By the time Reed arrived, this time in a dark green T-shirt and the sexiest worn-in jeans I'd ever seen hug a man's ass, I knew we needed to go out in public somewhere or I was going to embarrass myself.

Greg straightened his work area, helped me cover the day's ingredients with plastic wrap, and unceremoniously left me alone with Reed.

As soon as the chimes signaled Greg's departure, Reed stalked around the counter. He wrapped one arm around my waist and threaded the other hand into the back of my hair, fisting it. He pulled me into him and gave me a kiss in the middle of the store that had my knees buckling and the rest of me aching for more.

I really shouldn't have shaved.

"Hey babe. Since I never got to play you the last

song, I thought maybe we could go to your place and order in, and I could play it for you there?" He twirled my hair in his fingers and waited for my answer.

My first instinct was to say *absolutely*. Spending an evening alone with him, letting him play for me…what could be better? Then, Morgan's damn words rang in my ears about how he didn't take me out anywhere, like he was afraid to be seen with me. I hated myself for allowing her words to enter my brain. I hated myself more for giving them validation by wondering if she was right.

But I had to keep my ground. I couldn't get so swept up that I forgot whom I was and what kind of relationship I needed. So I said, "I was thinking maybe we could go out somewhere." I waited for his answer, praying he didn't act like he didn't want to be in public, because what could that mean really? Nothing good.

He thought for a minute. "There's a cool museum I know not far from here. It might be open 'til eleven. Want to check it out?"

A museum sounded wonderful. A public place where people don't wear ratty clothes and aren't creeping around. Screw you, Morgan, for making me doubt my gorgeous Music Man.

"Do you want to drop your sax or your bag in your car?" I asked. He had both over his shoulder.

"Nah, I'm good. Never know when you'll need to bust out in song."

Before I could question how strange it was to carry these things everywhere, his mouth was on mine again and his large, strong hand was cupping my ass, pulling me up against him. The underwire in my bra poked my skin, reminding me of the view Reed might have later.

My toes tingled and I thanked God for museums that stayed open late.

The walk was on the long side. It took almost twenty minutes to get there, and it was humid, even though the sun had long since set. Reed held my hand as we walked and I hoped he didn't mind my sweaty palm. Beads formed at the back of my neck and on my forehead. I didn't want to be a mess before we even got there.

Reed asked if we'd heard from my brother again. We hadn't of course, and I didn't expect to. Hearing from Tristan twice in a month was unheard of these days, though I wished with everything in me that weekly check-ins were the norm.

"What was he like, you know, before?" He released my hand and brushed his palm on the back of my neck. He rubbed my nape with his thumb as we walked. I squirmed, self-conscious about the moisture there, but his eyes were warm with the sporadic streetlight casting a shine on them. It amazed me how seamlessly he shifted from sexy and flirty, to tender and caring when we talked about my family.

"He was…" I thought back. I rarely allowed myself to do that. All it did was cause me pain and long for the brother I'd never have again. The brother I loved, hated, adored, admired, wanted to kill—all the things close siblings feel. All the things they take for granted until one day when that disappears in an instant and you know the person you love more than yourself has been taken from you forever. "He was a huge pain in the ass." I laughed through eyes that welled without warning. "He used to torment me like crazy. Any time he found out I had a crush on a boy, he teased me and threatened to tell the boy until I did something for him, like clean his room or buy him a present. When I was in high school, he found out I hooked up with a guy my best friend liked. He blackmailed me into doing his math homework for two weeks to keep him from telling her. Good thing I was in advanced math."

"A typical brother," Reed chuckled.

I sighed and stopped walking. I faced Reed, toe to toe. "He never would have, though. Sure, he tormented me, but he was all talk. He was my biggest protector. When my father was irritable when we were young, Tristan would tuck us away in his bed and tell me gruesome ghost stories. They creeped me out. I'd yell at him, not understanding why he'd say such awful things to me. He'd snuggle me up and say, *See, Jolie, that's the scary stuff. If you can handle that, this is nothing. Dad will get past this. Tomorrow will be fresh, you'll see.* He'd hold me all night while we slept, keeping me safe from my thoughts and fears. He would never have let anyone hurt me. He was allowed to make my life hell, but no one else was. That was his thing. He was my protector."

God, how I missed him. An invisible vise squeezed my lungs.

Reed palmed the side of my face. "Somewhere, I'm sure he still is, Jolie. He just can't show it to you."

That did it. It sent the tears pooling in my eyes overboard. They fell on Reed's hand and he wiped them with his thumb. How many times was I going to allow myself to cry in front of this guy? How many times would he stick around for more? If he'd just stop asking me about my brother I'd be fine. If I used my usual deflection tactics, I could avoid all of this.

But it felt so good to share with him, to finally let it out, to talk about the brother I loved so much my bones cracked into a thousand pieces just thinking of him. Mourning him, even though he was alive. Reed made me want to whisper my memories about Tristan to him, even when they hurt so much I wanted to scream in anguish.

Reed did that. I didn't know how, but I was grateful for it. His lips grazed the top of my head as he held my face.

I shook my head against his lips. "I shouldn't keep doing this in front of you."

"He's your blood, Jolie." His words vibrated into my hair. "He's your brother. This is exactly what you should be doing."

Did he understand more than I knew? I lifted my head from his tender kiss. "Do you have brothers?" I wiped a stray tear away with my pointer.

Reed shifted from foot to foot and adjusted the straps on his shoulder, hopping a little as he fixed them. "Just one. Come on, we're almost there."

When we arrived at the museum, Reed tried in vain to open the doors. The sign on the door said they closed at nine. We weren't even close to making it. I was disappointed. Spending the evening strolling around a museum, holding Reed's hand appealed to me. I liked the idea of hearing his interpretations of the artifacts in there. It would have given me some insight to his thoughts, which he didn't readily share. Now, any hopes of that were shut down, just like the doors that forbade our entrance.

"Now I'm the one who's sorry." He sat on the top step, where a landing led to the doors. "I thought they'd still be open. I'm surprised they're not."

"It's okay." I didn't know of any museums open that late. I wasn't sure why he thought this one might be different. I sat next to him, close; our legs and hips brushed. "We can do it another time."

He nodded and unzipped his sax case. "Want to hear the song now?"

My smile probably lit up the dark, desolate side street. "Yes."

He hooked a strap onto the instrument and threw it diagonally over his shoulder.

I think our sitting, in the quiet of the night, after a serious conversation, made me assume I was about to hear a sad tune. Instead, his song was fast with a lot of zips and zags and was fun and even a little silly.

"I wrote that in anticipation of picking you up for our date. I guess I was a little jittery." He shrugged like a little boy admitting he put glue in a girl's hair, embarrassed but pleased at the same time.

"You were jittery? Mister Suave? You never look jittery. What's your secret?"

"Never let 'em see you sweat." He pushed the sax strap to his side, leaned in mere inches to close the gap between us and kissed me. Deep, slow, easy and long. Nothing like the song I just heard. Then he pulled away. "Want to hear some more?"

I nodded because I didn't know if my lips were ready to form a coherent word.

"These aren't mine, but I love them." He lifted the sax back to his mouth. These next songs were what I expected before. One after the other was soulful, melancholy, slow, and gut-wrenching. His eyes were closed. I was, once again, entranced by the way his lips surrounded that mouthpiece and the way he rolled them and wet them with his tongue as he played. His fingers pressed into the keys seductively, the way I imagined he'd touch a woman, and his chest heaved against his T-shirt as he found the air he needed. He was the single sexiest thing I'd ever seen, sitting there in the dark, making love to his sax.

I wanted to be that saxophone.

I took a microsecond to survey the block. Small, empty shops that had probably been closed for hours lined the street. We had walked far off the beaten path to get to this museum, and we hadn't passed a person for the last ten minutes on our walk. A flickering street lamp was the only sign of movement. There was no reason for anyone to come down here.

At least that was what I was banking on.

My heart beat through my ribcage, and heavier drops of sweat pricked around my hairline. My hands shook. He had to touch me or I might explode.

"Stop," I blurted.

He stopped playing mid-note, with his mouth hanging on the mouthpiece; he opened his eyes. "What?" It came out garbled. This was much less sexy than I intended.

I removed the sax from his mouth and touched my lips to his, just enough to pique his interest. Then I ran my tongue over them. Very slowly.

He pushed the sax aside. I traced my hands over his hard shoulders, up the back of his neck and into his hair. I whispered into his lips, "You're incredible, Reed. I've never heard anyone play like that."

"You inspire me. These days, I picture you whenever I hold my sax."

Then we were kissing. Deep throat, raw, uncontrolled kisses. We pulled each other closer, needing more, but Reed's hands stayed on my back and in my hair, over my clothes, the way any decent guy's would on the step of a store.

I broke our kiss and he leaned into me, his mouth following mine to not let go. I pulled back more, so I could lift my blouse up over my head. I threw it to the side and watched his face, hoping for the effect I wanted.

He gaped at me, then his head whipped side to side. No one was there. "What are you doing?"

I grabbed his face and yanked his mouth to mine. "I want to be with you. Now."

His fingers and hands shook against my bra strap as he kissed the parts of my breasts that were spilling over my bra.

"Jolie," he said, unsure.

I reached under his T-shirt and let my hands roam his chest and back. They were a little obstructed because of the sax strap that ran across his chest, and I wanted to feel all of him. I grabbed the sax and lifted, but one of the keys got caught on the lace of my bra. I tugged a little but without tearing the whole thing, it wouldn't come free.

"Damn," I huffed. As much as I wanted to rip it off, this bra had just cost me sixty bucks and I intended to wear it again. I did not want to destroy it.

"Wait," Reed breathed, his voice husky with want. "I've got something." He reached over into his backpack, careful not to pull away from me. He dug through the bag without looking in it, and after a few seconds, produced a pocketknife. "Here, let's try this."

He cut the tiniest piece of lace off the bra, freeing it from the instrument. He studied my breasts. "Good as new." He lifted the sax over his head, and placed it in its case. Then he stared at me, questioning how to proceed. Was the moment over? Was it time to come to our senses, get dressed, and finish what we started in a sensible place?

Not for me. My entire life was sensible. All the slight pause did was frustrate me. I leaned forward, pressing my chest into him and kissed his neck. He shivered, making me kiss him harder. I unzipped his jeans; he flinched when I reached inside. Then I leaned back on the landing, pulling him on top of me.

He resisted. "Jolie, not here. Let's go to your place."

"Why?"

Silly question really. We were in public, we'd never even seen each other naked, we were in *public*. He didn't need to answer.

"I don't want it to be like this for you. You deserve to be pampered." He stroked my cheek, pushing my hair away from my face.

"I've been pampered plenty, Reed. You make me want to do things I've fantasized about but would never consider. We can go to my place next time. Right now, I want you to touch me the way you touched your sax. You have no idea what watching you play does to me. Please," I breathed into his mouth as I stroked him.

"Shit," he panted.

He reached into his bag again. He took out his work shirt, balled it up and placed it under my head. Then he pulled out a pair of khakis and put them under my hips, laying me flat on the step. It was cold against my warm back, which was moist from both the humidity and adrenaline. The cement was rough against my skin, but that made it more exciting.

"You're sure about this?"

"Yes." It was an order.

He positioned himself above me with his knees resting on the khakis to protect him from the cement. As he lowered his weight onto me, slow and controlled, every muscle in his body pressed against me and took my breath away. "What about your rule?" His voice was back to rich chocolate, delectable. I wished it were a tangible object so I could devour it.

This was officially date three. And I couldn't give one flying fuck.

"Forget the rules for now."

"Rules?" he asked, stilling himself against me.

Rules, with an S. He didn't know I had more than one. He didn't know that, aside from worrying about Tristan, my biggest fear was that the schizophrenia would be passed on to me as well. That I used devices so I'd know my behavior was consistent with my personality, and that I wasn't slipping into a fantasy world, with conspiracies and paranoia where I'd worry about the surreal and not know the difference between the voices in my head and the ones spoken aloud.

I'd have to tell him. If I wanted him to know me, I'd have to tell him. But not now. Right now, I just wanted to be a normal woman, doing something spontaneous and a little dangerous. Right now, I just wanted Reed, and I wanted him to have me. The *me* I wanted to be, not the worried, conscientious, calculated me. The *me* I felt like when I was around him. The *me* that needed to get lost in his touch, in his mouth, in his body. The free *me*.

"Forget all of it." I yanked down his boxer briefs between us and he bit my lip in response. He fumbled in his bag one last time, pulled out a condom, then took me on the steps, between the cold unforgiving concrete and the hot, slick, raw muscles that made up every inch of his body. He played me with the same skill he did his sax. I sang out into the dark of the night the same way, and I loved every second of it.

Chapter Ten
Device: Know Who You're Dating

After you have sex outside the entryway of a closed museum, there's not a lot of time for snuggling and whispering sweet nothings in your lover's ear. So as soon as Reed and I caught our breath, we scrambled to put on whatever clothing had made it all the way off. The whole experience was exhilarating and my hands shook as I adjusted my shorts.

"Well, that was…unexpected." Reed laid his hands over mine to help me button the shorts.

"Unexpected good or unexpected bad?"

"Unexpected incredible, as long as you know I'd never ask you to do anything you're uncomfortable with." He balled up his khakis, the pocketknife, and our trash, and stuffed them into his bag.

"I know that, Reed. If I thought that's what you were going for when you brought me here, trust me, there's no way I would have wanted to do that."

He laughed and shook his head. "Women are so confusing. So, it was okay since you initiated it but if I had, it would be a turn off?"

That was kind of a double standard. "No, not if you initiated it in the moment. But if you came here with the explicit intention of getting me naked, then yes, turn off."

His laugh deepened. "Lots of rules."

He had no idea.

He shook out his polo, which had gravel on it. "Shit," he grumbled when he noticed a stain across the front. "I need this for tomorrow."

"That should come right out. It's just a smudge." I ran my finger over the stain.

He stared at the shirt as if he had no idea how to do a load of laundry.

"Want to come back to my place and I'll throw it in the wash for you?" It was only fair. It was my fault his shirt got dirty.

"You don't mind?"

"Of course not."

We hiked back to my car with Reed's hand on the back of my neck again. It was like he had found a comfortable resting place for it. We reached my car first and Reed asked if I minded driving, because his car was still a ways away. I was happy to drive. If he didn't have a car at my house, it meant he didn't plan on leaving.

I couldn't stop myself from stealing glances at him on the way. Who was this man who had me asking for sex in public, defying my normal logic, and breaking my rules? Was I comfortable with it? Could I be with someone who made my fear of the possible future slowly disintegrate, or was that a dangerous false sense of security? What if I dropped my guard and then I didn't realize I was headed down the same path as Tristan and my father until it was too late?

His focus was on the empty road, but he felt me on him. "What have I told you about keeping your eyes on the road, beautiful?"

I blushed, happy he wasn't looking at me. I needed

to be more discreet about the way I couldn't stop taking him in.

"What are you thinking?" Now he shifted his weight in the seat toward me.

I didn't want to tell him that I was wondering if this was good for me. I didn't want him to believe I had any regrets about what we'd done, because I didn't. I loved it. I was just afraid that my love for it might cloud my judgment.

"I was just thinking about tonight. I can't believe we did that." I kept my tone light, with any traces of worry shoved far out the car window, into the black night.

He stroked the back of my head. "Yeah, I think you might keep me on my toes."

"Me? You didn't fight me too hard."

It was true. As soon as he had my okay, Reed was comfortable being half naked and all buried on that barren block, lost in what we were doing. "Aside from the fact that, hello we were in public, it wasn't exactly sanitary out there," I joked.

Reed lowered his hand and placed it in his lap. "Yeah, the streets can be that way." He was quiet for the rest of the ride. My words may have implied regret after all.

As soon as we got back to my place, I collected my darks. "Let me get your clothes. I'll throw them in the wash with my own stuff."

I went to reach for his backpack, but Reed grabbed it. He pulled out his polo and khakis. "Thanks Jolie. I really appreciate it." He handed me them in a ball.

He was still quiet when I came back into the room after putting up the wash. I wanted to lighten the mood.

"Hey, do you purposely order those shirts a size too small to accentuate your muscles?" I swayed my hips as I strolled by him with the empty laundry bag slung over my arm like Santa's bag of presents, all delivered.

"You noticed my muscles, huh?" He yanked the bag from behind me, and I fell into his lap.

I rolled my eyes. "Please, don't act so innocent. You flaunt your body all over the place."

"Flaunt it?" he laughed. "I don't think I'm flaunting as much as you just can't stop ogling me."

We were back to this. His cocky act and my appalled one. It was a game I enjoyed. I put my hands on my hips.

"Excuse me, I have not once ogled you. In fact, if your shirts weren't so damn tight, I probably wouldn't have noticed you at all."

He knocked my hands off my hips and grabbed my waist. I thought he was going to pull me into him. Instead, he tickled me. He threw me onto the couch and his hands found my armpits, neck, waist, and inner thighs all at the same time. It was like he had eight hands at once, and each one was torturing me to a death by tickle.

"Stop," I laughed. "I can't stand it. I'm too ticklish." I squealed and squirmed, trying to free myself of his grasp, but I couldn't.

"Admit it," he teased, yelling over my laughs that had my eyes watering. "Admit you love the way I wear my shirts."

"No way," I choked. "It's ridiculous. You need to go up a size. You look horrible."

His tickles grew more persistent and I fought to breathe.

"Reed, I'm gonna die. Stop."

"I don't think anyone was ever tickled to death. Admit you've been plotting ways to get me out of that shirt for weeks, and I'll let up."

He targeted my thighs again. I tried yanking them up with all my might, but he had me pinned with his own legs. I was stuck between laughing and crying, and I thought he might be wrong; people could get tickled to death. If not, I was about to make history. But no way I would admit to all my fantasies about getting him naked.

"Uh-uh." I struggled get out the words. "In fact." I paused to steal some air. "You might want to hit the gym a little more."

I figured this last one would do it. He would dig his fingers into me so hard I'd definitely die of tickle torture, but his entire body stilled. His legs pinned mine and now his hands were around my wrists, restraining them against the couch.

"Is that so?"

I nodded and panted, trying to shove air back in my lungs.

"Hmm. I might have to use a different tactic then." He leaned down and nipped my neck between his teeth. "How about now?"

"Hideous," I breathed but I wasn't laughing any more.

He pushed my legs apart with his own, and lowered his hips into mine. "Now?"

I gasped. "Like you're wearing your little brother's clothes."

"I see," he whispered. He scooted lower down my body. He released one of my hands and pushed up my shirt, just below my bra. With the patience of a man who has nowhere to go and nothing to do, he kissed my torso. He slowly worked his way down my ribcage until he reached my belly button. He kissed and licked it, and the skin just below it, for an eternity. It might have been more torturous than the tickling. I was beginning to think the man was a sadist. I squirmed under him but had no leverage.

When he opened my button and took about five years to unzip my shorts he looked up at me. "And how about now?"

My words were shaky, but they came out. "I can barely stand to look at you."

"Mmm hmm." When he yanked down my shorts as I lifted my hips to help him, I broke my rule for the second time that night, but I didn't tell him that I was praying my drier would shrink his shirt a little more.

The washing machine finished right around same time as we did. I threw on Reed's T-shirt and went to put his clothes in the drier. When I came back in the room, he was already in his shorts.

"Do you mind if I take a shower?"

I was a little surprised at how abruptly he was up and ready

"Um, yeah, sure. It's through the hall." I pointed. "There are towels in the linen closet.

"Thanks." He kissed me on the cheek before disappearing into the bathroom.

I was left sitting on the couch, alone with his bag and sax. The guy sure liked to shower a lot. This was the second one I'd seen him take. It was like he had an obsession with showering.

Morgan's image appeared before me again. Why

would a man need to shower before leaving you, her critical voice asked. What was he washing away?

A shiver ran through me. I didn't want to think it. I couldn't be dating a man who had a girlfriend, or worse, a wife. Could I?

His bag sat on the floor next to me. I wasn't in the habit of snooping. I'd never wanted to pry into the life of a guy I was dating before. Then again, I'd always gone in with my eyes open and my information gathered.

I scooted a few inches on the couch toward the bag. It was zipped shut so I couldn't sneak a peek. I'd have to intentionally open it. I leaned over a centimeter at a time, as if someone was recording me and I was trying to be sly. In my own home. How silly. My hand fell to my side, closer to the bag. My nail scratched at the couch, creeping its way toward the zipper. My stomach knotted into itself and my palms got clammy. I wiped one against the couch. This was very unlike me. Besides, I wasn't even sure what I was looking for, or if I wanted to know the answer.

Before my hand could make its descent from the couch to the backpack, the bathroom door opened. My hand flew into my hair and I sat up straight. Rigid even.

"Forgot my stuff." Reed strutted toward me, in all his shirtless glory, with his shorts undone and hanging. He leaned over, scooped the backpack, and withdrew to the bathroom. He didn't notice the plank of wood rammed down my back or the word guilty scribbled across my forehead.

I should have been disappointed. My snooping opportunity had passed. Instead, a cool ocean breeze seemed to blow through the room. I guess I didn't want to know as much as I thought.

Reed didn't leave after his shower or when the clothes were dry. He hung out for a while and we watched TV. But when I threw out some suggestive bait that I wanted to go to bed, and hoped he'd join me, he didn't take it. He said he had to get going and gathered his stuff.

"Let me drive you back to your car." I slipped on my shoes.

"No, you look beat. I called a car service." He kissed my nose before he walked out the door. Funny thing was, I didn't see him make a call and I didn't hear a cab pull up to my building. Maybe I should have unzipped that bag after all.

Chapter Eleven
Device: Maintain Habits

If I didn't know I was standing at the foot of the Atlantic, I would have been sure it was the bay instead. The ocean was smooth and flat, resembling a sheet of glass more than a gigantic body of water. Its only movement was at the shoreline, where the tiniest of waves trickled over my bare toes. Seaweed washed up on the sand, and salty fish filled the air, as was often the case at low tide like this. If I came here later, no doubt the tide would bring larger, angrier waves. But I wanted to visit him this way. Calm and at peace. I liked to think he finally found that.

"Hi, Daddy," I whispered into the sea. The gentle waves kissed the ground in response. I sat in the wet sand and let the water ripple around my hips. I opened my hands, a finger at a time, to allow their contents to cascade into the water—sugar in my left and salt in my right. "It's me. Your sweet and sassy girl," I said as the water washed away the white crystals. "I miss you."

We closed the store on this day each year; the day after Tristan was diagnosed; the day my father decided he couldn't take the guilt of passing the disease onto his otherwise strong, healthy son. The day he walked into the ocean and drowned himself.

I always came to visit him on this anniversary, because he chose to give himself to the ocean. So although being here on this day brought me great sorrow, there was also nowhere else in the world I felt as close to my father as here with the water giving me the tender caresses he no longer could.

I waited for Mamie, with my back to the boardwalk. She always met me here and sat without speaking until the beach became crowded with sunbathers. I couldn't begin to imagine the pain she felt at his loss, not only on this day, but every day. She never showed it. She just held my hand and sat staring into the horizon.

When she didn't show by ten, and the early birds started spreading their blankets across the warm sand, I scratched at my thumb. After another hour and still no sign, the hives on my neck told me it was time to find her. I checked the shop first. Maybe she'd forgotten the date. But she wasn't there. I drove to her house. I didn't want to give her the chance to tell me I was making a big deal out of nothing. This was the first time she failed to meet me, and on top of the other strange ways she'd been acting, I was concerned.

No one answered her door. I pounded on it, thinking maybe she couldn't hear the bell, but got no response. A panicked thought occurred to me that she might be in there and unable to answer. I used my spare key, doing the steps two at a time to race to her bedroom. Overwhelming relief swept over me when she wasn't either lying on the bathroom floor or in bed, unconscious.

Where the hell was she, and why did I have to keep searching for her?

I pulled my cell from my purse. My finger was about to hit *call*, when voices echoed from the porch.

I yanked the front door open. Mamie's shock at finding me inside her house was evident, as was that of the woman standing next to her.

"Jolie, what are you doing here, honey?" She walked past me and took off her shoes, replacing them with the house slippers she kept by the door.

"Hi, Bea." I waved as Mamie's best friend of over sixty years entered the house. "Where are you guys coming from?"

"Hi, sweetheart." Bea kissed me on the cheek. "How've you been? I hear you're seeing someone new." She smiled at me and the apples of her cheeks looked like small golf balls. Her voice was small and brittle. She and Mamie were opposites, and complemented each other to form a beautiful lifelong friendship.

Mamie walked into her kitchen. "I'm making some coffee. Who would like?"

"Me," Bea chirped.

"No thanks." I waved off the horrible offer, following Mamie into the kitchen. "Where were you?"

Mamie set up the coffee to brew a full pot for the two of them. "We were at breakfast. Why do you look so tense?"

I walked to within a few inches of her, because as much as Bea was her best friend, she wasn't mine. "You didn't meet me at the beach."

Mamie's stare was blank.

"Do you know what today's date is?" I asked.

Her eyes cast to the side for a few moments and then it struck her. Her mouth dropped into a somber line. "I'm sorry, *ma petite-fille*. I didn't realize."

I shook my head and swallowed a lump. I wanted

to say it was okay, no big deal. But it was a big deal. How was breakfast so important that she'd forget?

As usual, she read me like the simplest of children's picture books. She took my face in both of her hands. "Jolie, I am truly so sorry. We made this appointment two weeks ago and I guess I just didn't think of the date. Please don't be upset. We can go to the beach now, okay?"

"No, no, it's okay." I choked back my disappointment. "Don't let me ruin your coffee with your friend. I've already been there. I have some other things to do. I'll give you a call later." I rushed out before she could insist.

I didn't realize how much I depended on sharing the burden of this day with Mamie until I couldn't. I needed some outlet. My first thought was to call Reed, but I dismissed that idea. He'd already witnessed enough of my emotional turmoil. Morgan was my next thought, but since we'd given her the day off, I didn't want her to feel obligated to spend the day with me. That was the problem with being someone's friend and boss; it was hard to find the line. Besides, I'd never told Morgan how my father died. I couldn't release any part of my burden without sharing that detail.

So I walked along the boardwalk. Crowds were still thin on account of the recent crimes, and there was little wait for my cheesesteak and fries. I threw a couple of dollars away on an impossible basketball game before winning a stuffed penguin from a ring-toss game. The games weren't lifting my mood at all. If anything, they reminded me of when my parents brought Tristan and me there for hours.

I made my way off the boardwalk. Before I knew

it, my feet led me toward the park. Hanging out with Crooked Curt and the others could be exactly what I needed. I had almost reached the Palace, when a hand on my shoulder sent me flying a foot off the ground. I whipped around with my hands in front of me, ready to defend myself.

"I'm sorry, Jolie," Brett said.

I must have been more on edge walking around there than I realized.

"I didn't mean to scare you, but I called your name and you didn't answer."

"Oh, hey Brett. I'm sorry, I guess I was lost in thought. What are you doing here?"

"I'm covering the Slasher story." Brett's puffed out chest indicated how proud he was to have been bumped to a real story, but his words frightened me.

"Has there been another one?"

"No, no," he answered. "We're just doing a piece on the effect the crimes are having on the park."

"Oh, thank God." I sighed. "Hey, great that they have you working this story, though."

"Thanks. Is that a new pet?" He pointed to the penguin resting in the crook of my arm.

I laughed. "Ha. No, boardwalk prize."

"Did that guy win it for you?"

I felt a little bad at the mention of Reed, but made light of it. "I won it for myself, thank you very much," I teased with my chin high in the air.

Brett chuckled. "Want to grab some food and sit for a few minutes? Or are you heading somewhere?"

I had nowhere to go, nothing to do and though I'd already eaten, was dying for a distraction. His idea sounded great. I got a hot dog from a vendor; Brett ordered a knish and we sat on a wooden bench in the shade.

"So what is the story reporting?" I asked, through a mouthful of fake meat and mustard.

Brett shook his head. "Nothing good. No leads and a lot of scared people. The local stores need their summer traffic to sustain them throughout the rest of the year, but people aren't shopping. Or even coming to Seaville for that matter. People don't want to expose their families to potential risk when there are a dozen other shore towns two miles in either direction." He ripped off a piece of his knish and popped it in his mouth.

"I know what you mean. Stuff Your Crepes has been pretty empty since the second one happened." I took another bite and a dollop of mustard dripped onto my fingers and mouth. The flimsy napkin the vendor gave me barely wiped it away.

"Uh, there's some in your hair." Brett pointed.

I pulled at the strands near my shoulder, but my hair was too short. I couldn't see.

"Here." He took a wad of my hair between his thumb and forefinger and ran down it with a napkin. He paused when he reached its tip. If we were dating, or hoping to be, I would have called it a moment between us, but as it was, this was Brett revealing that he still had feelings for me. Intentionally or not didn't matter.

"What's wrong with me?" I laughed to end what could have been an awkward interaction. "Can't take me anywhere."

He let the moment go, and moved on as if it hadn't happened. "How's your grandmother?"

"Oh, she's fine. You know, she's Mamie. She

hasn't stripped anyone lately, so I guess that's a plus."

He laughed. "Is she always like that?"

"Oh god, you got the tame version. Be thankful you didn't order anything from her. She uses food to test the resilience of the guys I date by sticking something unexpected in their crepes. If she'd made it, your Mr. Basic may have tasted like strawberries with pickles and onions."

He gulped. "Seriously?"

I laughed. "Oh, yeah. You should have eaten the one she made for a biker I once dated." In high school. Before Tristan was diagnosed. Before I had my devices.

Brett let out a bark. "Oh my god. I don't even want to know."

"No," I shook my head. "You don't."

Much to my relief, the rest of the day passed easily. After leaving Brett, I went to the Palace. Curt wasn't around but some of the others were, and I talked to them for a while. I was aware that I could never truly understand their lives, but the more I saw them, the more I wanted to spend time with them. I liked to think it was more than pity at that point, that I would have cared about these people, even if I didn't know about their situations, but there was no way to go back and un-know information you were already given.

Around dinnertime, I drove back to Mamie's. I was sure Bea would be gone by that time, and I felt the need to connect with Mamie before the day's end, even if it wasn't on our spot at the beach.

A white sedan was parked in her driveway. I was disappointed that Bea must have still been around. Maybe it was selfish. Maybe Mamie needed a distraction from the day as well. I walked up the steps, anyway. They'd spent the entire day together, after all. I needed a little Mamie time.

I knocked on her door. Mamie answered wearing the same floral blouse and beige shorts as that morning, but her wrinkles were more pronounced, and she was paler.

"Hello, sweetheart. What are you doing back?" She stood in the doorway, blocking it.

"We didn't get to hang out before, so I figured we could now. Will Bea mind?"

"Bea?" Mamie looked confused.

"Yeah, isn't that her car in the driveway?"

Her eyes shifted to the driveway and back to me. "Oh. Bea left hours ago, Jolie." Still, she didn't move from the door. "Can we do something tomorrow, honey? I'm kind of in the middle of something." She winked as if she had a man inside.

"Okay," I stammered. It always threw me when she talked about guys, though I wasn't sure why. "I'll see you tomorrow." As I walked down the porch steps, it occurred to me that she'd removed all of her makeup and her fine hair was pulled up in a messy bun.

There was no way a man was in that house.

I shot back up the steps and threw open her door before she could lock it behind her.

"Mamie..." I froze after the word.

Standing in the living room behind Mamie was my mother.

Chapter Twelve
Device: Validate What's Real

She stood poised and at attention, as if she was both expecting to see me and shocked at the same time. Logically, she couldn't have been that shocked. She had to know I saw Mamie every day. If I hadn't needed to distance myself from some of the memories, I'd probably still live with her, in the house where I grew up.

"Hello, Jolie." My mother's words were emotionless, allowing me to take the lead. She wore a pink satin blouse and a white flowy skirt. A glass of iced tea rested in her hand. You'd have no idea it was in the nineties outside. She looked cool and summery. On this day, she looked absolutely fine.

"Why are you here?"

"Do you know what today is?"

The urge to throw the nearest object at her overwhelmed me. "Do *I* know what day it is? Of course I know what day it is. I'm surprised you do." She was the one who missed the first seven anniversaries. Not me. I fought the fury rising in me. I had to stay even. My chest rose and fell with rapid speed and heat warmed my neck under my hair, but I would not yell at her. I would not give in.

"I always remember, Jolie. Moving away doesn't change anything."

"It changes everything." My nostrils flared and inside I fumed, but I didn't raise my voice. "Mamie, I will see you at work tomorrow. Alone." I strode out of the house and clicked the door shut behind me.

I would not even slam the door.

I couldn't look at Mamie the next day. I worked around her, muttering an *excuse me* now and then when I had to get by to grab a filling, but I didn't make eye contact. Not even once. Shockingly, she didn't call me out on my immature and rude behavior.

My phone vibrated against my leg in my apron pocket. I checked the text and stuck it back in the apron.

"Was that Reed?" Mamie didn't lift her head from the crepe she was making as she asked me the first question of the day.

"Yes." I offered no more.

She was quiet for a few minutes as she finished preparing a hazelnut spread crepe, the one that filled the shop with the most delicious smell of a succulent, chocolate dessert. Then she wiped her hands on her apron and faced me. "Would you like to tell me what he said?"

"Would you like to tell me why she's here?"

If this had been any other situation, Mamie would have exploded at my snide tone, but I guess she gave me a free pass on this one because she just sighed. "Now?" She glanced around the shop. There were few customers, but we'd be airing dirty laundry in front of them, nonetheless. If Morgan had been there, we could have hidden in the back for a few minutes, but as slow as business was, there was no way to justify all three of us working. What a difference from a couple of weeks before when business was the best it had ever been.

"No. Later."

She nodded. "Then would you like to tell me about Reed now, or are you going to continue this juvenile silent treatment?"

I smiled down at my hot stone. I couldn't help it. I couldn't stand not talking to Mamie, even though it had been just a few hours. "He said he can't wait to see me tonight."

"Where are you going?" She placed her hand on her hip, but not to sass me. She was in pain.

"Mamie, sit." I dragged a chair to where she was standing. "Close your line. I can handle it."

To my dismay, she listened without arguing. "So, where are you going?"

"He's bringing me to his job so I can see where he works."

I couldn't wait to see his store. He was so connected to music. It was the only thing he openly shared, even though we talked and texted regularly. I might have been reluctant to see him too often, but I couldn't resist the urge to hear his voice, or flirt with him over text.

Seeing the place he worked would allow me to share that connection.

"That'll be nice." She lowered her head as she massaged her hip.

"Why don't you go home, Mamie?" When she was in pain, so was I.

She fanned her free hand in the air, as if to shoo away the idea. "I'll be fine. Just give me a few minutes."

A few minutes turned into an hour, and when I

couldn't watch the grandmother I loved more than anything wriggle on the chair to ease her pain, I insisted she go home. She offered to call Morgan, but I didn't need the help. Unfortunately.

"Let me close up for a few minutes so I can drive you. I'll shoot right back over. We won't even be missed."

"No. I'll get a ride." She stood to grab the phone.

"From who?"

She didn't have to answer, because her frown told me everything I needed to know. She would call my mother to come get her.

"I'll—"

"Abby will pick me up and you will let her or I'm not leaving until closing time." She crossed her arms in front of her chest. The conversation was over.

When my mother arrived, she texted Mamie, who walked out to meet her at the car. I promised to call her in the morning and tell her how my date went. When the chimes went off two minutes later, I thought she'd forgotten something, but nope. My mother's frame blocked the sun from coming through the doorway.

How fitting.

"No."

"No what?" she asked in response to my single syllable. "I haven't said anything yet." She approached the customer-less counter.

"No to you being here. No to me talking to you. No to all of it."

"Jolie, I know you're angry."

I'd heard that sentence from her lips so many times before, I could have spoken it before she did.

"But you're going to talk to me. We have things we

need to discuss."

I lowered my voice so the remaining customers couldn't hear me. "The only thing we have to discuss is the fact that you abandoned your family when we needed you most. That you are selfish and thoughtless, and that leaving was the most cowardly, hurtful thing you could have done. Other than that, I have nothing to say to or hear from you."

"We have things to discuss that have nothing to do with that. It doesn't have to be now, but it does have to be soon. You asked why I'm here and that's why. You'll have to listen." She turned on her heel and walked away.

Once more.

****

Reed picked me up at closing and we walked, hand in hand, to the music store. It wasn't that far from the boardwalk, but it was off a couple of side streets, so it wasn't surprising I'd never seen it before. It *was* surprising though, that I'd never seen him around. Not even grabbing a bite to eat or walking to his car.

Smells of wood and metal hit me as soon as Reed unlocked the front door. He flicked on the lights and even though they lit the room, the steel shutters that had been pulled down over the windows for security made it feel like a private cave. Guitars hung from the walls. Brass instruments, some of which I knew, and some I'd never seen before, huddled in a corner on my left. Bins of sheet music stood in the middle of the room. It was easy to see Reed working here surrounded by every instrument he loved.

"My boss, Hector, wanted to meet you but when I told him you couldn't get out of work 'til nine, he bailed. We closed at seven."

"He's okay with us being here?" I slipped my purse down my arm and rested it on a stack of old records.

"Sure." Reed shrugged as he locked the door. He closed the empty space between us. "I've missed you." He dragged both hands through my hair and pulled my face in to kiss me, showing me how true his words were. I'd missed him too, although I didn't realize how much until he showed up in my doorway that night, still in his work clothes but looking sexy as ever. My pulse raced at my first glimpse of him. When he complimented my pastel sundress, checking me out from head to toe at such a slow pace I shivered, it accelerated to lightning speed.

He must have spent some time outside during the week because he was tanner and his cheeks were slightly sunkissed with a pink twinge. The bruise he'd had when I first met him was gone; all that remained was a chiseled jawbone. When we finally came up for air and I needed a second to breathe, I ran my thumb over it. "Your bruise is gone."

He raised his eyebrows as if he was surprised I'd ever noticed it. "Yeah."

"How did you get it, anyway?"

He backed up just an inch or two, but enough to make me sorry I asked the question. He angled his shoulders away from me and dropped his focus to a nearby music stand. "Stupid bar fight."

"What was it about?"

He cut off my last word before I'd spoken the second syllable. "I want to show you something. Come." He held out his hand and I let the subject go, like he intended. I put my hand in his and he led me to the back of the room, the percussion section. Drums and cymbals of all different sizes filled the small area. Off to the side were two drums covered with some kind of towels. On each sat a plate of food and a glass of wine.

"We won't tell Hector about me using the snare drums as tables. He might not appreciate that part." He gifted me with a wink that had my belly turning to Jell-O. "Here, sit." He pulled out one of the drum stools that had wheels on the bottom. I sat and, without warning, it scooted me away. I let out a giggle.

"Hey, come back." Reed pulled me from behind my knees, sliding me closer. He brushed one of my knees before removing his hand. I wondered how I'd make it all the way through dinner without another kiss.

"So." He opened a napkin and laid it over his lap. "We have a different theme tonight."

I took stock of the place setting. Chicken parm, risotto and another red wine.

"Italian?"

"Yep." He leaned to the side and lifted a bottle off the floor. "Brunello." He held one hand on the neck and the other underneath, as if he were a sommelier educating me. "Hopefully, this will make up for the last one."

"But I like drinking out of the bottle. Didn't you say you like watching me?" I tilted my head and feigned a pout, jutting out my bottom lip. My cheeky response had its intended effect.

"Damn, Jolie." He yanked my stool until it clinked against his, palmed the back of my head and sucked my lip into his mouth, before enveloping the rest of my mouth with his. After a minute, he pushed back the wheels of my stool with his foot. His breaths were as heavy as mine. "Stop teasing me or this lovely dinner I've prepared will go to waste and you'll never learn what I intend to tell you."

I considered telling him to forget dinner and to drive right back to my place. But he wanted to share something, and after the couple of digs I'd texted during the week about him being a complete mystery, I couldn't turn that down.

"You cooked this?" With a sprinkled parsley garnish, it was plated as if a professional had done it.

"I had some help."

"Whose?"

"My cousin is a good cook." He took his first bite of chicken. "A damn good cook."

I tasted my thick, creamy risotto. It was spectacular. I was a sucker for Italian food. I let out a loud hmm that sounded like a sigh.

His eyes shot to mine. "What did I tell you about teasing me? Sound effects aren't fair play, Jolie."

I giggled again. I hadn't meant for that to sound sexy at all. "Who says I'm teasing you? Or that any of my actions have anything to do with you? Really, Reed, you give yourself far too much credit." I couldn't contain my ear-to-ear grin to even pull off that I might be serious for a second.

"There's that gorgeous fucking smile. Rotating is definitely an understatement." He took another bite and I was relieved that his reference to my father felt natural and pleasant, instead of a topic I needed to bury. I wanted to be the person who made him feel like that, too.

"So, is this your way of telling me you're Italian?

There are easier ways, you know."

"Easier isn't necessarily better. And yes, Italian on both sides. My father's off the boat, my mother's family has been here for years."

"And your brother?"

He lifted a brow in question. "Uh, yeah. He's Italian, too."

I laughed. "No, I mean, what's he like?"

"Oh." He shoveled in more food. "Vinny's a typical brother. You know, really competitive."

"That's funny."

"Yeah, well, brothers are like that."

No," I said, thinking. "I mean he got such an ethnic name and Reed is so not ethnic."

He stopped chewing and stared at me. "So what's been going on with you this week? Anything that didn't make it into the texts?" He wiped his mouth with his napkin and it reminded me of Brett wiping the mustard from my hair. That definitely didn't make it into the texts. Neither did one other piece of information. "My mother's in town."

"Oh, that's nice," he said, lightly. Then he saw my unpleasant expression. "Or is it?"

I shook my head. "My mother moved to California right after Tristan took off the first time. She said she couldn't go through it all again and had to get away. She's tried to keep in touch with me, but I have no desire. When I needed her, she left. Now I don't need her. That's just something she has to deal with."

He nodded. "Where is she staying?"

"With my grandmother. Technically, the house is hers and my grandmother's. My parents moved us all in with Mamie when my father got too bad for my mother to handle on her own. Mamie put the house in both of their names, in case anything ever happened to her, to make sure we'd always have a place to stay. My mother can live there any time she wants."

"How does Mamie feel about her?" He rubbed my leg as he waited for my answer.

I scoffed. "Mamie loves her like she's her own daughter. I think she always felt sorry for my mother. She had no idea what she was in for when she married my father. They didn't know what was wrong with him for years."

God, it felt good to talk about this. In some ways, it was like I was outside my body listening to a stranger talk about someone else's memories. In other ways, it was like I was confiding in my own soul. What was it about Reed that made me feel like he could understand my hardships?

Reed took my hand and extended my fingers. He put my palm to his lips and kissed it gently. "I can't begin to imagine what you've all been through, but I can tell you this. It's made you and Mamie into incredibly strong women the likes of which I've never seen before, Jolie. Everything you do to help people." He shook his head. "You could have become a recluse and chosen not to deal with any of it. Instead, you feed the hungry and truly care for them. You're not an anonymous donor. And look, I'm not saying that's wrong either. Any kind of charity is wonderful, but you let them know they matter to you. You're fucking amazing." He kissed my palm again, as Crooked Curt and his friends flashed through my mind, but Reed had to be talking about the people who used the tokens. No one outside of those involved knew about my weekly stops in the park.

"I wish I was as strong as you," he whispered, with a voice as thick and creamy as the risotto, as he trailed kisses onto my wrist. His lips shot currents up my entire arm, into my chest.

"I don't know," I breathed, steadying myself by placing my other hand on his thigh. "You seem pretty strong to me." He chuckled against my wrist and the volts grew stronger. But I had him talking and I wanted more. "What's your relationship like with Vinny these days?" I huffed.

His lips reached my forearm, and he mumbled against it. "We don't talk much. He hates me."

"I'm sure he doesn't," I managed to say. Now I was torn between letting his mouth continue its exploration and learning more about him.

"No, he does. He told me." He sucked on the skin where my elbow bent and I gasped. "I was an asshole. He's right to hate me. I deserve it." He skipped the rest of my arm, went right for my neck, and the rest of the story went up in flames.

I climbed off my stool and onto his lap, straddling him. My sundress pooled around my thighs. He ran his hands up them, raising the dress until his middle fingers reached the lace of my thong at my hips, revealing the entire length of my legs. He drew the lace a fraction of an inch down and slid his pointers back and forth over the curves of my hips, underneath the delicate material. My legs clenched in anticipation. The tips of my toes reached the floor and I used them as leverage to boost myself into him. My push forced the stool to slide backward and we crashed into the cymbals, which made a raucous clanking noise. Reed laughed in my mouth as I sealed it to his. We kissed like we hadn't seen each other for a year, not a week.

I ground into him, needing to be closer. Under my dress, he grabbed at my thighs, my ass, my hips, anywhere he could get his hands. With labored breaths, he slid the thin strap off my shoulder and replaced it with his mouth. "I'm so into you, Jolie, I can't believe you made me wait a whole week to see you again." He nipped and bit and I couldn't take another second.

I scooted back just enough to wedge my hand between us and reach his zipper. I had no qualms about being with him there. With the metal shutters closed, the only exposed area was the door, and we were off to an angle. No one could see us. Besides, after our last encounter, inside the store was conservative.

I couldn't believe I was comfortable with this. I felt more alive than I'd felt since Tristan was diagnosed. Maybe more alive than I'd ever been before.

I lowered his zipper and this time he didn't stop to check if I was sure. He lifted his hips a little so I could lower his jeans and boxers to his knees. He let out such a deep groan when I pushed myself against him that I almost didn't wait until he reached into his wallet. But I wasn't stupid, even if I was consciously defying my own rules. I waited for him to cover up, albeit impatiently, and when he pushed my underwear aside and I lowered myself onto him, I threw back my head and sighed. This was it. *He* was it. He was my passion. My release. My freedom.

We didn't move for a long time. I sat on Reed's lap on the drum stool with my legs wrapped around him while he talked about his childhood and his brother. It sounded like they had a love-hate relationship, one filled with ruthless competition and battles to the bitter death. Sports, board games, anything they could bet on. Vinny was always determined to win, but Reed, a year younger yet a touch stronger, usually came out ahead.

While he spoke, Reed rested his forehead against mine, or peppered my cheek and shoulders with kisses. His memories were goofy and pleasant, but there was also an underlying sadness. I didn't ask, but assumed it was because Vinny didn't speak to him anymore.

Eventually, it was time to go. There was only so long we could sit on a stool. We gathered the garbage and headed toward the front door.

I scanned the room.

"Your sax and your bag. Where are they?" This was the first time I'd seen him without them.

"Oh, they're outside," he pointed. "In my car."

Before we reached the door and Reed unlocked it, I could have sworn I saw a tall, dark shadow glide past it. When Reed opened the door for me, no one was there.

"Did you see that?" I asked.

"No, what?"

"I think someone was outside."

He turned his head in both directions. "I don't see anyone. Must have been your imagination."

I flinched at his words, but he couldn't know how they'd bother me. I shook away the thought.

He motioned his hand in front of us. Parked two feet away was his navy SUV. "I have to move it soon. Alternate side," he answered, as if in response to my silent question about why there were no other cars on the block.

Except for one...a black two-door sedan.

A door slammed. The tinted windows prevented

me from seeing inside, but my heart raced as it pulled out of its spot and flew down the road. I turned to Reed to see if he thought it was strange that someone would be here after midnight when no stores were open and there were no homes around, then speed away like a bat out of hell. He just took my hand and walked me back to my car, noticing nothing strange.

I tried to be subtle as I scratched my neck and over my chest. I tried not to let him hear my quick, clipped breathing.

I did not imagine someone watching me in that store. I did not fabricate a car pulling away like they were caught spying on me.

It was not all in my mind.

It couldn't be.

Chapter Thirteen
Device: When in Doubt, Ask

"What the hell is with you? You're making me crazy."

There was that word again. *Crazy. Paranoid. In your imagination.* They all made me want to put my fist through the face of the person who muttered them. Morgan was lucky I loved her or, despite my pledge to keep calm, I might have done some damage to her.

"Nothing's with me. I just have some things on my mind."

The fact was, I hadn't slept at all the night before and I couldn't stop pacing now. Was there or was there not someone on that block last night? My chest pounded and I felt like I was going to vomit. I had to get a grip.

"Have you ever been down Sixth Street?" I filled some trays with condiments and tried to sound nonchalant.

"I don't know. Why?" She handed a customer her order.

"Reed's store is on that block. I'd never been. I was just wondering if you had." I don't know what I expected her to say. *Yes, I frequent that block and there's usually a sports car with tinted windows and a peeping tom driver lurking around.* Would that answer have made me feel better?

146

"Can't say I've been there. Is that where he took you on your date?" The air quotes she put around the word date pissed me off.

Okay, so it occurred to me, during my night of no sleep and lots of worry, that Reed once again planned a date that was not out in public. But it was romantic and thought out, and he even said his cousin helped him with it. I doubted his cousin would help him cheat on any wife or girlfriend. If there was something shady going on, I didn't want to know.

Besides, I had more important things to think about. Like whether I was losing my mind.

I could have asked Reed. I'd picked up my cell no less than six times during the night to ask, casually, if he'd noticed that car drive away. When he texted me an hour after I got home to tell me how our evening was the most unforgettable one he'd ever spent, I almost did.

But he would have wondered why I asked. I'd have to give him the reason. I may have opened up to him more than anyone else, but I wasn't ready to tell him that yet. What if he didn't want to take the risk of being with someone who could have the disease? I wasn't ready to let him go. Not yet.

Worse than that…what if he said no? That there was no car. That no one pulled away.

That was a reality I was not ready to face. Not yet to that either. Maybe not ever.

"Yes, and it was wonderful," I said. If I got defensive, she'd only push back. "What ever happened at Crimini's that night?" Asking about Chase was the best way to deflect her next statement.

"Nothing." She took some bills from the cash

register to give a customer his change. "It was…" She shook her head and didn't raise her head. "Nothing happened."

There was more to that story, but I wouldn't dig. Not when I didn't want her shovel in my backyard.

I was deciding where to take the conversation next when the door chimes clattered with a bang and Mamie raced into the store. "Jolie, I need to talk to you in the back." She grabbed my arm and yanked me into the storage room with the speed and strength of a twenty-year-old woman. "Sit."

I figured this had to do with my mother's failed attempt to talk to me and crossed my arms over my chest, defiant in my refusal to sit.

"Fine," she said. "But you'll wish you had when I tell you."

That made me nervous. I'd only need to sit if she had news about Tristan. I backed into a chair.

She pulled her chair next to me and placed a hand on each of my knees. Her beautiful gray eyes filled with clouds and worry while she contemplated her words.

"Just say it," I prompted her, sweat beading at my temples.

"Your friend." She cleared a quiver from her throat. "The one you call Crooked Curt. He's been stabbed."

The words were a flutter in the wind that suddenly filled the room. They took a second to register, a little at a time. What did she say? She wasn't talking about Tristan. She was talking about Curt. He'd been stabbed.

Everything went still.

Curt had been stabbed.

No.

"How do you know? Maybe it's not him. There are lots of people in that park."

"It's him, *ma petite-fille*. His picture is on the news."

Mamie had met Curt once or twice when he came into the shop. I introduced them. His wasn't a face you forgot. I had no doubt she was right.

"Is it bad?" A tiny croak escaped my lips.

"They're saying it's not good. Critical, I think is the word they used. I'm so sorry, honey."

My cheeks were wet before I realized I was crying. I stood and ran my hands through my hair. Curt. Poor, poor Curt. I started to pace.

"I need to see him."

"I'm sure it's limited to family, Jolie."

"I can at least try. Do you know what hospital he's in?"

Mamie shook her head. "That's not released."

"I need to find him, Mamie. Can you take over for me?"

"Of course." She stood and untied my apron, which was helpful because my hands were a shaky mess.

I hurried out of the back room and nearly ran into my mother, standing in the middle of my store.

"Jolie." She reached out to me, but I swatted her arm away.

"No," I barked as I barreled out the door.

There were three hospitals within a twenty-mile radius of the park, and on my second try, I got lucky. Sort of. The reporters outside confirmed that Curt was there, although no one would let me in to see him. When I told them I was his sister, they asked me his last name.

Shit.

Why had I never asked his last name?

I paced the waiting room for over an hour before a hand on my hip sent me flying.

I almost burst into tears when I turned around and Reed was there, arms open for me. I fell into them, but didn't cry. I just shook while he stroked my hair.

"How did you know where to find me?" I asked into his chest.

"I stopped by Stuff Your Crepes to see you. Mamie told me what happened and suggested I find you. Not that I wouldn't have figured that out on my own." His chest rumbled against my cheek when he laughed.

God, I wanted to feel this man against me forever.

"Thank you for coming."

"Of course I'm here, Jolie. Where else would I be?"

"Um…at work?"

"Nah, I got fired for breaking in last night."

I ripped my head away from his chest and gaped at him in horror.

He laughed. "I'm kidding." He kissed the top of my head. "I told you, I don't get that many hours. I'm off today."

I sighed and slapped his rock-hard chest. "Not funny. I've got enough to worry about right now, don't you think?"

"I'm sorry." He stroked my face. "Why don't we get you some coffee or lunch? Standing around here won't do anything. Especially if they won't let you in."

We went to the hospital coffee shop. Reed bought me an egg salad sandwich and nothing for himself.

"Aren't you hungry?" I offered him some of my

sandwich after I took a bite. I didn't realize how starving I was until the hospital food tasted good.

He waved it off. "I ate before I came. You enjoy."

I told him the few stories I had about Curt. My limited information made me realize how little I actually knew about the man I delivered food to every week for who knows how long. The eggs curdled in my throat. I made a silent vow to get to know the man better, if I had the chance. *Please, let me have the chance.*

Reed massaged my knuckles with his thumb. "Crooked Curt sounds great, Jolie. I'm ashamed to admit I was a little jealous of the time you spent with him."

"Ha, jealous? Of Curt? Why would..." I stopped midsentence. "What did you say?" My heartbeats froze all at once. I'd never mentioned Curt to him before. And I never called him Crooked to Reed. That was for damn sure.

"What?" Reed's tan face turned a shade of white a bleached sheet would have envied.

I yanked my hand from under his. "I never told you about Curt."

Reed pulled at his collar. "Sure you did. Don't you remember? Or maybe it was Mamie the night we were at her house. I can't recall." His voice sounded shaky, but I wasn't sure if it really was, or it was my interpretation. Had I told him about Curt and didn't remember? Would Mamie have mentioned him? What the hell?

"Reed, I—"

"You know, about the crepe deliveries and stuff," he added.

So he knew what he was talking about. I just didn't know how.

"You know what? I'm actually really tired from all of this." From getting no sleep from the night before. From going over things in my head. And now from not remembering for sure if I had a conversation or not. "I'd like to go home."

Reed walked me to my car, before heading to the other side of the lot to find his. I was tentative when I kissed him goodbye, though I wasn't sure if I had a reason to be.

****

Mamie picked up the phone. "How's Curt?"

"I don't know," I answered, distracted. I had put on the news, hoping for any information they'd give about the crime. "They wouldn't let me see him."

"I'm sorry, honey. I'll keep listening to see if I hear anything."

"Thanks, Mamie. Do you want me to come back into work?"

She paused on the other end. "No, it's okay. We've got things under control here."

"Okay. I guess I'm going to try to take a nap then."

"That sounds like a good idea. I'll let you go." Mamie almost hung up.

"Wait, Mamie?"

"Yes?"

I hesitated before asking. "Did you ever mention Crooked Curt to Reed? Like the night he came over your house for coffee?"

"No, Jolie. Why?" Her swift answer left no room for doubt and my stomach sank.

"I was just curious. Bye, Mamie."

"Good nap, dear."

The information from the news broadcast only made me feel worse. I turned it off. As soon as I rested my head on the pillow, I fell asleep to a whirlwind of worries, swirling like a tornado in the confines of my brain.

Chapter Fourteen
Device: Write Shit Down

I had to organize my thoughts. I had to figure out which ones made sense and which ones didn't. If any didn't. Some had to not make sense, because the thoughts I'd been having right before I fell asleep…well, they were just insane.

So I made a list. Three lists, in fact.

List number one: *Things I know for sure:*

1. There is a person called the Seaville Slasher stabbing homeless people in the park.

2. Three people have been stabbed within the last couple of months.

3. Reed keeps taking me on "dates" where no one else is around.

4. Reed said he's jealous of Curt.

5. Reed carries a switchblade in his bag—a bag he never lets me touch—that he used to cut my bra.

I added one more bit of information I'd learned from the most recent news story:

6. The crime occurred around 2 a.m. About an hour after I left Reed.

List number two: *Things that may or may not be real:*

1. A stranger was watching me inside the music store with Reed.

2. The same stranger sped away in a car after I saw him.

3. I told Reed about Curt.

List number three: *Things I fear:*

1. There was no stranger.

2. I told Reed about Curt and don't remember.

3. Reed is keeping me a secret because he's committed to someone else.

4. Reed is the Seaville Slasher.

5. I am losing my grip on reality.

I rocked back and forth as I read the lists over and over. They made no sense. Something on these lists made no sense. I twirled a plucked eyelash between my fingers as I forced myself to take deep breaths, and tried to figure out which items I could cross off.

There was no way Reed was the Slasher. That was impossible. Not the wonderful, sexy, sensitive, talented man I was dating. So what if he carried a knife for no apparent reason? So what if this last crime happened not long after we separated, in an area close to where we were, to a guy he admitted being jealous of? Those things didn't mean anything. And that didn't explain the other victims anyway. It was probably all a weird coincidence. I was just being...that horrible word: paranoid, because I didn't know that much about him, yet I was opening myself up to him completely. It was normal to have doubts.

Doubts, yes. But these kind? The attempted murder kind? I ran my pen over the list item, wanting to cross it off. My hand wouldn't move and on the list it stayed.

I got up to get a glass of water. Even with the air blasting, I was dripping wet and dehydrated. I guzzled the entire glass and went back for another. My doorbell rang. I was tentative as I crept toward the door, as if the answers to all my list questions were on the other side, waiting to reveal themselves.

What would have been the worst reveal? That Reed was married? That he was the Seaville Slasher? Or that I was exhibiting signs of schizophrenia?

As sad as it was, married was my best option. I'd even choose dating a criminal over the disease. Dread crawled its long legs over every pore of my skin and I shivered. None of these was tolerable.

Against my will, I looked through the peephole on my door. Reed's beautiful face greeted me on the other side, and I knew in an instant there was no way this man would hurt another person. I couldn't be misjudging him on such a huge scale. That left two options. But my need to be close to him and release some of my inner anguish had me opening the door before I could hesitate.

He took one look at me and pulled me into him. He had no idea how close I was to collapsing in his arms. "I knew I shouldn't have let you go home alone. I regretted it the second you drove away. He's going to be okay, Jolie. I know it."

He thought I was distraught over Curt. Of course he did. It was the last conversation we had. And I was. Just not *this* distraught.

He walked into my apartment, with me tucked under his arm. He sat me on the couch and stood in front of me. He was like a giant, towering over me. A gorgeous giant with ripped arms and a too-tight shirt. "How about a glass of water?"

I was about to tell him I'd just had some, when the sheet of paper I'd written the lists on taunted me from the table. I gulped. "Water would be great," I blurted. As he walked away, I snagged the paper off the table and jammed it under a couch cushion.

He returned with the water and drew me against his side with his arm around me. "We're going to watch TV to get your mind off Curt. Then I'm going to hold you in bed until you fall asleep. How does that sound?"

"Amazing. You can stay?" I asked, hopeful his answer would put some of my worry to rest.

"Until you fall asleep. I sure can." He kissed the top of my head and I had a fleeting thought that he was going home to a beautiful woman when he left me.

Reed was gone when I woke up in the morning, but there was a text on my phone, telling me how hard it was to leave. Then another telling me he'd stop by the shop today to check on me. Then a third detailing things he would do if I still didn't feel better and needed cheering up.

I blushed reading the third text but found the courage to respond with some suggestions about how I might return the favors. I'd never sent those kind of texts before, and the experience made me giddy with anticipation.

Reed was not the Seaville Slasher. The idea was ludicrous. As the hours passed the night before, and Reed spent every second caressing me, kissing me tenderly on the lips, the forehead and the face—and never trying anything else—I just knew. All the other questions remained unanswered, but in the light of a new day, things didn't seem as bleak and horrible. I was sure there had to be reasonable explanations for all of it. Explanations that didn't have to do with me being sick. I'd find them out eventually.

Just to be sure, I took an online screening test for schizophrenia. The tests didn't replace a doctor's evaluation, but they could give you an idea about whether you might need to be concerned. Whenever I felt nervous, I took one to show myself that I was okay. I knew all the questions by heart, but as long as I answered honestly, it should still be accurate. The screening came out fine and I was able to rest more easily.

For the time being.

With a clearer head, I left for the gym. As it turned out, I enjoyed the cross-fit class much more than the yoga class I'd replaced. The training was hard and it kicked my ass, temporarily relieving me of my burdens.

It was gorgeous out, the perfect summer day. It wasn't even that humid and I took my time getting to work. I decided to visit the Palace to see if I could get any information, but when I got there, the grounds were almost empty. I didn't recognize a soul.

After searching the area, a figure at a rusty water fountain caught my attention. His hand shook as he pushed the button to dispense water. It was Crooked Curt's friend, Ronnie, the Slasher's second victim.

"Ronnie." I was careful in my approach. I didn't know if Ronnie would recognize me and I was sure he'd be jumpy after his attack. He held up his hand to block the sun. He squinted, trying to place me. "It's Jolie, from the crepe shop."

Those words turned his uncertain expression into a familiar welcome. "Jolie, well how the hell are you?"

"I'm good." I moved closer. "How's your shoulder?" His arm was wound up in bandages, wrapped close to his body. The bandages had already turned a dirty shade of gray.

"Eh, not suh great. May not heal. But I couldn't

stay in the hospital. Don't exactly have coverage for physical therapy." He let out a harsh chortle.

I didn't know how to respond. It sucked that he couldn't get the care he needed, but he already knew that. I didn't have to tell him. "Have you heard anything about Curt?"

He shook his head. "I tried to visit, but it must have been a different guard at the desk than when I was there. This lady didn't give a rat's ass if I was as good as family or the goddamn president. She wasn't lettin' me in. In fact, if I'da tried to walk past 'er, I think she would have trampled me to the ground." He lifted the bottom of his shirt to wipe excess water off his mouth. "'F I see him I'll tell him you was asking about him."

I nodded. "Thanks, Ronnie. You should come by the store sometime. I'd be happy to see you. I've got some bandages we can replace that one with." I had no medical bandages at my crepe shop, of course, but I'd be sure to buy some in case he took my up on my offer.

"Maybe I will. Thanks, Jolie." He turned and walked down a path with overgrown shrubbery hanging over the walkway.

I headed to work. The closer I got to the boardwalk, the stronger the smell of the saltwater grew. I inhaled, taking in as much of it at once as possible. That smell was a source of energy for me, and with every step I took toward it, I felt more positive.

At Stuff Your Crepes, behind my counter, my mother was cooking. With one of my spatulas. Wearing one of my aprons.

I stormed to her. "What are you doing?" I asked through a clenched jaw.

"I'm helping out, Jolie. Mamie has something to do

today, so I offered to come in."

I struggled to keep my composure as heat traveled up my neck like a slow moving train. It may have taken a while, but when it got there, it was loud and powerful. "What does she have to do?"

"An appointment." My mother's dismissive answer, as she poured batter onto the stone, caused my body temperature to further increase. She had no right to know more about Mamie's whereabouts than I did. And how the hell did she know how to make crepes? She never worked the store with us. Not even when I was younger. It was always Mamie and me.

"What kind of appointment?"

"We can discuss it later, Jolie. For now, we have customers."

"No," I spat, louder than I intended. "*I* have customers. This is my restaurant. Mine and Mamie's. I'm not sure what you're doing here, but don't get comfortable." I tied on my apron, yanking at the strings as if my grievance was with them.

My mother didn't engage in the fight. She was polite while serving her next customer. The way she was able to just go on with the work and not be affected by my insult made me angrier. But I'd learned from the best. I could be cool. I could maintain my composure. I'd staked my sanity on it.

For the next few hours, my mother and I worked side by side, without uttering a word to each other. I refused to even look in her direction. When we were super slow and no one had to be served, I retreated to the back and pretended to take care of the supplies. She might have thought I was being childish, but she'd lost the right to have any opinion of me long ago.

This store was my joy. I would not allow her to ruin it for me, and I sure as hell wouldn't share it with her.

It wasn't a minute too soon when Reed stopped by in the late afternoon to check on me. He was puzzled, frowning a little at the woman behind the counter. He didn't say anything until I stepped outside with him.

"Who's that?" He bit into the steak and pepper crepe that I insisted he take for free. His lips puckered and he moaned. "Holy shit, Jolie, this is incredible."

"I know. It's Mamie's *au jus*. She's my mother." I switched gears and for a second he stopped chewing, confused.

Then he got it. He pointed inside. "That's your mother? Why is she working?"

"I don't know but I'm going to find out tonight."

"Are you okay working in there with her?" He licked the sauce off his fingers, with pleasure written all over his face. I was about to tell him he better not get more pleasure from the damn sauce than from me, but I refrained.

"What choice do I have?"

"Leave?" His brows rose in question. "Hang out with me. Let her handle things."

Leave her short-handed? In the middle of the day? I'd never do that. Except. Things were very slow. And it would punish her a little.

"What do you want to do?"

I didn't even tell her I was leaving. I just sauntered back inside, hung my apron, turned off my stone, grabbed my purse and left. Again, childish? Maybe. But she deserved it.

I didn't know how long I could stand to be away.

After all, my business would suffer if she couldn't hold down the fort. So Reed and I stayed close by, walking the boardwalk for a while. It was much more fun playing the games with him by my side than when I was alone. He didn't play, though. He stood behind me and watched me win a prize for filling a balloon with water the fastest. And another for throwing the most frogs on a leap pad. It wasn't fair. I grew up playing these games every week. I had a distinct advantage over these summer renters.

"Don't you want to play?" I asked, my arms full of junk I'd hand off to the first interested taker.

"Against you? No way. You're clearly a shark. Poor little kids don't know what they're up against."

"Hey!" I swatted him with a stuffed snake. "I wouldn't beat any kids. You're just a coward." I stepped closer and leaned into him. "Come on. Play. *Please*." I gave a little pout, remembering the way he liked it last time.

He took a step back and lifted his hands in front of him. "Nope. I will not try to overthrow the Boardwalk Queen."

"Ooh, I think I like that title. First Boardwalk, then Queen of the World. That could grow on me." No matter how much I tried to persuade him with flirtation, he insisted he'd rather watch than play.

Eventually, my guilt at leaving my mother alone wore on me. It was time to go back to work.

When I got there, she was helping a customer and a few others were at tables, already eating their food. She had everything under control. That shouldn't have irritated me the way it did.

I heated my stone and resumed taking customers

without acknowledging her.

"Your guy is certainly handsome," she said from next to me.

I didn't answer.

That was the last thing she said to me that day.

"Another appointment? What was it for?" I demanded when I got Mamie on the phone later.

"It's good for you to spend time with your mother, Jolie."

"So you didn't have an appointment?" I scowled at the phone. Mamie's ambiguous answers brought my frustration level to an all-time high.

"It doesn't matter. What matters is, you need to learn how to accept your mother back into your life."

No, that answer frustrated me more. We'd been through this too many times. She knew how I felt.

"Mamie, can you please answer me? Did you or did you not have an appointment today?"

She sighed. "I did, sweetheart. It was a doctor's checkup." She paused. She gulped like she was drinking something. "Jolie, I'd like you to come by tomorrow before work. Let's all have breakfast together. There are some things we need to talk about."

Chapter Fifteen
Device: Keep Your Eyes Open

Things we need to talk about. *Things we need to talk about?* There were no things we needed to talk about before my deserting mother came to town. Mamie's words were an annoying song on repeat in my mind all night long.

The next morning, I took a never-ending shower, giving myself the excuse that I had to shave in case I saw Reed that night. While that was true, I generally didn't take forty minutes to shave. The water was so chilly by the time I got out, I almost regretted my stall tactic. Then I went to three different stores to find acceptable crescent rolls. Never mind the fact that Mamie didn't eat them because she watched her cholesterol intake. Then I walked around until I found a nice florist, because I figured you bring flowers to your hostess. Sure, it was probably my twentieth brunch at Mamie's that year, but who was counting?

When I couldn't find another single errand to use to procrastinate, I made my way to her house, giving myself a pep talk the entire way. I would not let my mother get under my skin. No matter what feeble excuses she offered for leaving us all those years ago, I'd let them go with a grain of salt.

Confident I could handle whatever bullshit she tossed my way, I turned the corner and approached

Mamie's house.

Then I spotted it. My pulse raced and my breaths became shallow. Beads of sweat drenched my hairline. I needed to breathe into a bag. Or Reed's mouth.

The same car with the tinted windows that was in front of the music store sat parked in Mamie's driveway, behind the car I recognized as my mother's rental. But that couldn't be. Why would that car be here? Why would its owner be in Mamie's house? I had to be imagining it.

I couldn't be imagining it. It was too real. So real. But the only explanation would be that it had been following me, and that was too...too...paranoid to be real. Who would want to follow me?

I dropped my purchases on the sidewalk and leaned over, placing my hands on my knees. Darkness shaded my peripheral vision. There had to be an explanation.

I needed an answer. With as deep a breath as I could draw, I ran toward Mamie's. I ran my hand along the car as I booked up her driveway. The metal of the car was warm from the sun. If I was able to feel that, and the car really wasn't there, things were worse than I thought.

I threw open Mamie's door and grabbed her arm as soon as I saw her. "I need you to come with me." I panted. I pulled her out the door and stood at the top of her porch.

"Jolie!" she reprimanded, but I didn't care.

"Tell me what you see," I commanded.

"What's wrong with you?" She touched my forehead with the back of her hand. I jolted my head away.

"Please, Mamie. Just tell me." My croak was

desperate.

For the next beat or two, she inspected my face with narrowed eyes. Then she followed the direction of my finger, which was pointing at the car I prayed sat in the driveway and was not a figment of my imagination.

"I see Abby's car. And a black one behind it."

I drew a breath from deep inside my chest and released it in a long, loud huff. "Oh, thank God." I hadn't meant to say it out loud, but it escaped anyway. Now Mamie would give me the third degree, insistent on knowing why I acted like identifying the cars was of the utmost importance.

I searched for a quick cover. I didn't want to tell her what I'd suspected.

But she didn't ask. In fact, she didn't seem to notice or register how panicked I'd been. Instead, she scratched at her ear and was lost in her own thoughts for a moment, attention no longer on the cars. Or on anything, as far as I could tell.

"Mamie?" I lay my hand on her shoulder. Where had she disappeared to, all of a sudden?

My voice brought her back. She blinked. "If you're done dislocating my arm, can we go inside now?"

"Yes." I hung my head. "Sorry."

Mamie went inside while I collected the things I'd dropped all over the sidewalk. As I knelt to gather the flowers, I lifted my head toward the car. I was so relieved to find that it was, in fact, a tangible object, that I forgot to ask why it was there.

I made my way back into the house. The aroma of coffee filled the air. It might have tasted like thick dirt, but the smell took me back to the warmth my grandmother brought to a sometimes otherwise chaotic home.

Mamie was placing a tray with the cups on the living room table. My mother was on the sofa. Sitting next to her was a man who had to be in his sixties. His gray hair formed a horseshoe around his freckled head, and his slight paunch was covered by an untucked button-down shirt. One of his arms was draped over the back of the couch. The other rested on his stomach. His feet, loafers and all, were planted on the table next to the coffee.

I had no idea who this man was, but I couldn't for the life of me understand why Mamie wasn't having a fit over the fact that his filthy shoes were on her furniture.

My mother said hello and Mamie asked me to sit, but I stood in the center of the room, staring at this ill-mannered man. When I found my voice, it was anything but welcoming. "Who are you?"

"I'm Tim," the stranger answered, as if that explained anything.

My head swept to my mother, whom I assumed could offer more of an explanation.

"Jolie, join us and have a cup of coffee." My mother lifted a cup and held it in my direction.

"If you would have been around for the past eight years, you'd know I never go near that stuff. See? Three cups." I motioned to the table, where Mamie hadn't placed coffee for me.

My mother set the coffee back on the tray with a sigh. "Okay, Jolie." She rubbed the side of her face.

I sat in a side chair and Mamie took her place at the end of the couch. She reached for my hand.

"Tim came here with your mother, sweetheart."

Oh. He was her boyfriend or something. As if I cared who she was dating. I didn't need to be sat down to have that news broken to me.

I shrugged. "Okay."

"I hired him a few years ago."

My ears perked at her statement. Hired him? "For what?"

My mother found a thread on the seam of her shorts and twirled it in her fingers. "To keep tabs on Tristan. Tim is a private investigator."

It's a good thing they made me sit because my spine sagged in the chair like the bones had been removed all at once. Like I'd been filleted. How could a private eye have been keeping a watch on Tristan? We almost never knew his whereabouts.

"I don't understand." The harsh tone I'd used with her a minute ago was replaced by a small mutter.

My mother scooted back on the couch and straightened as if to gather confidence to speak. "About three years ago, Tristan told me a friend got him some kind of job with a mechanic. He told me he was taking new meds, although when I pressed him, he didn't give me any details. But he sounded good, so I felt at ease for a little bit. Then I didn't speak to him for a while, which was unusual. A few months later, out of the blue, he called. He sounded horrible. Just like your father when the voices were louder. When they were more dangerous." A child rode his bike outside and my mother watched him through the window as she got lost in a memory. She shook the thought away. "Anyway, I hadn't heard him like that in a long time."

My head reeled from her words. He had a job? It was unusual not to talk to him for a few months? What the hell was she talking about? Since he left, it was always months between points of contact. Sometimes even years. "I don't understand why you're saying that was a long time. That was normal. He wasn't speaking to any of us."

My mother's face melted into a guilty sag from her forehead down to her chin. She found the thread again. "He talked to me. Regularly."

Rage boiled low in my belly. "What do you mean, regularly?"

"Regularly. Every couple of weeks."

I stood. My face was hot and my body was shaking. The chair was too small to contain me. "How can that be? We didn't hear from him for months. We had no idea if he was alive or dead. There's no way you could have been in touch with him, because you would have told us. You wouldn't have made us worry sick every single fucking day."

"I'm sorry," she mumbled.

"What do you mean, you're sorry? You knew where he was all along?" I shrieked.

Mamie took my hand again and rubbed it, attempting to soothe me. "Jolie, let her finish."

I spun to her. "Did you know, too?"

If she said yes, I knew I'd never be the same. She was with me, watching me drive myself crazy with fear for my brother, year after year. That kind of a deception would have been unforgivable.

"She didn't know. I never told her," my mother answered as Mamie shook her head. "Please sit so I can tell you the rest."

"No," I snapped. "You talk. I'll listen. Then I'll never need to see you again." I wrapped my arms around my chest and paced back and forth in front of Mamie's couch.

My mother hesitated, but continued. "Anyway, he was very agitated on the phone. He was going on about how he had to stop working at the garage because one of the mechanics was reading his mind and now he had to find somewhere far away to live because the mechanic was using his thoughts to turn the city against him. A lot of what he said was incoherent. He was a mess. I could hear it through the phone. I asked him which medications he was taking but he said something about the mechanic messing with his meds and how they were the gateway to his mind, so he had to stop taking them. I tried to get him to tell me where he was. During the last conversation, he told me the name of the garage in New York, but he wouldn't tell me if he was still there. I flew in from California the next afternoon. But when I spoke to the mechanic, he told me he hadn't seen Tristan in weeks. He said he left after screaming about how no one would ever be able to get his secrets and making a mess of the shop in a fit. Then I didn't hear from Tristan for months.

"Too much time had passed. I'd never gone that long without talking to him. Even when he was in a bad way, somehow he still managed to call me. The complete silence was torture. It was deafening."

"I can imagine," I snapped. I'd been living with complete silence for most of eight years. I could not believe she hadn't been.

She ignored me. "I had to do something. So I found Tim. He was based in California, but traveled all over the country for cases. I had him try to find Tristan."

She took a long sip of her coffee, and held the mug

to her mouth even after she finished drinking. It was a stall tactic. I was familiar with them.

Finally, she set it on its saucer. "At first, he didn't come up with anything. It's hard to find a ghost. Eventually, Tristan withdrew cash from an account I'd set up for him. He always hated to use it when he was agitated because he was sure the money was being traced, but sometimes we'd get lucky, or he'd get desperate, and he'd make a withdrawal. Anyway, as soon as he did, Tim flew to New York. Tristan had been in the Bronx at the time, staying in a shelter. Since then, Tim's been keeping track of him. He wasn't maintaining much contact, but at least I had some idea about where he was. Until his last call."

"What happened after that?" I was furious, but I'd get to that. First I had to hear the entire story.

"He took off and none of the people who knew of him had any idea where he'd gone. He hasn't withdrawn any money from the ATM. He's disappeared. I'm terrified."

Nausea welled in my throat. It was like I'd found and lost him all over again. I had so many questions I didn't know where to begin. "How could you not tell us you were in touch with him?"

Tears welled in my mother's eyes. "He begged me not to, Jolie. He said he thought you'd have him committed."

"Of course I would have! At least until he could get sorted out," I yelled. "You should have, too, if you knew where he was living. He needs help!"

Her voice became a quivering whisper. "He didn't want that, Jolie. He told me"—she swallowed the tears in her throat—"he told me he'd kill himself if we forced him to go away. I couldn't have another…" She put her head in her hands and her shoulders shook. Though I knew she was crying at the thought of losing another loved one to suicide, I couldn't console her. She knew where he was all along and she didn't tell us. Now, he was lost, or worse. We could have gotten him help, if she'd told us sooner. This was her fault.

Tim rubbed her back, irritating me more.

"I was trying to protect him," she sobbed.

"Protect him?" Her idea of protection was appalling to me. "What else?" I snarled.

She lifted her head and wiped the tears with her palms. "What?"

"What else haven't you said?" I didn't know if there was more, but now was the time to ask, while she was vulnerable. Obviously she was good at concealing information when she wasn't.

She gulped. "The last people Tristan had contact with told Tim something disturbing." Her tears made her eyes look like glass and I thought they might crack into shards.

"What?" I bit.

"Tristan was doing drugs."

I fell back into my chair. By educating myself about the disease, I'd learned years before that drugs exacerbate the symptoms in schizophrenics. People often turn to them as an escape, but they make things worse. Much, much worse. No matter how bad my father got, my mother always made sure to keep him away from drugs, or any kind of alcohol. He never had a single drink that I could remember.

But if Tristan was taking drugs, there was no telling how bad his hallucinations and paranoia had become.

"No." I rocked in my chair, still hugging myself. "No, no, no," I repeated again and again.

Mamie came up behind me and wrapped her arms around my neck, clasping them in front of me. She rested her cheek against mine. "We're going to find him, *ma petite-fille*. Tim is going to help us and we'll find him. I promise you."

"I'm going to do everything I can to locate your brother." Tim pulled a cigar out of his shirt pocket and hung it from his lips. "Don't worry, sweetheart, we'll get him back."

I hated Tim's familiar tone that implied he was part of the family and had been dealing with this for years. Even more, I hated the fact that he had more knowledge about my brother than I did, more than I could probably even imagine. I had to talk myself down from exploding. I would not yell. No matter how much my rage threatened to burst from my mouth, nose and ears, I would keep my composure. It's what I did.

Instead of screaming all the profane accusations bubbling up, I took a step toward him. "You can't smoke in here," I said, my voice calm and monotone. "And get your damn feet off the furniture." I stormed between the sofa and the table, knocking his feet down with my knees.

I left. There was no way I could sit across from my mother knowing she'd kept such important information to herself all this time, while Mamie and I lost sleep and could have encouraged Tristan to get help. It was better when I just thought she wrote us all off.

I stood stone still, in front of Reed's music store before I realized I'd gone there. Part of me was shocked

I remembered the way. A couple of customers were inside browsing at the instruments. I found a man in a light blue shirt identical to Reed's and asked if Reed was in.

"Reed's not working today but I can help you with whatever question you have." The guy gave me an obligatory customer-service face, one I'd worn many times. I forced myself to return it before excusing myself. I didn't know I wanted to turn to Reed about this new information before I got here, but now that I couldn't share it with him, I almost felt a compulsion to do so.

I walked toward the door to leave the store and a car sped by. My memory flashed with Tim's car parked outside the other night. In my heated rush to escape the house, I didn't ask an important question. Why had he been following me?

I texted Reed. I needed to vent about what I'd learned and I didn't want to spill family secrets to Morgan. Besides, even if Morgan knew about the situation, the person I wanted to share it with was Reed.

He didn't text me back right away, so I headed to Stuff Your Crepes early. On my way, I catalogued my thoughts. I often found that when there were too many racing around, it helped to file them into mental folders. That way, I could put them away for the time being. It helped abate the nerves and worry until I could productively deal with each issue—another useful technique from therapy. While doing that, I wasn't paying attention to where I was going, and when I looked around, nothing was familiar. I tried to retrace my steps, back to the music store, but that only confused me further. The town wasn't that big, and if you could find the ocean, you could head in the direction of the boardwalk. But somehow I'd become so spun around I couldn't even do that.

It wasn't surprising. I paid no attention when Reed walked me to his job. I was much more concerned with the way he rubbed his thumb over my hand while we walked, and with the stories he told me about his childhood. He could have walked me into Canada and I probably wouldn't have noticed. Now, my horrible sense of direction and I were paying for it.

No stranger to getting lost, I tried to use GPS on my phone. My service was spotty and the app wouldn't load, so I walked into the nearest coffee shop. My stomach growled as I walked through the door. It smelled of bacon and after not eating anything at Mamie's, an egg and cheese on a bagel sounded amazing. Some sweet, flavored coffee that I could tolerate, would be good, too. I stepped onto the short line and allowed the soft music to lull me. The store wasn't jam packed, but the tables were almost all full. I felt a fleeting wave of envy.

I inspected the customers. Customers that could also potentially be mine, assuming I hadn't strolled too many miles from the boardwalk. I always viewed strangers as potential patrons and wondered how I could get them into my shop. Career hazard.

My gaze came to a screeching halt when it fastened on a back. A back that was too familiar. A back I'd run my hands over on more than one occasion. A back whose muscles rippled when I dug my nails into it. Sitting across from that back was a beautiful woman with long fire red, satiny hair and large, green eyes.

I almost walked over to their table to say hi. If my

suspicions about Reed were true and he was with someone else, it was better to know now. Before I got in deeper.

I sucked in a breath. Or two. Or five. I instructed my foot to take a step in their direction. Just as it lost contact with the ground and was about to listen, the woman placed a white, folded envelope on the table in front of Reed. He shook his head and slid it back toward her, but she placed her hand on top of his, pushing it back. This reverse tug-of-war lasted for a few more seconds before the woman got annoyed. She frowned and said something to him, in a voice too low for my straining ears to hear. Reed lowered his head, but accepted the envelope, sticking it in his duffel, which sat on the floor next to him.

Satisfied, the woman gathered her coffee and plate and brought them to the garbage. She returned to Reed, who still sat with his back to me. She kissed him on the top of his head, but when he didn't lift it, she raised his chin with her forefinger and said something. What I would have done to have the hearing of a bat at that moment.

Reed nodded and the woman left.

"What can I get for you, miss?" the girl behind the counter asked, invading my snooping.

I whispered my order and scurried out through a side door before Reed knew I was there.

Chapter Sixteen
Device: Surround Yourself with Trustworthy People

To ask him or not to ask him? I questioned myself over and over before responding to his text. He didn't get back to me until later, and when I asked him what he spent the day doing, he answered *not much*. While it may not have been a lie, it definitely wasn't forthcoming. How far did I want to press?

At first, I was sure that woman was a wife or girlfriend. But why would a wife or girlfriend pass him an envelope in a café? The way she touched him told me she was no business associate—how much more was she exactly? No matter how many times I went over it in my head, I couldn't make heads or tails of it.

So I sat, deliberating about whether I should tell him I saw him, and come right out and ask my question. Or if I should continue along the path we'd been on, where he revealed information at a pace that made him comfortable. Everything else was turning to shit at that moment. He was the one thing that made me happy. He was a private person, but we'd been making headway. Every time we spoke, he told me a little more about himself. Did I want to ruin everything by asking?

Yet, if I was so happy, why was I wondering if he was a husband or a slasher?

Before I made a decision on which way to take the

next text, a new one from him appeared.

—*I want to take you out tomorrow. I need to see that smile of yours.*—

I hated how those few words had me forgetting about getting to the bottom of what I saw and almost dizzy with anticipation. Knowing I'd see him later did that to me every time.

I wrote back:

—*Oh yeah? Just my smile you need to see?*—

I could almost hear his growl at my teasing on the other side.

—*For starters. I plan to see a lot more…*—

My face heated even though no one was around, remembering the drum stool. I was about to ask him if he had any other instruments to introduce me to, but his text beat mine.

—*I wrote you another song, though it's on paper, not a napkin. I'll play it for you after dinner at Crimini's. I'll pick you up at 9, when you close. Okay?*—

My heart fluttered and my fingers trembled. This was not Reed trying to hide me. This was Reed bringing me to the most romantic restaurant in town, out in public, writing me another song. Even thinking of Tim searching for Tristan couldn't ease my excitement.

"You must have heard from Reed," Morgan said when I returned to my stone, after taking a short bathroom and texting break.

"Why?" I asked. How did she know?

"Because you're all flushed and giddy like a fool." There was no pleasure in her comment, just judgment.

"He's taking me to Crimini's tomorrow." Why did

I feel like I had to justify myself to her?

She stopped working to stare at me. "It's very expensive there."

I shrugged. "Okay?"

She said nothing but turned back to her stone.

"You never told me how your date with Chase was, aside from fine."

Morgan and I hadn't been talking a lot, ever since she went out with Chase. Part of me knew it was because I felt like she was judging me, assuming Reed was in a relationship and thinking I was a homewrecker. The other part felt like it was because she didn't want to talk about Chase. Maybe I was pushing it by even asking now, but I wanted my friend back. If she wanted to accuse me of doing the wrong thing with Reed, so be it. We could have it out. At least we'd be talking. I could explain to her that he made me feel more like the me I wanted to be than anyone I'd ever met. If I found out he was married, I'd break it off, but I hadn't asked yet because deep down, I knew I was afraid. I was afraid this part of me would disappear as soon as he was gone, and I wasn't ready to let him, or that part, go yet.

At least I could tell her. It would be better than the silence.

Instead of making a snide comment, though, her eyes filled with tears. She practically shoved a crepe at a customer before running into the back room. I had to finish serving two more people, but as soon as I was done, I went after her. "Hey, what's wrong?"

Morgan sat on a stool. She was wiping away tears with a napkin, which she used to blow her nose. She shook her head. "Nothing. Sorry, I'll be right out."

"There's no one out there. Tell me what's got you so upset."

She lifted her head. "How do you do it, Jolie? How do you overlook everything and enjoy him? Doesn't it bother you?"

There it was. She was implying Reed had a wife. "I don't know of anything that should bother me, but I'm asking about you, not me."

Morgan sniffled. "I care about him, Jolie. I really, really do. Much more than I want to. I have for a long time now. But that's not everything, you know?"

I waited for her to wipe her nose and continue.

"My parents have nothing. Every month, they scrape by to pay their mortgage. I could never have new stuff when I was little, I was jealous of all my friends who had nice clothes and toys. I promised myself that wouldn't be me as an adult. I'd never be with someone who would lead me into a life of scraping by. I'm taking loans out for college because my parents can't pay and I work here for spending money. But that's just until I graduate, Jolie. I want things. I want a nice house and nice clothes and to travel. I need to be with someone who wants the same things."

All of a sudden, I understood. "You don't want to be with Chase because he's a teacher?" I had no idea Morgan was so shallow. It must have been written all over my face.

"Don't look at me that way. He's a grown man who needs a roommate to pay rent. He has to tutor to earn extra cash because his salary isn't enough. I wish I wasn't like this. I wish I didn't feel this way, but I do. No matter how much I love being with Chase, he can't give me the kind of life I'm looking for."

I was appalled. Actually, physically appalled at what she was saying. Chase was a good, honest, hard-working guy who obviously cared about her. If she didn't want him because his income wasn't high enough, if she couldn't appreciate those things about him, then she didn't deserve him.

I turned toward the door.

"He kissed me, you know."

I turned back.

"As soon as dinner was over. He took my hand and walked me out of the restaurant. There's a beautiful patio out back. It's lit with white lights and is covered by a canopy. Very romantic. Anyway, he led me to it and told me how he's been crazy about me since we met. Then he leaned in and kissed me."

"And?" I asked. After what she just told me, I knew there wasn't a happy ending.

"I kissed him back. I'd never felt that kind of tenderness before in a kiss. He was so sweet." She wiped a new tear off her cheek. "Then I told him I didn't feel the same way. Even though I do. I just thought it was kinder that way."

There was nothing kind about what she was doing, but it wasn't my business.

"I don't know what to tell you, Morgan. I don't think that would make a difference to me. I think if I truly cared about someone, the numbers on his paycheck wouldn't matter."

Her expression grew dark and cloudy. "You don't know, Jolie. You don't know what your reaction will be until you're in the situation. Don't judge me. Wait and find out for yourself." She wiped her face on the bottom of her apron and went back out front to serve our customers.

Before Reed came around, Morgan never showed such animosity toward me. It was growing tiresome.

I straightened my apron even though it didn't need straightening, and headed back out to join her. I wouldn't allow her petty comments and digs to make me uncomfortable in my own store. My chimes jingled at the same time.

Ronnie from the Palace stood in the doorway. He didn't enter any farther, and I felt like he might need a nudge. I waved to him from behind the counter. "Hi, Ronnie. Welcome."

He took a few slow steps, rubbing the back of his neck. He searched the room and then made it the rest of the way to the counter. "Hi there," he said.

"What can I get you?" I poured out some batter, so happy that he'd come in.

"Oh, nuthin'. Nuthin'." He waved both hands in front of him. "I just wanted to let you know I heard sumthin' about Crooked Curt." His hollow eyes swept over all the crepe fillings behind the counter.

My heart raced as soon as he mentioned news about Curt, but it also ached at the hunger in his face. "Well, first tell me what you want to eat, then tell me about Curt."

"Really, you don't need to give me nuthin'." His open mouth, almost salivating, said otherwise.

I heated another stone. "Ronnie, please, it's my pleasure. I'd much rather you tell me what you like than for me to guess." I pointed at the menu over my head.

He glanced up for a tenth of a second before shrugging. "Whatever you think, then."

It occurred to me that Ronnie might not be able to

read my menu.

"Okay." I loaded up two crepes. One was my *South of the Bord-walk,* with chicken, beans, cheeses and Mexican toppings. The other, stuffed with shrimp salad, was ready sooner. "Here's a *Sea You Later.*" I handed him the crepe and he engulfed almost half of it in his mouth in one bite.

"Let's go sit and discuss Curt." I wrapped the second crepe and motioned to an empty table, bringing a lemonade with us.

"He's doing a little better," he said through a mouthful. He wiped his mouth on his arm. "They said he was in 'tensive care, but not anymore. They moved him to a diff'rent hospital."

"Why?" I asked.

"It's a veteran's hospital. So he can get whatever he needs, I guess."

"Curt's a veteran?" I was ashamed of the question. How did I not know that?

Mayonnaise smeared in Ronnie's facial hair. "Yup. Gulf War, Desert Storm." He took a long gulp of the lemonade. "Anyway, I heard Marilyn is with him. He can get other visitors now, but the hospital's a ways away, so I won't be going. Thought you'd like to know, though." He finished his crepe and crumpled the wrapper in unsteady, soiled hands. He held up the other crepe. "Thanks for the food."

He told me the name of the hospital and started to disappear out the door, but I caught him before he was gone. "Ronnie, wait."

He turned back to me.

"Can you come into the back for a minute? I've got those bandages we talked about."

****

Visiting hours were until nine, so I had to get coverage for the store. When I called Mamie, my mother answered and offered to take the shift. I didn't want her anywhere near me, or my store for that matter, but she said Mamie was tired, so I couldn't argue.

Curt lay in bed with the covers pulled up to his chest. He looked frail and weak, but also the cleanest I'd ever seen him. His hair was lighter than I'd realized, and he was younger than I thought. He couldn't have been more than forty, forty-five.

When he spotted me in the doorway, he sat up a little. "Oh no way! The cat lady's here. You didn't have to come." He smiled and revealed his half-empty mouth.

"Who?" I asked.

A nurse checking his vitals chuckled. "They've got him on some good pain meds."

Curt scoffed. "I'm not high. I know Jolie when I see her. Come on over, darlin'." He tapped the bed next to him and I knew the nurse was right. The only times I'd made physical contact with Curt, he'd flinched.

I sat on the side of the bed, careful not to invade his space. "How are you, my friend?" I asked. Maybe it was presumptuous to call him that, but I did care about him and wanted to be a friend to him in any way I could.

"Been better. Although right now I feel really good."

We chatted for a bit. Curt told me that if the hospital kept taking care of him this way, he might never leave. He told me about the food they were serving him. He didn't bring up the attack.

"Do you remember what happened?" I finally asked.

"Nope. Coward got me from behind. Pierced my neck. Lucky for me, he didn't get any arteries or anything, or else we probably wouldn't be having this conversation."

The knife's tear was jagged and long, down between his shoulder blades. He'd lost a lot of blood and had come down with an infection at the wound site, but was taking IV antibiotics and improving every day. "I'd love to get my hands on this guy," he said. Then he released a long, loud yawn. He was growing tired.

"I won't stay and wear you out. I just wanted to come by and see how you were." I stood from the bed.

"That was awfully thoughtful," a voice said from behind me.

I turned to face a woman with a gentle, round face and dark wavy hair. "You must be Jolie," she said. "Curt has told me all about you, and your drop-offs. I'm Marilyn. Curt's wife. Ex-wife," she corrected and offered me her hand.

Her statement took me by surprise. I had no idea Curt was in touch with family, or had a wife, ex or not. And I would never have imagined that he would talk about me. I extended my hand in a fog of confusion. She must have noticed my shock. She motioned for me to join her outside the room.

I said goodbye to Curt, and Marilyn walked me out, to the other side of the door.

"Yes," she whispered. "He keeps in contact with us. It's just hard for him to stay home. He feels like we're better off without him." She wrung her hands together.

"Can I ask why?" It was none of my business, but she reminded me so much of myself, concerned for a man she loved.

"Curt's got PTSD. He tried to get some help when he first came home from the war, but it didn't do much. Eventually he grew frustrated and embarrassed and stopped. He felt that he was putting us in danger, so he took off. He comes home from time to time to see our children, but he never stays long."

"He has children?" I couldn't believe it. I never pictured him with a family. Then again, I really never pictured his life before the streets.

She nodded. "Two. One born during his time there, one after. I explain things the best I can. They try to understand, but even though they're grown, it's hard. They just want their dad home safe."

"I had no idea." I hoped my voice didn't sound as hollow out loud as it did inside my head.

"I'm sure not. He doesn't talk about his time there." She looked at her watch. "Wow, it's late. If you don't mind, I'm going to say goodbye to him. I have to go home and call my kids. I like to check on them daily."

"No, of course. It was so nice meeting you, Marilyn."

She scurried back into Curt's room. He was already asleep but she kissed him on the cheek. He flinched.

I said my own silent goodbye before going home.

Chapter Seventeen
Device: Demand Honesty

I must have been on hundreds of date in my life. Hell, I'd even been on a few with Reed. But none made me as nervous as this one. For some reason, I felt like this was a turning point.

So when Mamie called and asked me to stop by, telling me there was more we needed to discuss, I refused. Whatever it was, I knew it wasn't good. I was so down about Curt, I was having a hard time picking myself up, and didn't need more bad news to ruin my night. Besides, I'd already subjected Reed to enough family drama. I wasn't getting some bomb dropped on me hours before our dinner.

The restaurant was every bit as beautiful as its reputation promised. Somehow, Reed got reservations on the patio, under those dim lights Morgan mentioned. The food was spectacular from the first bite of my grilled artichoke appetizer, to the last spoonful of the tiramisu Reed and I shared. He held my hand, or touched my hair intermittently throughout the meal. We joked and laughed and the entire thing would have been like a dream.

Except Reed wasn't himself. I couldn't put my finger on it, because he was still flirty and joking around, but something was off.

When the check came, I offered to split it. This was

a nice place and the prices were hefty. He wouldn't hear of it. He placed his cash in the checkbook and set it aside. He helped me with the shawl that the weather made unnecessary, but that complemented the dress I'd painstakingly chosen.

We strolled for a while, fingers linked. He was quiet. Contemplative. Whatever was bothering him, I wanted to find a way to ease his nerves. As we approached a quiet corner, I stopped walking and stood close to him, so my chest was pressed against his. I ran both hands through his hair.

"Are you okay? You seem quiet tonight."

His gaze landed on my lips, before lifting back to my eyes. He grabbed my hips in his large hands and pulled me closer. "I'm okay."

"Yeah? Does this help?" I gave him a slow kiss.

He returned it for a moment before pulling away. He twirled a few strands of my hair between his fingers. His olive, sun-kissed skin had grown paler. "I've been feeling guilty about something, Jolie."

My stomach tightened. I should have been waiting for the other shoe to drop. Guys like Reed didn't exist without a whole slew of problems.

"Okay?" I wanted to cover my ears with my hands. I didn't want him to relieve himself of his guilt. Not now, when everyone else was unburdening themselves on me. Not if it made me walk away.

But I wasn't three years old and denying the truth didn't make it any less inevitable.

"You don't deserve what I've been doing."

I dreaded his next words. I wanted to run before he could tell me about her. Any *her*.

"You deserve this." He took my hands and spread

my arms, as if to put me on display. "You deserve gourmet food and a reason to wear that dress." His eyes raked over my body in a way that heated me everywhere. "And"—he lowered his voice and leaned closer to me—"you deserve sex in a bed, where I can take my time exploring every inch you. Not rushed sex in random places."

"Reed—" This was his big guilt? That we were having too much exciting sex? Relief swept over me like a fantastic summer breeze.

"Don't get me wrong." He didn't let me cut in. "The music store was fucking incredible. And the museum? God, Jolie, I want to rip your clothes off right here thinking about it. But I don't want you to think that's why I went after you. I just...it's just..." His eyes grew dark. "Do you remember that couple sitting next to us?"

I did. The woman was adorned in diamonds. They were drinking expensive champagne. Everything about them said money. I nodded.

"I want that for you. I know you said you've already been pampered, but not by me. I wish..." Again his voice trailed off as he was lost in thought. "Let me pamper you tonight, Jolie. Let me show you that even if I can't do other things for you, I can do that."

"Reed, where is this coming from? I never said I wanted that. I'm perfectly happy with how things are going." If he knew how I lay in bed at night, reliving what we'd been doing, I didn't think he would've given that speech.

"Please, let me show you who I am. It's important that you know the real me, before—"

A headlight flashed from somewhere behind Reed.

Though the night was dark, I could make out the damn car. It was Tim. Even though I couldn't see him through the tinted windows, I had no doubt.

Like a bolt, I freed my hands from Reed's and ran toward that car. It tried to pull away, but I jumped right in front of it. He'd have to hit me if he wanted to get away.

I pounded the hood of Tim's car with both palms. "Why the hell are you following me?" I yelled.

Now I could see his round face through the front window. He shrugged.

"No." I walked around to the driver's side of the car. "Not this," I mimicked his shrug. "Tell me why."

He rolled down his window so he didn't have to raise his voice, the way I realized I was doing. "Your mother wants me to keep an eye out."

"My mother? Well you can tell my mother she lost her right to keep an eye out for me years ago. And if you were as conspicuous at following Tristan as you are with me, it's no wonder he ran. You must have spooked him. You even had *me* thinking *I* was crazy. Great private detective my mother found."

I walked back to a confused Reed. "What was that?"

I didn't want to talk about Tim. Or my idiot mother. Or my lost brother. Or my grandmother, who kept coming up with weird reasons to have my mother work with me. All I wanted was to hear more about what Reed thought I deserved. I reached up and threaded my fingers behind his neck.

"Take me home and pamper me," I whispered in his ear.

I didn't realize I'd cut off his sentence until much

later.

****

We drove back to my place in Reed's SUV. Each time he turned to glance at me, I couldn't tell if his serious expression was laced with desire or the same emotion I couldn't read earlier. When his gaze trailed down my body and halted on my bare legs, I assumed it was the former.

Despite his speech, I expected a replay of our previous dates. I expected the same raw desire as soon as my apartment door closed, but Reed was true to his word. He led me into the bedroom and laid me back on the bed. He kissed me for so long, and so tenderly, that my lips were deliciously swollen and worn out. As he peeled each article of clothing from my body, he replaced it with soft kisses and caresses, doting on every inch of me, until I couldn't take it anymore.

Eventually, I slapped my palm into the mattress. "Come on!" I huffed, then let my hands roam his body. I expected him to get excited and speed up.

Instead he dropped his forehead into my chest and sighed. "God, Jolie. I still can't believe you're really touching me."

I looked at the top of his head. "What do you mean? When did you ever have a doubt about a woman wanting to touch you?" Where had my cocky Music Man gone? Humility was not one of Reed's strengths.

He lifted his head and rested his chin on my chest bone. "Nothing. I don't know. You're just incredible and I'm very happy to be here with you." With that, he ran his hands through my hair and kissed me, giving me exactly what I asked for, exactly what I needed.

****

I dreamt of a stranger, desperate to reach me, pounding on my front door. As I came out of my groggy sleep, the stranger disappeared, but the knocking continued. I rolled onto my back to answer the door, and felt like I was still dreaming. In my bed, sleeping soundly on his stomach, was the most beautiful man I'd ever seen. His bare, muscular back rose and fell with each of his soft breaths. My sheet covered him from the waist down, outlining his perfect lower half.

The entire night before flashed through my mind in a matter of seconds. The tender care he took when he made love to me. The agonizing, sad song he played for me as we lay in bed, with my sheets serving as our clothing. My elation when he asked if he could stay the night. The words he whispered when he thought I was asleep on his chest as he rubbed my back. *I've loved you for so long, Jolie. I'm so sorry.*

Though I'd never been happier to hear a person say he loved me, the second half of that statement was disturbing. I'd put this off for long enough. I was going to find out everything that day. I'd sit him down and ask him questions until I was satisfied I knew enough. If that meant we had to be over, then so be it.

That's what I told myself. It's what my head swore. My heart feared I wouldn't be strong enough to leave, even if it was the right thing.

The banging on my door grew louder. I threw on a T-shirt and shorts, huffing that we were being intruded on at this early hour. This was the first time Reed was waking up in my bed. I wanted to savor it a little before having the dreaded conversation. Whoever was on the other side of the door was ruining that for me.

"You're avoiding me," Mamie said as soon as I opened the door. "So I came to you." She pushed her way inside and stormed into my kitchen. She opened and closed cabinets with a bang. "Where is your coffee?"

"I don't have any," I whispered, hoping her intrusion didn't wake Reed. When she scowled, I added, "I get it around the corner."

She walked back into the living room and plopped herself on my couch. "Now, I have things I need to tell you, and you must listen. No more of this scurrying off like you did when you were thirteen and didn't want to hear what I was saying." She crossed her arms in front of her chest. She meant business.

I sat next to her on the couch and tucked my feet under my legs. It was so easy for her to revert me into an adolescent who had to listen to her. Maybe it was because she was the only consistent authority figure I ever had. My mother was there until she wasn't, but my father had to be her priority. It was easy for Tristan and me to fall by the wayside.

"Okay. What is it?"

She cast me a hard glare. She was preparing herself to tell me something I didn't want to hear. Her pink lips pinched the way they did every time she broke bad news. Like to tell me the voices were louder and my father was agitated. Or that he'd been arrested for making a public disturbance. Or that Tristan's test results had come back.

I didn't want to hear anything that was on the other side of that expression.

"I've been seeing a doctor."

For a split second, the air around me disappeared,

making it impossible to breathe, but Mamie took my hands in hers and spoke immediately.

"I'm okay. I've just been forgetful lately. Getting things wrong. Losing words. It's unlike me. I thought it was the early signs of dementia. That annoying WebDoc app had me convinced."

The word dementia pounded in my head with such tenor I forgot to appreciate how my eighty-something year old grandma was looking up symptoms with an app on her phone.

"It's not," she quickly followed with. "I've had an MRI. My doctor said it's just..." Mamie's face scrunched into an awful, angry scowl. "Aging," she spat out the dirty word. "He says it's normal aging, but none of it feels normal to me."

Mamie prided herself on being sharper than a tack. A diagnosis of "old age" must have hit her like a hard slap in the face. I was surprised she didn't slap the doctor who gave it to her.

"Plus, I'm having more trouble with my hip. Standing all day and working the register and making the crepes isn't working for me anymore, Jolie."

I nodded. "I understand, Mamie. It's too much. I'll take on more hours. Maybe we'll hire someone new." It was inevitable. Mamie wouldn't be able to keep at the pace she was used to forever. Still, the idea of working without her filled me with an immense weight of sadness.

"No, dear," she said.

"It's not a problem. I don't mind working more."

"No." She shook her head. "You work enough, and we can't take on more help. It's already been decided."

For a reason I didn't know, a sharp chill ran up my

spine.

"What has?"

"I'm selling my portion of the store to your mother. She and Tim are going to live with me until…well, they're going to live with me."

I jumped from my seat. "No way! I'm not working with her. I'm not going to be in business with her. She's taking that terrible PI and going back to California where they came from. Do you know she even had the audacity to have him follow me? As if she has a right to know anything about my life! You cannot sell the store to her, Mamie. You just can't!"

She stood to take my hands again and pulled me back down to a sitting position. "Sweetheart, those are the facts. That is what's happening. Now you have to listen to the advice. I'm not just selling her the store because I'm too old to manage it anymore. Believe me, if that was it, I'd fight this bitch they call age tooth and nail to keep what's mine. I'm doing this because I know it's good for you." I opened my mouth to protest, but she held up her hand. "There isn't a soul in this world who is perfect. Now, I may be close, but believe it or not, I even have my little idiosyncrasies."

I chuckled but she was deadpan.

"You want people to be perfect. You use your "devices" to manage yourself, but all they do is keep you at a distance from people. I understand why you are afraid but you've seen doctors. They've told you you're fine and the older you get, the less likely you are to develop that damn disease.

"Reestablishing a relationship with your mother is the first step. Yes, she did wrong. But, Jolie, people do wrong sometimes. It doesn't mean they're bad people.

It means they made a bad decision, or in some cases, a few bad decisions. You are willing to be so kind and generous to all the strangers you know, who may or may not have contributed to their own circumstances, but you're not willing to pass that same generosity to the woman who birthed you. It's not right, dear."

My bedroom door opened and Reed peeked out. When he saw Mamie sitting in my living room, he blushed. "I'm sorry to interrupt. I just wanted to make sure everything is okay."

"Come out here, darling. You should hear this, too."

Reed was tentative in his approach to the couch. I was grateful he put his clothes back on. Otherwise, my hands might not have been the only thing Mamie grabbed.

"I was just telling Jolie that she needs to be more understanding and forgiving. That sometimes people do things they might not be proud of, but they have their reasons and she shouldn't cast them aside without trying her best to put herself in their positions. Wouldn't you agree, Reed?"

A look passed between them. It reminded me of that other time they shared a moment. I was certain at that second, Mamie knew something about Reed that I didn't.

"I'd say that's probably true," Reed mumbled.

I hated that they shared something. I hated even more that Mamie was lecturing me on forgiveness. She and I weren't the same. Her mother hadn't abandoned her after consecutively losing her father and brother. Having her daughter-in-law walk away wasn't nearly as hurtful. She had the luxury of forgiving Abby.

I looked back and forth between them. What did they know?

"What is this?" I barked.

"What's what?" Mamie asked.

"These looks you keep giving each other. Like you're hiding something. It's bad enough you barely tell me anything," I shot at Reed. "Except to apologize to me in my sleep for some mysterious secret. What, do you have a girlfriend? A wife? And Mamie knows? Is that it?"

"What?" Reed asked, eyes wide, looking stunned.

"And you"—I turned my attention to Mamie— "I've been telling you to stay out of my relationship with my mother for years. Instead, you decide forcing me into a business partnership without even consulting with me is the way to go? Why don't you two go off and talk about me somewhere where you can plot against me some more?"

"Jolie." Reed reached for me but I pulled away.

"What is it you're hiding, Reed? Why don't you tell me things? Like why haven't I been to your house? Why do you carry that damn bag everywhere you go? Why can't you normally spend the night? Who were you having breakfast with the other day when I texted you and didn't hear from you for hours? And why the hell does Mamie look at you like she knows you better than I do?"

If I'd plotted out every word I was going to say when I confronted him, not one of those words would have exited my mouth that way, but this wasn't planned. Not a word of it. All my questions just spilled out as if I had no control over them, and now I looked like an insecure, jealous girlfriend. But they were questions that needed answers, and even if I asked them the wrong way, I was still anxious to hear what he had to say.

Chapter Eighteen
Device: Honesty is the Only Policy

Reed's jaw bobbed as if he were talking to me, but no sound emerged from his lips. He ran a hand through his hair and shook his head in silence. He disappeared into my bedroom, came out with his bag, and gave me the most despondent look I've ever seen, right before walking out my door without uttering a single word.

I stood, frozen in a stupor. He just left. That was an admission of guilt if ever there was one. I fell into my couch, with the wind knocked out of me. "He's married," I whispered into the air.

"He's not," Mamie answered, even though I wasn't talking to her. In fact, I'd forgotten she was there at all.

"What do you mean, he's not?" I faced her. "I asked him point blank if he has a wife and he bolted out of here like a bat out of hell. Of course he's married."

She shook her head. "You don't know everything, *ma petite-fille.*"

Her pet name enraged me and I couldn't keep from bellowing. "Yes. I'm your darling granddaughter. So where's the loyalty, Mamie? It's supposed to be me and you against the world. The two of us. You're off plotting with my mother behind my back for God knows how long and now, with a stranger. What the hell is going on? You are *my* grandmother, *my* blood. Not Abby's and certainly not Reed's. Where is your allegiance?"

Raising my voice to my grandmother was a big no-no. Even though she fought to keep her demeanor because I was distressed, her clenching jaw told me I'd broken an unspoken rule.

"Allegiance is not the same as disclosure, Jolie." She shot me an all-knowing, condemning glare. "I can be loyal to you without telling you every piece of information I come across. Especially if I deem hiding the information beneficial to you." She stood up and stepped in front of me, knocking her knees into mine. She leaned over me and pointed between my eyes. "Don't you ever question my loyalty. Since the day you were born, every one of my actions has been what I thought was best for you and your brother. You may not understand my motives all the time, but someone needs to save you from hiding inside yourself until you're nothing but a shell, too afraid of a diagnosis that will never come to let yourself experience true emotions. Don't dare condemn me for trying to be that person."

She threw her purse over her shoulder, turned on her heel and left, slamming my door. She was the second person in less than five minutes to run from my home, leaving me with a cluster of emotions and a laundry list of unanswered questions.

My immediate response was to recoil at having spoken to Mamie in such a way. Her words were true. She did spend her life helping Tristan and me, and my father too. After all, she'd sacrificed her privacy and independence when we moved in with her.

On the other hand, she was withholding information from me. Important information, because she assumed either I couldn't handle it or wouldn't handle it properly. I was no longer the child she needed to rescue from the instability of her son. Hiding things from me for my own good was no longer an acceptable behavior. My guilt quickly gave way to an unfamiliar heated anger.

It made me uncomfortable. I was handing over too much power to my emotions lately. I had to regain control.

I decided to catch a class at the gym. It didn't matter which class. Anything that could get my heart rate up and my heat level down would do. After that, I'd decide what my next step should be with Reed, and how I wanted to handle the store situation with my mother.

It turned out to be a great decision. I walked in just as a cardio sculpting class started. Since I'd never taken one before, it challenged me in a slew of new ways, forcing me to give complete focus to the class. I worked out so hard, I felt it in my legs as soon as the class was over and I walked down the steps to leave the gym. I temporarily forgot the problems I'd face when I arrived home.

****

One of my problems sat with her legs crossed and her purse in her lap, in front of the door of my garden apartment. Her flaming hair hanging over her shoulders was unmistakable, and my throat closed as I reached in my pocket to find my key, not taking another step forward. What would I possibly say to this woman?

I contemplated pivoting and scurrying away to avoid contact altogether, but Reed's wife spotted me before I could escape. She stood tall and stared me down in a way that made Mamie's speech from a little while ago feel like a pep-talk. She adjusted her watch; her diamond wedding band sparkled in the sunlight.

All at once, I felt guilty and dirty, yet jealous and resentful. He may have belonged to her and I may have been the *other woman*, but I didn't become one knowingly. My feelings for Reed couldn't suddenly disappear because I found out about her. Still, it changed nothing. This was the woman he was with in the coffee shop that day and she was about to call me out for sleeping with her husband.

And she would be right.

I willed my stomach to stop churning as I tore at the skin around my thumb. The pain of tearing at fresh skin didn't even make me stop.

The woman approached me. "Where is he?" she spat.

"Who?" I asked. My voice was a soft squeak, an admission of my guilt, even though I had not intentionally done anything wrong.

"Don't bullshit me. He never came home last night. A friend of mine saw him at Crimini's. I cannot believe you let him take you there. What the hell is wrong with you? Of all the places in this town, you let him take you there? To the most expensive restaurant in Seaville? Are you kidding me?"

I must have looked like a mute, standing in front of her speechless. This woman knew who I was, she knew where we'd been, she knew we'd been out together before…and somehow, she knew where I lived. She didn't seem nearly as appalled that I was seeing Reed as she was with the location of our date. Was she more embarrassed that people could have seen us in public together than angry at us?

I summoned some coherent words, but couldn't think of anything remotely appropriate for the situation. It was one I certainly never thought I'd find myself in.

"I'm sorry," I muttered, for lack of anything better. I wasn't sure what I was sorry for, though. Sleeping with her husband, or not wanting to give him up even though she was standing inches away from me?

"You're sorry? Don't you care about him at all? I mean, the way he talks about you, you sound like a compassionate, considerate woman, but this behavior is the exact opposite."

If I'd been at a loss for words before, now it was as if I'd never learned any in my entire life. The way he talked about me? He talked about me—to his wife? Never before had I felt as clueless as in that moment. This didn't make any sense. Situations that didn't make sense caused me all sorts of discomfort, and I scratched at the palm of my hand trying to figure out what the hell was going on.

The beautiful redhead didn't waste time continuing her tirade, though, so I had some time before I had to answer. "He told me the money was to fix his car. You must know how important that car is, so I had no problem giving him the money. When he dumped all of his things at my house, it made complete sense if he had to put the car in the shop. But what? He just wanted to cart you around in style so you wouldn't be embarrassed by the fact that everything he has to his name was sitting in the trunk as you let him pay a couple hundred dollars for dinner? Is that the kind of person you are, Jolie? Because if it is, my cousin has certainly misjudged you."

I was about to tell her he wasn't wrong. I strove to be as compassionate and considerate as possible. Before I could, though, I processed one of her words.

Cousin.

This woman was Reed's cousin.

Thoughts shifted in my head, like a seesaw with a child added to one side. I was no longer the other woman, afraid of being called out. Something else had come to light.

Reed never brought me to his house. He carried a bag of belongings everywhere. His most prized possession was always strung across his chest. He left his things at his cousin's house before taking me out. She was complaining about money she gave him.

Reed wasn't married. He was…

I stood there in shock. I must have looked like a deer in headlights, because she turned sheet-white. "He didn't tell you?" she suddenly asked, her mouth hanging agape.

Mine probably was, too.

"He told me he told you," she said. "He told me you were okay with it."

I gawked at her.

She took a step away from me and ran a hand down her face. "He didn't tell you," she whispered, though her glossed over, unfocused eyes made it clear she was informing herself, not me. After a few beats of coming to her own realization, she found me again. "Where did you think he lived?"

"I…" I was too ashamed to admit what I thought.

"He's going to be furious that I told you." She shook her head. "Serves him right," she said, but it wasn't convincing.

Still, she hadn't actually told me anything. I had to be sure. "Reed is homeless?"

"*Reed*?" She chuckled his name. "Yeah, Reed is homeless."

"But you said home. You said he didn't come home." I may have begun piecing things together, but a lot of the puzzle was missing.

"I meant to my home. To pick up his things and maybe stay for the night. Sometimes he does that."

"But—" I hadn't formed my next question, but I knew it was there somewhere.

"Look, I've obviously said too much already. I thought you knew about his situation and were taking advantage of him. That's why I came here. I've got to let him explain the rest. But I don't want you thinking I don't try to take care of him. He knows he's welcome at my house whenever he wants to come. He's just a stubborn bastard who doesn't listen to anyone but himself. I guess that's part of the problem." She adjusted her watch again before walking past me. She craned her neck back as she left. "I'm sorry, Jolie. It seems I'm the one who misjudged you."

As she pulled away in a sports car that matched her hair, I tried to make sense of what just happened. My Reed, my beautiful, talented, mysterious Music Man wasn't being mysterious after all. He was just hiding the fact that he was homeless. Homeless. How could that be? How could I have missed it? All the times he took the opportunity to shower. The fact that he carried a pocketknife around for protection. The way he responded when I mentioned getting dirty after our time on the steps. How the places he took me for dates, with the exception of last night, were all inexpensive. I thought he was being creative but it turned out they were strategic. There must have been a thousand other clues that I didn't pick up on and couldn't call to mind as I stood in front of my house, unable to move.

I remained standing outside for what had to be a ridiculous amount of time, paralyzed by the information. When a woman walking her dog stared at me, I knew it was time to bring my confusion inside.

Lying on my couch, I replayed every minute I spent with Reed, from the first time he walked into Stuff Your Crepes. I went over the glances Mamie and he shared, the way he looked guilty when she spoke to him privately. She knew about his situation. There was no doubt. With each memory, I became more irate at being lied to and deceived. He had countless opportunities to tell me about his situation and yet, he chose not to trust me enough to believe I'd stand by him. Did he think I'd walk away because he was on the streets?

My thoughts came to a screeching halt. Would I have? Would I have embarked on a relationship with someone who could offer nothing stable? With whom a life would have been a definite string of uncertain events? A man whose entire existence would force me to disregard every one of my devices?

I calculated how many of those devices I'd already compromised for him. I was a ball of nerves half the time questioning what was real and what wasn't. As it turned out, I had every reason to question. I wasn't paranoid or crazy, the two things I feared most, but the two things his lies most often made me feel. Fury bubbled and boiled inside me at being kept in the dark, forced to turn into someone I wasn't, and abandoning the things that kept me most in check—all at the expense of falling for a man who was keeping his true life a secret from me.

I didn't go to work that day. The urge to strangle my grandmother was too alive in my hands and fingers, and I feared I couldn't contain myself enough to be polite to the customers. I paced my apartment before taking a shower to cool off and then heading back to the gym for a second class. This time, it was yoga. I needed to be centered, grounded, to get back to the me I was before. The conscientious me. Not the me I'd recently convinced myself was the new, shiny, better version. That version was nothing but a lie.

Part 2

Reed

K.K. Weil

Chapter Nineteen

She thought I was married. *Married.* It was such a ridiculous idea that I might have laughed out loud if the truth hadn't been so much sadder.

I didn't have an answer ready, though I should have. I'd been preparing for the moment of truth for weeks. In fact, I'd decided the night before that it was time to come clean. I couldn't keep pretending. I was lucky she even tolerated my evasive behavior up to that point. It was easy to see she wasn't used to opening herself to someone like me.

If her grandmother hadn't come over, jabbering in thinly veiled code, I would have told her the entire story as soon as we woke up. I didn't have the chance, though, once Mamie started with that whole forgiveness shit. I understood she was trying to be supportive, and I truly appreciated her keeping my secret for all that time, but she wasn't even close to subtle. I hated the way she looked at me like we were in cahoots. It made me feel like I was betraying Jolie's trust even more.

I must have wished a million times that I'd never stepped foot inside Stuff Your Crepes before I met Jolie face to face; that I'd ignored the pangs of hunger during those weeks when Hector offered me few hours and cash flow was a problem; that I'd never used their generous tokens, giving Mamie, and worse, Morgan, something to hold over me. But that wasn't the reality of life. You couldn't wish away your past mistakes. If you could, I would have been in a very different position.

So when Jolie questioned me, I left. Without giving her an ounce of explanation, I bailed.

Again. It's what I did best.

This time was different, though. This time, with Jolie, I didn't want to escape without answering for my fuck-up. I needed to make her understand.

With my belongings stored at my cousin Victoria's house, I was free to park my car without worrying about who would break into it this time and steal what little I had left in this world. I walked the perimeter of the park, maybe a dozen times, taking comfort in some familiar faces and figuring out what to say to Jolie.

I played my speech over and over in my head as I shuffled my sneakers against the pavement. I'd tell her my story, in my way, on my terms. Voluntarily dishing out the entire truth, in all its ugliness, would prove I was ready to open up to her. She'd forgive me for deceiving her, because I was admitting everything, even though I could have just told her I wasn't married and left it at that.

That was my plan, anyway. Given the shape of my life, I should have realized nothing went according to plan. When I finished my trek and drove back to Victoria's house, I knew I'd lost my chance for a preemptive confession.

Her cheeks were the same color as her hair. She didn't even give me a chance to ask what was wrong.

"This is not my fault." She held her hands in front of her, on the offensive, as soon as I closed the door.

"What isn't?" I slipped off my dirty sneakers and

tucked them to the side of her foyer.

"You told me she knew."

My stomach tightened. "Who knew what?" It was an unnecessary question. Victoria could only be talking about one *she* and there was only one thing she thought she knew.

"Jolie," she sighed. "You told me you told her about your life. I would have never gone there if you hadn't."

"You went to her house?" I couldn't believe it. From day one, Victoria had been my advocate, going to bat with my brother when she thought it would help me. Her temper was as fiery as her hair and she didn't mince words, which was why it was easier to tell her Jolie accepted my life. It didn't occur to me that she might go there and discover the truth herself.

"I found out you were at Crimini's last night and I was incensed that you wasted money you borrowed from me on such a meal. You didn't come home so I thought you felt guilty and maybe took off again, so I went to find you. When I got there, my anger transferred to Jolie, for letting you spend that money on her. I may have yelled at her a little."

I threaded both hands through my hair. I was familiar with Victoria's yelling. I'd been on the receiving end once or twice in recent months. I hoped it was a muted version.

"Anyway, it was obvious she didn't know what I was talking about."

My stomach fell to the floor. "But now she does."

Victoria nodded. "You shouldn't have lied to me. This would never have happened if you'd been honest and told me you didn't want her to know."

"Shit!" I ran my palm over the few-day-old scruff on my cheek. I'd have to find a place to shave soon. I couldn't go to work looking like I was sleeping in my car. "Shit, shit, shit." I paced her living room. Some quick damage control would be necessary if there was any hope of having Jolie forgive me. It was bad enough I'd been lying to her all along. Now I wasn't even telling her on my own accord. I was going to have to give an after-the-fact admission, which didn't have much value.

God, if only I could go back to that day and never sit down at that fucking table.

I shook off the thought. There was no going back. I had to figure out how to move forward. Just like I'd been trying to do for the past ten months.

"I have to go." I threw my shoes back on.

"Where are you going? You just got here."

"I have to tell her the whole story and hope for the best." I opened the door.

"I'm sorry, Anthony. I really, really am."

Her rarely seen remorse barely registered as I left, already reworking my explanation in my mind.

****

Another answer to the question of "why you."

I had a lot of qualities that worked with women for most of my life. Looks and charm weren't the least of them. But that was then. I had more to offer then, and less to lose.

How can you have less to lose when you have nothing? Simple. You find some*one* you can't stand the idea of losing. You adore her before you even speak to her and when you finally get that opportunity, you can't believe she might feel the same. So all the gifts you had before, the swag, the killer smiles—they become insignificant and you need to find something else. Something that's only meaningful to her, not something you've shared with countless others before her.

I decided to start there, with the conversation we had on our first "date" under the boardwalk. I jeered at myself, remembering the way I'd thrown that date together. When I saw her with that preppy, perfect, dullard in her shop, I morphed into a green monster and knew I had to act fast. If I'd lost my chance with the woman I'd been craving from afar, I would pound myself into the ground. I had wanted to get back on my feet before asking her out. I thought the songs would buy me some time, but then he appeared and my hand was forced. I had to make my move.

I had little cash on hand. Creativity had to be my friend instead. I knew more about her than I had a right to, more than I could reveal, but showing her I was paying attention by making a theme for the date seemed safe enough. I hoped it would distract her from the fact that I wasn't taking her anywhere. When I rummaged through the back of my car, searching for my favorite T-shirt and came across Victoria's tent, it all fell into place.

After sending her this message, I held my breath, waiting for her to respond, but I refused to let my fate rest with a possibly unanswered text. I shot off another one before she could decide not to bite.

—Because the first time I saw you in the park handing out crepes, the most exquisite song played in my mind. It spoke to me about your sparkle and your love, about your energy and your passion. Even though you did your best to maintain your distance, these

things poured from you in every look you gave those people. I doubted I'd ever meet you, and was jealous of anyone who got to have you in their lives.—

I read over the text, making sure it served its dual purpose: acknowledging that she knew my secret, and admitting I saw her in the park before we met. I admired her, long before she even knew I was alive.

I just prayed she'd pay close enough attention to my words to find their meaning.

—*Where are you?*—

She responded as soon as I hit Send. That had to be good.

—*At your apartment. Can we please talk?*—

She opened her door within seconds. I stood before her with my shoulders slouched and my back hunched. It was the posture I'd worn ever since I started living in my car, that of a man who felt he was no longer worthy of being the cocky, confident bastard he once was. My reflection in the mirror on her opposite wall told me the Reed Jolie knew was nowhere to be found.

"Can I come in?"

She opened the door and I walked past her, dragging my feet. I sat on one of her chairs, far from the couch.

"My father owned a music store," I started, without waiting for Jolie to ask questions. She hadn't even sat yet. She stood before me, exhausted, worn and absolutely beautiful. She had no idea how long ago I fell for her, but her welling gray eyes and shaking hands told me I wasn't alone in feeling what was between us. This could not be the last time I got to speak to her. I had to make her understand the shame I felt, and why I kept my truth from her.

"He built it from scratch. It wasn't huge but to him it was enough. My brother and I spent hours and hours there, fiddling around and imagining the day it would be passed to us. I had plans. Big expansion plans. I wasn't interested in keeping it as an immigrant's mom and pop store. I wanted our name to be synonymous with Sam Ash. Vinny was more conservative. He said as long as the store could support us and our future families, it was doing its job.

"We argued about it for years, but it was all in fun. We figured we wouldn't be in any position to make decisions for a long, long time, because our father wasn't looking to retire. We'd have forever to debate. Three years ago, though, out of the blue he had a heart attack. We lost him."

"I'm so sorry," she whispered. She sat on the corner of the couch, leaned across and reached for my hand. If anyone knew how painful it was to lose a father, it was Jolie. But I buried my hands between my legs. I didn't deserve her pity or her empathy. She did nothing but respect her father's memory. I did nothing but destroy mine.

"Right from the start, Vinny and I saw things differently. Like I told you, we were very competitive, and neither of us was willing to concede to the other. It became a daily battle, with Vinny trying to maintain the family store feel and me trying to branch out. I wanted to advertise, offer big deals, and most importantly, I wanted bands to perform in our store, bringing in crowds who would talk about our store and grow our business. But you need money for that.

"Eventually, Vinny couldn't stand all the fighting, so he conceded to try to expand, but he was giving so little, it wouldn't have made any difference. He only agreed to let me use five percent of our profits for my ideas. He was thinking too small. My motto had always been go big or go home. It would have taken a decade to make any progress Vinny's way and I've never been a very patient person. Never had to be. Before that, everything had come easy."

I slouched over and buried my head in my hands. My voice was muffled but I made sure to speak loud enough for her to hear me. The last thing I wanted to do was repeat myself. It was bad enough to have to tell the story out loud at all. It was my first time discussing it with anyone outside of my family.

I shook my head in my hands. "I was so sure I was right, Jolie. So sure."

I paused, trying to summon the strength to admit the rest. To acknowledge what an impulsive, selfish piece of shit I was. I sank lower into the chair. Jolie leaned forward to hear my next words.

"Vinny had given me complete access to our accounts so I could start advertising right away. All I wanted to do was grow our business, make us some money and turn us into a profitable company. I never thought I would hurt my family." I sighed into my palms, trying to hold back the vomit welling in my throat.

"I always gambled a little too much, like in college we'd place bets on football games and even video games we played. Other than losing my extra spending money, it had never been a problem. I had actually become pretty good at it. In fact, I'd become exceptional at blackjack."

Just the word blackjack heated my entire body with

shame. The clinking of chips was still a sound that almost brought me to my knees. Jolie had no idea how much the sound of the boardwalk tokens in her jar reminded me of that day.

"I figured five percent of hardly anything wasn't nearly as good as five percent of a lot. I was determined to make our small profit into more." My hands shook as I lowered them.

"I did a stupid thing. A ridiculously stupid, selfish thing. I took it all to the blackjack table. All the money we'd made. That night, I played as well as anyone could have. Doubling down when I should, splitting my cards whenever possible. I played like a pro. I never lost big at blackjack. I knew all the rules, all the odds. Yet no matter what I did that night, things didn't go my way. My stack of chips kept shrinking. The more I lost, the more desperate I became and the more determined I was to win it back. I bet, bigger and bigger, into the morning, until it was all gone. Every fucking cent." My voice cracked, which was nothing compared to the cracking inside of me. Even as I spoke to her, I could almost feel the sweat that dripped down my back, forehead and temples that night, the pounding in my gut that increased with every hand I lost.

"I disappeared for three weeks after that. I couldn't face my brother, or my mother, who had entrusted the store with us, considering it our birthright, instead of running it herself. I couldn't tell them that in one night, I'd singlehandedly lost everything my father had built with the change he had in his pocket when he came here. How do you look people you love in the eye and tell them that?"

"You were trying to do something good," Jolie

said, but her words were as empty as the pit of my stomach.

I shook my head. "My intentions don't matter. Only the end result does. I knew better. Hell, everybody knows better than that. I was just so determined to show Vinny that my way was the right way I became irrational. We couldn't pay our vendors since there was nothing in reserve. We couldn't buy any supplies. Vinny and I tried to use our own money to keep afloat for a bit but it didn't work. We lost the store in a matter of months. I lost my apartment. And I lost my brother."

"I'm sure—"

"We haven't spoken since, and I'm sure we won't ever again. He despises me, and he's got every right to. I stole from him and his wife and child. He can't look at me. It was a long time before I could even look at myself. In fact, it was until I met you in your store. For the first time since this happened, I felt like myself again, not the gambler who lost his father's business."

"Reed—"

At once, I couldn't stand to hear her call me that. Another fucking lie. "I'm sorry, Jolie. I'm so sorry I couldn't tell you the truth."

"But I don't understand. You have a job. So why don't you have a place to live?" She was confused, of course. Up until this moment, when she looked at me she saw an employed, creative musician. I knew all too well how that could change in an instant.

"I was lucky my brother didn't sue me. I'm sure he could even have had my ass thrown in jail. All he wanted, though, was to be free of me and to cut ties. So, after that I couldn't ask Vinny for a reference. There was no way I would hurt him like that and then ask for his help. How could you do that to someone you love?"

Jolie nodded in thought. "Tristan said something like that, too, before he left."

I was grateful for any connection she could make between her brother and me. I continued. "I was lucky to get the job I have now, but I can't save enough at minimum wage, working part-time, to pay first and last month's rent plus utilities and food and all that. So for now, I live out of my car. You have no idea, Jolie, how many homeless people are out there. People with jobs, whose rent increased more than their paychecks. People with PTSD, or who were bankrupted by so many bills they drowned. People you'd never think are homeless. You have no idea."

"Crooked Curt," she whispered, but I was too caught up in my own thoughts to wonder what she meant.

This time, I didn't pull away when she reached for my hand. Her simple touch was a consolation. I wanted...no I *needed* her to understand how much I regretted what I'd done. My brother would never forgive me, but if Jolie could look at me as something other than the jerkoff I was pretending not to be lately, it would do me a world of good.

Yet her eyes told me she now saw me as everyone else did. Not with the anger my brother felt, but not the way she looked at me before either.

"So the bruise you had when we first met?"

"There was a fight, but not in a bar. Someone had broken into my car the night before. I caught him in the act. I got him pretty good, but he got me better and made out with some of my things. That's why I try not to leave my car unattended at night anymore. And why

I carry my guitar with me, and the few essentials I can't live without. It's not that I didn't want to stay with you every time I had the chance, but I have to protect what's mine."

She nodded again, letting everything sink in. She rubbed my hand with her thumb as she thought.

"You know, if you want, you could—"

I didn't let her finish. "Don't offer me a place to stay. Thank you, but no." I squeezed her hand to assure her I was appreciative.

"Why not?"

"You and I are far from ready to live together. I won't allow my issues to become anyone else's. If I were going to do that, I'd stay with Victoria or my mother. They've offered too many times to count. Once in a while I even take them up on it, but this is something I need to figure out on my own if I'm ever going to forgive myself. Besides, I couldn't stand to stay with someone, knowing they were pitying me every minute I was there."

"I don't pity you."

Her facial muscles betrayed her.

"Your lips are telling me exactly what they're supposed to say, Jolie. I appreciate that. But would you like me to tell you the story told by the slight creases in the corners of your eyes? Or the story behind your tight lifted shoulders, or the tilt of your head? Because those are the honest stories, Jolie. Those are the tales about sadness, the ones great songs are written about. And pity? That's the one that really gets you. Pity is a demon all its own. It's not like hatred or jealousy or vengeance. You can't be mad at someone for pitying you. In fact, more than likely, they care about you.

They break you with their pity, nonetheless. I'd rather you punched me clear across the jaw than look at me the way you are right now. That I could deal with. If I messed up and you were pissed, which is what I was preparing for, you'd cool down and it would blow over. But once you feel sorry for someone, that's a look that can never be forgotten."

On the way over, I was preparing an explanation, in the hopes that she'd forgive me for lying to her. As I was telling her this now, though, what I really wanted was to never have had to tell her at all. What I would have given to be able to keep this from her until I had a better job, more money, and a home.

"That's why I lied." I wrapped her hand in both of mine, now. "I just wanted to be the guy I was before for you. Once I was back on my feet, this would all be a memory and you'd be none the wiser. You'd never have to know about this blip in my life and we could have been happy. I'm so sorry you found out."

I was taken aback when the pity in her pout mutated into anger. She yanked her hand from mine. "What did you say? Am I hearing you right? You're not sorry that you lied, you're sorry I found out?"

If this was one of those semantics things with women, it wasn't a fight I wanted to have at that moment. Whatever way she needed to see it was okay, as long as she forgave me.

"I don't know, Jolie. I just meant I'm sorry about the whole thing."

"Reed," she said, standing. "This is important. If you had to do it again, would you tell me right away?"

I thought for a second. I hated the way she looked after I told the story. I needed to be honest. "No. I would have fixed the situation first. Then dealt with telling you. But I would have been more careful so you didn't find out from someone other than me. That was wrong."

She wrapped her arms around herself and walked away from the couch, giving me her back. When she turned to me again, her eyes were filled to the brim with tears. "I was so upset when you left here. Between you and Mamie…" She paused in thought, then shook her head. "I thought I needed you out of my life."

Panic rose in my throat as I held my breath, waiting for the *but*.

"But then…"

I sighed with relief as a tear rolled down her cheek.

"When your cousin came and I found out about your situation, I was shocked. I didn't know your story, but I understood why you'd be afraid to tell me right away. When we met, you didn't know what kind of person I was, or if I'd date you or whatever. So after I spent a little while letting it sink in, all I wanted to do was come find you and hold you, tell you everything was going to be all right and see if there was any way I could help you."

More tears fell, meshing the fury behind her eyes with undeniable sadness in the forefront. "But if you can stand there and tell me that you'd do it all again, now knowing why I need stability and truth and consistency in my life…if those things don't make you see that lying is the absolute last thing you should have done to me, then I can't be with you anymore, Reed. I can forgive the lying. I may not like it, and I may not be good at forgiving, but I promised myself that if you came here and apologized, I'd work on that shortcoming of mine, because you were in a bad situation. But I can't forgive the fact that you'd do it the same way, given the chance. You'd deceive me again, even though you know about my family and what's most important to me. You didn't know me when you started lying, you didn't understand me. Now you do, and that makes what you just said a thousand times worse."

"Jolie, please…"

She was right. I wished I could take back what I said, even if it was the God's honest truth. Telling her I'd lie all over again was stupid. Another mistake.

She walked toward her door and opened it. "I need you to leave."

I couldn't leave that way. "Please. You were going to give me a second chance. You said it yourself. Please let me show you it wouldn't be a mistake. I won't hurt you again. I'll be honest about everything from now on. I swear to you."

I stepped toward her, leaving little space between us. She backed into the door. "I can't," she whispered.

"You can." I spoke against her mouth, hoping to gain back some of the emotions my songs brought out in her. "You're afraid because you're used to protecting yourself and I did an enormously stupid thing. So I get it. But Jolie," I said. It was time to lay everything on the line. "I've been crazy about you since I heard about you from the guys at the Palace. I hadn't even seen you yet, but I knew from the way they spoke, you were extraordinary. Then, when you came to the park, I stayed back and watched you delight in helping people, gaining nothing. The day we met sealed it for me, the way you tried so hard to keep your decorum and gave me a hard time, even though I knew you felt it too. I've been falling deeper and deeper in love with you every time I see you, touch you, or even just talk to you. I'm not this kind of guy, Jolie. I don't write music for women and I don't spend time conjuring up dates. Only for you, because of you. I've fucked up a lot recently and I'm having a tough time finding my way back to normal. Please don't leave me before I can."

I closed my lips over hers in a soft kiss. Her tears rubbed my cheek as she kissed me back. She opened her mouth and I took full advantage. I slid one hand around the back of her head and the other around her waist, pulling her into me. She wrapped her arms around my neck and kissed me desperately for a minute. I was getting through to her.

Then she sobbed into my mouth.

She pulled her head back and released me from her hold. "I can't, Reed. I wish I could, because I love you, too, but I can't. I can't let myself be with someone who makes me ignore all my devices and ignore what I know is right for me. I can't be with someone who changes me into a person I don't know, even if I fooled myself into thinking for a second that the change might be good. It's not safe for me. And I definitely can't be with someone who, deep down, would do it all again if he had the chance."

Shit. Why did I say that? Why did I need so many do-overs? Why couldn't I get things right the first damn time?

I took the ends of her hair between my pointer and thumb and twirled it slowly. The way it fell at the edge of her chin reminded me of old movies my mother watched when I was growing up. The women in them had a sex appeal and sophistication I'd never seen in girls my age, until I met Jolie.

"Please, Jolie," I whispered as I swept a finger over her jawbone.

"Reed," she whimpered. Her head wanted me to go but her body was leaning toward me. She laid a soft hand on my chest and inched her face closer. Her gaze fell to my lips as tears fell from her eyes. She was losing her resolve.

I could have taken advantage. She paused for just long enough that a few more words of apology and warm kisses might have brought her back over to my side. But when she said the name I'd given her, I knew she was right. I had deceived her, and I'd do it again if it would have kept me on the fictional pedestal we'd created—one where I was a man of intrigue and mystery. I'd intentionally confused her and if it meant never exposing my faults, I'd do it all again.

She deserved better. If I wanted to deserve *her*, I had to be better.

I took her hand from my chest and kissed the top of it. "You're right, Jolie. But one day, I hope you can be wrong." I kissed the tear dripping down her cheek, and walked out of her apartment, praying it wasn't for the last time.

Chapter Twenty

For the next few days, I tried my best to figure out how a guy who was used to getting his way all the time, then suddenly had nothing and still couldn't seem to fix himself, might do better. No matter how much soul searching I did, how much saxophone playing, how many laps I walked at the park, I couldn't find any answers.

Things had always come easy to me. School, music, especially women. I'd never had to fight for anything I wanted, which was probably why I'd been such a baby about getting my way about the store. Even when I lost all that money, though I'd carried a boulder of guilt on my back, I never acknowledged to myself what a spoiled brat I'd been. Did I acknowledge it to anyone else? I couldn't remember.

Jolie was the first thing I wanted and couldn't have. It was more than her charity work for the homeless and her undeniable beauty, of which she seemed oblivious. It was her general passion toward everyone and everything in her life. She *felt* people deep in her soul, even though she tried to bury that to stay even-keeled. I loved the way she was calm and passive around everyone else, but allowed her fire to come out when she was with me. I was honored to be the person she chose to share that side of herself with, so honored that it kept me up at night figuring out how to improve. We were good together. Good for each other. I just had to work past the part of me that was bad for her so I could give her all the good.

I was distracted enough at work for my boss to notice. Hector knew all about my car-partment, but he was generous enough not to ask why I lived there. I'd given him some information about losing the business, but didn't tell him I was solely responsible. Hiring me was risky. He didn't know me, or my past, from a hole in the wall. If he had, maybe he wouldn't have hired me at all.

I'd told him bits and pieces about Jolie. He must have read between the lines to see how much she meant to me, because when he offered me the store for my date, he was apologetic about not being able to offer more hours so I could spoil her. He didn't need to apologize. He'd already given more than enough.

So now, when he wondered aloud whether the brass would wear off the tuba I polished absently, I had to give some details. "How can I make it right, Hector? How can I stop messing up and be worthy of her?"

"Well, in my experience, you can't just want to be better. You have to actually be better, ya know?" Hector was in his late thirties. He had two kids and what seemed like a solid marriage. Hell, the guy was able to keep his store afloat, so any advice he could give me was better than I was doing.

"Not really," I answered.

He pulled up a drum stool. I couldn't help thinking of the night Jolie and I christened it. I didn't think that's what Hector was intending when he said I could have dinner here.

"Have you apologized?"

"Yes."

"Did you mean it?"

"I was sorry," I spoke the truth, "but I don't know if I was sorry about the right things."

He nodded. "Have you fixed what you did wrong?"

I shook my head. "That's where I'm getting into trouble. I want to fix it, but I'm not sure what to do."

"Well, if it's lying that's the trouble, you have to decide to be as honest a person as possible. Until you decide to do it for yourself, you can't ever do it for her."

I was confused. "What do you mean? I am honest with myself."

"Are you?" he asked, staring right at me. "Have you asked yourself why a man with your raw talent is working in this shop for a few dollars an hour, living out of his car, when he could be pursuing so much more?"

"You know why," I rebutted. "A failed business isn't exactly a strong resumé-builder."

"Well, there's that"—he tapped a finger on the snare—"or maybe you're hiding out from life because you don't want to fail again. Something tells me you're not accustomed to that. It's easy to blame external forces for your failures because they'll always be there, so why bother trying again?" He stood from the stool and walked over to a customer eyeing one of his most precious guitars while I let his words sink in.

Was I hiding? Victoria often criticized me for not trying harder to make amends with Vinny, calling me a coward. Was I doing the same with my career? And with Jolie? Had I been hiding the real me from her because it wasn't the perfect, charming guy I was used to being for everyone?

There was only one person who would know the answer to that.

****

"Why did you let me lie to her?"

It was possible that I shouldn't have shown up at the home of an eighty-something year old woman without calling or asking, but I decided to play the game the way she'd been playing me.

"Are you here for a booty call, because if so, I'll need to change." She fanned her floor-length nightgown in front of me.

I'd gotten to know Mamie's no-holds-barred ways over the course of the summer, ever since she showed up at the Palace the morning after my first date with Jolie, asking around for me. Somehow, she still had the ability to take me by surprise.

"Oh, stop being such a prude. Come in." She gave my ass a swift smack as I walked in the door. "Sit."

I wondered what made people do everything she said as I plopped myself onto her couch.

"I didn't *let* you do anything. You did what you did yourself. Don't lay blame on me." She sat next to me and crossed her legs, draping her nightgown over them.

"You can't say that, Mamie. You told me not to tell her, to let her get to know me before she found out I live in my car. You told me I was good for her, that some things take time. You compared my story to that of a flower with an ugly seed, saying not everyone could appreciate the seed; they couldn't see the seed for a gorgeous flower until *after* it germinated. They didn't need to know it came from an ugly seed until they loved the gorgeous flower. Remember how confused I was? But you insisted it was right. Why?"

"My mother-in-law likes to be in control, Reed."

The voice startled me, but I knew as soon as I turned that it was Jolie's mother. Jolie hadn't inherited her gray eyes from this woman—she got those from Mamie—but she inherited everything else.

"Abby." She extended her hand.

I shook hers, but didn't feel the need to offer my name. "Nice to meet you."

Abby sat with us.

"It was not about control," Mamie spat at Abby.

"Then what?" I asked. "Why would you encourage me to deceive her when you knew she'd hate me for it?"

Mamie walked into the kitchen and emerged with a pot of coffee. She poured out three cups. Did the woman always have that dirt-like coffee on hand? I sipped, pretending to love it the way I did weeks before.

"My granddaughter doesn't know what's good for her. Something tells me you don't either."

"I know what's good for her," I answered, regretting that I might not be the answer to that.

"No, I mean you might not know what's good for you," she corrected.

"How's that?" I sipped the mud.

"You always came into the creperie on Thursdays, the day Jolie wasn't there. At first I thought it was a coincidence. I actually wished she would see you, not because she loved when customers used her tokens, but because I had a feeling she'd like you if she could get past the fact that you needed a free meal every so often. But you always looked forlorn. Your eyes were downcast. You were ashamed. At least that's how I saw it. The night you came in when Jolie was working, though, something changed. Morgan said she recognized you right away, but when you looked at my granddaughter, you morphed into a self-assured, confident man. I knew as soon as I heard that, it wasn't the first time you'd seen Jolie. You recognized her, but you weren't ready to reveal yourself. Am I right?"

I ran my hand through my hair and shrugged. This woman was too perceptive.

"She needs someone like you to open her up to the beauty and life inside of her, Reed. But you need her, too, to show you that you can still be that confident man, even if you're in a bad way. You also need her to knock you down a few pegs when you're in a good way and you forget you're imperfect. She's good at all of that. If you two can find ways to make each other accept the parts you want to hide, I've done my job."

There was that word again.

"You had no problem with your granddaughter dating a homeless man?" I'd wondered that all along, but hadn't wanted to hear the answer until now.

"I learned a long time ago not to define a man by his current situation. I saw more to you than that, Reed. In time, Jolie will, too."

"I don't think that's the problem right now."

"I know. She's been here to yell at me. Second time in a week. I don't like it, but in a way, it's good. It means she's letting her emotions out. You need to prove that you're honest and true and consistent. If you can do those things, you'll win her back. If not, you're probably both doomed to eternal unhappiness."

"Thanks," I spat. "Your coffee sucks, by the way."

She leaned over and kissed my forehead. "That's a

start. Go get her, *bel homme*."

****

Ordinarily, being called a handsome man had little effect on me. My looks were something I'd used to my advantage many times, but they weren't a source of pride. I was smart enough to know a person's appearance was, at best, skin deep. It didn't give you the ability to successfully run a business and it certainly didn't make you worthy of the most amazing woman you'd ever met. When Mamie called me that, though, it wasn't about whether or not I could make women fall over me. It was a pet name. It meant she gave me her stamp of approval, her consent to be with the thing she prized more than anything in the world. Her granddaughter.

Her words gave me confidence. I still had no idea how I would prove to Jolie that I could be trustworthy and reliable, but if Mamie believed I could do it, then I did too.

Spending time with the guys in the Palace seemed like the perfect way to end my day. Even though these were some of the most down and out people I'd ever met, they managed to form a sense of community amongst themselves that was inspiring and elevated each one of them. I wasn't a Palace regular. I was an outsider who spent most nights in my car. But every so often, it was too hot or too cramped and I'd either find a remote spot to pitch Victoria's tent, or hang out at the park, where I could be anonymous, where I could be Reed. The people there spoke to me as if I were one of their own, never being territorial or making me uncomfortable. Finding that small patch of earth was the luckiest I could have been, given the situation.

Society assumed these people were dangerous, but in fact, it was the strangers who passed through that caused the trouble, never one of the regulars. They were a family. For someone like me, who'd alienated almost everyone he loved, being part of a surrogate family, even from the periphery, was a comfort.

As I approached the Palace, a small crowd gathered around the bench that sat in the middle of the park. Through an opening between two people, I caught a glimpse of a large hand shifting a brown knit cap on a man's head.

Crooked Curt was back.

An exultant tune played through my mind. Crooked Curt was a staple here. Even an outsider like me knew how important he was to this community. His return would bring back normalcy to a lot of people.

I strode over to welcome him home. The word was funny. Every one of these people lacked a home, yet this place was an indisputable substitute.

The crowd had their backs to me, all swarming over Curt. My gait had a little bounce as I made my way to them. I hadn't realized until that moment how concerned I'd been about this man who was practically a stranger to me.

From just a few feet away, Curt's baritone voice emanated into the trees. "Yeah, well, had to get back here and make sure you were all holding down the fort. Couldn't be getting out of that hospital too late to find out you'd all been moved to God-knows-where," he joked.

With all my personal drama, I'd forgotten there was talk about closing this area of the park. Thankfully, those seemed to be panicked rumors. My feet covered twice as much ground, decreasing the distance between the group and me. I was anxious to have my turn welcoming this man back.

They came to a halt, though, when a figure appeared out of nowhere, directly in front of me. He was taller and broader, which in itself wouldn't have bothered me. The way he leaned in, though, sent an unfamiliar sinking sensation in my stomach. A streetlight cast a shadow on him, and I wasn't sure if he meant for his eyes to be menacing, or if it was a side effect of the ominous veil of darkness.

Either way, the expression in his eyes that looked like bleak sockets from my angle, had a familiarity that I didn't have a chance to place.

"Leave them alone!" he howled into the darkness. One of his arms flew up to my face. I caught the flash of metal before a searing pain in my cheek blurred my vision and sent me crashing to the ground.

Chapter Twenty-One

Everything hurt. As soon as I lifted my hand to get a feel for my stitches, hot pain shot into my chest and radiated throughout my torso.

Apparently, when I grasped my cheek before I fell, the guy struck again and caught me in the chest, just below the collarbone. Then, as I hit the ground, the knife sank deeper, right before my head slammed into the concrete. At least that was what the witnesses' statements said. I didn't remember any of it.

"Don't touch that, honey. It needs to stay clean."

I nodded at the nurse taking my pulse and closed my eyes as I lowered my hand.

"You have another visitor," her soft voice said. In the two days I'd been there, drifting in and out of consciousness, Nurse Nancy's voice had been the one constant that kept calling me back. I heard her through the sedation the doctors gave me while they were working so close to my eye they feared I could lose my eyesight and I heard her as nausea from my concussion washed over me.

"Okay," I whispered. Speaking any louder hurt my head. Even the quiet beeping from somewhere by the nurses' station had bothered me the day before.

I wondered if it was another police officer coming to collect more information about the locally infamous Seaville Slasher, or another reporter trying to sneak in disguised as immediate family.

As far as real family, my mother and cousin had been by, but so far there was no word from Vinny. Though I deserved it, each time I was told I had a visitor, a small part of me expected him to walk through the door. When it was always someone else, I chastised myself for even hoping it was him.

I had to squint to focus on the visitor in the doorway. The first few stitches sewed the outside corner of my eye together. Though the plastic surgeon assured me there would be no permanent damage to my vision, I would probably have a scar, and right now, everything was a blur.

Blurry or clear, though, there was no mistaking Jolie's beautiful gray eyes and short, bobbing hair. She looked like an ancient goddess, standing there in some kind of flowing jumper, cinched at the waist. I hadn't called her to tell her what happened, but so many people had seen the crime, it wasn't surprising she heard.

"Hi." She took a tentative step into my room. "Can I come in?"

"Of course." I extended my hand. She took it when she reached my bed.

She scanned me, first the bandage covering one side of my face, then my chest where the stitches were hidden with gauze. "Are you okay?"

I tried to smile to reassure her, but even that pulled at the stitches. "I will be, thanks to some of the people at the Palace. They scared the guy away. Apparently, me hitting the ground and losing consciousness wasn't enough to deter the psycho. He was still leaning over me when I fell."

"My God, Reed." She ran her hand over the unharmed side of my face, with the gentle touch of Aphrodite. Her hand had a faint scent of batter. I breathed in the warm, homey smell that hid the hospital's disinfectant for a second. "I came as soon as Brett told me what happened."

"Brett?" I was a little groggy from the painkillers pumping into me, but that name didn't sound familiar.

Jolie blushed. "The guy you saw me with at Stuff Your Crepes? He's a reporter and they'd been giving him small stories, but I guess they bumped him up. He's reporting this one."

I didn't like the idea that in the few short days we hadn't seen each other, she was back in touch with that guy. "Lucky for me." My words stank of bitter sarcasm. Later, I'd blame them on the drugs.

She picked up on it right away. "We haven't been speaking or anything, but he remembered seeing you that day, so he called to tell me you were in the hospital. He assumed we were…"

Still together. The unspoken words hung over my hospital bed, like a canopy.

Could we still be together? Or together again?

"Want to sit?" I motioned to the chairs on the side of my room with my free hand. There was no way I was letting go of hers with my other.

Instead, she pulled away. She walked to one of the chairs that were meant to be comfortable for visitors, but were upholstered with a barf green plastic material that made them look anything but inviting. She dragged the chair across the smooth hospital floor and placed it next to my bed so she could sit next to me. She took my hand again.

"You scared the hell out of me, Reed. You can't imagine how relieved I am to see you, awake and talking, even if everything you say might be pure bullshit." She pretended to slap my leg and shook her head. A sign of initial forgiveness. I didn't like using my attack as a way to garner sympathy, but taking a few stabs to the face and chest had to come with some silver lining, didn't it?

She rubbed my face with her thumb, close to the bandage. She had no way of knowing how tender the entire side of my face was, or that even her soft caress caused me pain. I sucked in a small breath to conceal my discomfort.

"I'm so sorry, Jolie. I never should have lied to you, even if it was to protect myself. I swear, if you give me another chance, you won't have to worry about trusting me. I'm going to get back on my feet, and then I'll have more, I'll be able to give you more."

"I don't care about stuff, Reed. You know what matters to me. Honesty, reliability, me being able to depend on you. Those area the important things."

"I know. And I promise, no more lies."

"Or omissions," she specified.

"Or omissions," I agreed. That was the important distinction. I hadn't actually lied. Well, with the exception of one thing. I opened my mouth to clear up what I hoped she'd see as a silly white lie, but before I could, she leaned over and feathered her lips against mine. Her renewed touch played a soft ballad in my mind, one I'd have to remember so I could write it down after she left, if I could lift my arm.

"I didn't like not being in touch with you these last few days, you know. I even cut into Mamie pretty bad.

Told her I was furious that she betrayed my trust and I didn't see her gaining it back anywhere in the near future."

"She told me." I tried not to laugh. Laughing hurt worse than smiling.

"To my amazement, she didn't get angry. She just kissed my cheeks and said something about me taking a first step. I'm not sure what she meant."

"I might be." I ran a finger over her palm. The medication made everything tingly, and her skin felt prickly under my touch. "She meant she was happy you expressed yourself and that you should be the whole you. Jolie, who's selfless enough to dedicate her life to helping others, but also adventurous enough to blow off someone safe to be with me, undeniably the questionable choice. My beautiful, perfect Cat Lady."

"Cat lady?" she laughed.

Shit. Damn drugs. The guys probably didn't want her to know about that. Even realizing it, though, didn't make the blabber stop. I was so happy she was beside me.

"That's what they call you at the Palace, on account of those amazing eyes of yours, and your demeanor. You know how quiet cats are, but how they're always lurking, loyal to those closest to them, watching? That's you. They talk about you like a goddess dropped down from heaven. Cat Lady is their term of endearment for you. You're their legend. And now you're mine."

A throat being cleared in the doorway prevented Jolie from finishing a kiss she started to give me.

"I'm sorry to interrupt." Officer McAlister entered my room. "I just came by to drop this off."

The number of visits Officer McAlister had paid over the last two days almost equaled those of Nurse Nancy. He was itching to solve this case. It was plaguing Seaville, and since I was the only person, so far, to see the slasher's face, McAlister had become my new best friend.

"It's no trouble," I answered, even though I wanted to throw his ass out and finish that kiss, no matter how much pain it caused my cheek.

"Officer McAlister." He nodded at Jolie, lowering his eyes to our intertwined hands. It probably wasn't every day a homeless person had a girlfriend. Or maybe it was. What the hell did I know?

"Nice to meet you," she said. "Thanks for saving this guy. He kind of means a lot to me."

"Well, miss, I can't take any credit for saving him, but with his help, I hope to take credit for saving others by catching this criminal." He tipped his head in my direction. "Here's a copy of the sketch the artist did from your description, Anthony."

Officer McAlister handed me a piece of paper, but I didn't put my hand out to retrieve it. I was too busy cringing from his use of my proper name. Maybe she wouldn't notice.

"Anthony?" Jolie's head shot from the officer to me, confused as all hell.

Yeah, she noticed.

I crinkled my nose and shrugged.

"Why did he call you Anthony, Reed?"

"That was the last thing left to tell you." If I'd known where this was going, I never would have given her the name Reed. Hindsight was definitely 20/20, something I lacked both figuratively and literally at the moment. "When I went on the streets, I was so ashamed. I didn't want to identify as the old me, so I created a new me, one I used when meeting people in this world. I used a name kids called me in high school because of the way I played. Reed. Get it? Like a saxophone's reed?" Either the drugs or my nerves were causing me to babble, but I hoped I got enough out before she walked out once and for all.

She yanked away from me and planted her hands on her hips. She paced the room. "I can't believe I didn't even know your goddamn name. Even that was fake, Reed. Oh, I guess I mean Anthony. Ugh!" She threw her hands in the air.

"It's just a name, Jolie. One I used to use. One that actually fits me better than Anthony, anyway. The only reason I gave you that name is I'd already given it to Morgan once when I was ordering at your store and I had to wait aside for my order. She may not have remembered but I didn't want to take that chance. Please don't be mad. It was the first thing I was going to tell you when I made my ultimate, un-turn-down-able plea for you to take me back."

She stopped pacing and suppressed a laugh. "Oh, yeah? What exactly were you going to do?"

"I hadn't actually decided yet, but it was gonna be fucking amazing."

This time, she released a hard guffaw. She rolled her eyes. "I must be out of my mind." She grimaced when the words left her mouth, but covered it up with a cough. "Fine, whatever. Reed Anthony. That's it now. Don't do anything else that's going to piss me off."

"Never," I swore as I crossed my heart with two fingers.

"Okay, I'm going to be on my way," Officer McAlister reminded us of his presence. "But I want you to take a look at this, Anth—" He stopped mid-name. I was grateful. "See if it's a good likeness, or if there are any other identifiable marks you can remember." He held out the paper again, but it hurt too much for me to reach him.

Jolie took the paper from him to hand to me. She glanced at it as it drifted between us. Then she froze. Not just like when a person is surprised and pauses for a minute, a little shocked. She froze, as if a bucket of supercooled water had been poured over her and turned her into a block of ice. She didn't blink, she didn't swallow, she didn't breathe.

She screamed.

Chapter Twenty-Two

I'd seen her lose it before. When she had a panic attack outside Mamie's house, all I wanted to do was make her better. I felt privileged when her body responded to mine, calming with each passing breath. At least I was able to do something right.

This was different. No matter what I tried, her screeching didn't stop. I couldn't get out of the bed, so I reached for her and used my words to attempt to soothe her. It was like she didn't even hear my voice, though. I don't think she even inhaled. Her wail was one continuous siren.

"Jolie, please tell me what's wrong." I tried to hold her hand, but she clutched the paper so tightly there was no way I could make contact. By now, the entire nurse's station was in my room trying to soothe this woman.

"Miss." Officer McAlister gripped her shoulders. "You need to stop screaming and tell us what happened." His firm grasp brought her back to reality. She turned to me.

"This isn't true!" she yelled. "It's another one of your lies. Everything you say is one huge lie! You're a lying son of a bitch!"

"What isn't true? Jolie, you're not making any sense. I didn't even say anything." I was the one on painkillers, but she was the person acting irrational.

"This!" she screeched, shaking her fist at me with the crumpled paper inside it. "This is a lie."

Officer McAlister palmed her fist. "I'll have to ask you to let go of that." He tried to pry open her hand, but she let out a growl and yanked it away.

"How do you even know what he looks like, Reed? Have you been stalking my family? Is that it? You admitted to knowing me before I knew you. Did you know him, too? Is this some kind of weird revenge thing? And why does he have this scar on his chin? Did you throw that in for good measure?"

I didn't need her to say anymore, because as she yelled at me, the furious eyes that flashed in front of me a second before I was stabbed reappeared. I didn't have time to process it before my attack, but it was clear as day now. The gray eyes that belonged to Jolie also belonged to her brother.

Tristan was the Seaville Slasher.

Chapter Twenty-Three

I couldn't catch a fucking break. I was an odds guy, but as of late, they were definitely not in my favor. Seven and a half billion people in this world, and the one person I would never want to implicate in a crime stared me straight in the face and slashed it. This totally sucked.

After Jolie stopped screaming, she keeled over, unable to breathe. One of the nurses led her out of my room. She wouldn't look at me or respond when I called her name.

It had been three days and I hadn't seen her since.

I gathered my belongings into a blue duffel I'd used for camp when I was a child. My mother brought it by the day before, when she came to tell me I was coming home. She wouldn't hear a word about the music store or how I needed to make things right before I could be around the family again. Until I healed, I was staying home with her and that was that. I didn't have the energy to argue. I was physically and emotionally drained, and grateful that I had somewhere to go while the pain subsided. The thought of staying in my car while nursing these wounds was too overwhelming. The rest of the people I'd met on the street didn't have that option. I wouldn't be such an ingrate to not accept her offer.

The release paperwork was complete. As soon as

my mother came to collect me, we'd be on our way.

My movements were slow and deliberate. Though I was healed enough to be released, any sudden jerks could still cause me extreme pain and damage. The stitches in my face wouldn't come out for another two weeks, and my chest was in worse shape. I hesitated before lifting my bag, even though there wasn't enough inside to make it heavy.

"I'm driving you home."

The voice caused me to spin around and I regretted it instantly. My hand shot up to my chest, but grabbing it increased the pain. I fell forward, bracing my fall by putting my hands on the mattress.

Vinny lunged at me. "Are you okay?"

"Yeah." I straightened with caution. "What are you doing here?"

He glanced around and scratched his head, as if my spare hospital room was an art gallery. Anything was better than looking at me. "Mom had an appointment, so she asked me to pick you up."

I searched for a hidden message behind his words. Was he resentful that she'd sent him, or had he been looking for an excuse to come? I was unable to find one.

"Well, thank you."

He didn't say any version of *you're welcome*. He just stood, waiting for me. I unzipped and re-zipped my bag, desperate for something to fill the silence caused by his lack of response.

It was terrible to be so awkward around the brother I'd once shared a room with. The brother I'd loved, battled and loved again. We were strangers now. No…worse than strangers. Strangers could make small talk. Strangers could make eye contact. We couldn't even make empty gestures without the air between us feeling thick with discomfort.

I placed the bag on my left shoulder, with care. Though it wasn't the side that was cut, any movement to my torso had to be ginger. Vinny's eyes followed the strap on my shoulder, then shifted to my chest. He frowned, but didn't offer to help.

I didn't blame him. If I had to guess, he probably considered my pain a little bit of karma. He might have been right.

"I'm ready," I told him.

He turned on his heel and walked out the door. I followed.

He was silent all the way home. My fingers pressed imaginary keys into my shorts, my body's answer to unease. I tried to conjure a song in my head to make the ride more bearable, but for the first time, no music would come.

Finally, it was too much to bear.

"Vin—"

"Don't, Tony. After I get you home, I can be on my way. I'm sure Mom didn't have anything to do. This was a pathetic excuse to get us in the same place. But she's been too upset over you to argue. The last thing I want to do is give her more stress. She's got enough already." He glared at me before turning back to the road. "I'm glad you're going to be okay, but frankly, if I'd wanted to see you, I would have come to the hospital days ago. Let's not make this ride more than it is."

Shame filled me. My brother hated me so much that all he could muster was that he was glad I wasn't dead. I caused that.

My thoughts swept to Jolie and her brother. Was her love for him truly unconditional? If Tristan had behaved as I had and gambled away the crepe shop, would Jolie forgive him? What was she thinking right now, knowing he'd stabbed numerous innocent people?

We pulled into my mother's driveway where her car was parked. Vinny was right. She wasn't out running errands; she'd been looking for us to bond. Her plan didn't work.

I opened my door and slid off the seat. "Thanks for the ride." I hoped he would get out and come inside, but as soon as I closed my door behind me, he reversed off the driveway and sped away.

My mother and cousin were waiting when I walked inside. It didn't take long for them to hit me with a barrage of questions about the slasher. I told them about Jolie and they both looked at me with pity when I revealed the annoying twist that Tristan was the slasher. This time I didn't mind the pity because my situation was, in fact, pitiful.

"I don't know why he did it," I said, finishing my story. "They haven't caught him yet, but now they know who to look for. Thanks to me." I shook my head. I would have done anything not to be the guy who named him.

"It's not your fault that it's him." Victoria handed me a can of soda. I gave an internal laugh at how long it had been since I had one. Soda wasn't an extravagance I often allowed myself since losing my apartment.

"Jolie doesn't see it that way. She thinks I'm obsessed with her family or something, and that's why I identified him. I can't blame her. I haven exactly been the poster child for honesty since I met her."

"Yeah, well, I didn't help that." Victoria gave my leg a rough rub in apology.

"You're not to blame, Tori. I screwed this up from the very beginning. I should have just been honest about everything."

"So now what?" Victoria asked.

"Now we wait until they find him, and then I have to testify against him."

The thought of doing that while Jolie sat in the courtroom made me physically ill. How the hell did this happen?

****

Over the next couple of weeks, my mother doted on me like I was five years old. She brought me sandwiches on trays while I rested on the couch. The only thing she didn't do was cut off the crust. I told her I didn't want her waiting on me hand and foot, but she insisted that I allow myself to heal. The doctors said I couldn't do anything physical until the stitches came out of my chest, and she took it to heart.

So all I did was sit around. And think. And wait for the dreaded call telling me they caught Tristan and I'd have to come in and identify him as the slasher.

Every so often, my mother lectured me on how I needed to make things right with Vinny. She'd wanted to talk about this for months, but I was her captive audience now. Each time I said he made it clear he didn't want to talk to me, she countered with the fact that this was my fault. I caused it so I was the one who had to figure out how to fix it. What she didn't seem to understand was that I'd caused so many messes lately, no mop was big enough to clean up all of them.

The Vinny problem was too huge and overwhelming to solve, and honestly, as wrong as it was, it wasn't the one pressing hardest on my chest at that moment. I'd been dealing with the loss of Vinny for months. The loss I felt over Jolie, though, was raw and fresh and all-consuming. If I could have taken back my statement, if I could have broken into the police station and recreated that sketch; if I could have taken a dozen stab wounds in the back instead of the one in my chest so I wouldn't have seen him, I would have in a heartbeat. But there was no undoing what was done—a lesson I'd been slapped with over and over. The single difference was, this time it wasn't my fault. Yet I had lost the love of my life because of it. That knowledge was the thing keeping me on my mother's couch longer than I needed to be there. Not my physical wounds, though they were still tender, and not the fact that I'd insist on going back to the streets when I was healed. Losing the person who made me want to be the best version of myself was debilitating.

I called her a couple of times, but of course she didn't answer. I sent her a text, apologizing, explaining that my description of her brother was in no way the act of some crazy stalker. I had described what I saw, and that was it. My text got no response, which I'd anticipated. My other option was to show up in person, but how did going to her store to show her I wasn't a stalker, when she was intentionally ignoring me, not prove her theory?

The day the doctor removed the stitches from my chest, I told my mother it was time for me to go. Her pleading and tears didn't change my mind, though they did cause an ache in the pit of my stomach. I'd done enough, I didn't want to hurt her more, but nothing had changed. I was still the guy who lost the store and I wouldn't become a mooch living off his mother too. Until I could figure my shit out, this is how it had to be. She begged me to stay, at least until my eye had healed, but I refused.

I kissed her cheek. "I have to do this, Mom. If I can't do this on my own, I'm still taking from the people I love. I know you don't understand, and I'm so thankful I have you as an option, but for now I've got to go."

I went straight to work. Ever the upstanding guy, Hector promised my position was secure and told me to take as much time as I needed to recover, but I was an hourly employee. Every day I stayed away was a day without pay. The sooner I could get on the schedule, the better.

Hector raced to the door and shook my hand as I stepped inside. "You look good," he told me.

I doubted it was true, but couldn't care less. Only my hours mattered.

"Well, I'm glad to be back," I answered.

"Back? Are you sure you're ready?" He scanned my eye—still pink and inflamed where it was scarring—and rigid body.

"Can't sit home anymore. I need to start making things happen." Sheet music was stuffed in boxes next to me. I fanned through them with my index finger, trying to be nonchalant, but Hector caught my unspoken words.

"Things haven't been sorted out with the girl yet?"

"I'm afraid they're worse than ever."

He nodded. "Well then, let's get you back to

work."

Over the next hour, between customers, I caught him up on everything that happened with Jolie.

"Are you going to testify against him?" he asked, putting away some sticks a child had been using to play my favorite snare.

"I don't have a choice. I gave my statement before I knew who he was."

He turned his back to me and lowered his head. "There's always a choice, Reed. I'm not saying it's the right thing to do, but people do all sorts of things for the ones they love." He disappeared into the back room, leaving me wondering what this honest, hard-working man had done for his family, and contemplating whether doing something wrong could lead me to making everything right.

I had to see her. Stalker or not, I had to go by Stuff Your Crepes to decide if what I was thinking made any sense at all. Only having Jolie in front of me could tell me for sure.

When I got there after work, though, Mamie and Morgan, were working the counter. I almost turned and booked out of there. I had no idea what kind of response I'd get from Mamie. Dating her granddaughter while homeless was one thing. Naming her grandson as a slasher was entirely another.

She spotted me before I could make a swift exit. Her charcoal eyes hooked me and I was unable to move. Crepes weren't the only astounding thing Mamie had passed to Jolie.

"Come here," she demanded over the heads of her customers. "We need to talk."

I followed my direction and slinked across the

floor. Could she make me feel worse than I already did? Somehow, I was sure she could.

She grabbed my arm and a lingering ache in my chest reminded me of my stab wound. I flinched. "I'm sorry," she said when she realized she'd hurt me. She put her hand on my spine and led me into the supply room, letting the door slam behind us. She stood an inch away, and her nose would have bumped against mine if she'd been taller. "You're one hundred percent confident it's Tristan?"

A lump lodged in my throat. Not only did I feel like I was betraying Jolie, but now Mamie as well.

"All I'm confident about is the fact that the slasher looks like the sketch. I swear to you, Mamie, I had no idea that it was Tristan when I described him. I'm not a crazy man, obsessed with your family. I love her, Mamie. I'd never want to hurt her, although I know my actions may not make it seem that way."

"I know you're not crazy." She chopped some random lettuce sitting on a board. "I don't think Jolie believes you are, either, but it's easier than the alternative."

"Can I see her? Please? Is she home?"

She stopped cutting. "She won't admit she wants to see you, Reed. Or Anthony." She rolled her eyes.

My shoulders slumped. Of course Jolie had told her about my name. I'd just forgotten about that particular lie at the moment.

"I know she does, though. She's got a fierce pain brewing inside of her right now and the only person I've ever seen her expose herself to is you. Here's the problem. She can't be with you and acknowledge that Tristan did these things. As long as she makes it your fault, it isn't his. I've been strong for my family my entire life. I watched my son suffer with an unconscionable disease. I watched him kill himself on account of the suffering and I watched my grandson head down the same path before he disappeared. I've watched my granddaughter shut herself out from the world because she's so afraid it's going to happen to her she can't function normally. She makes rules for herself to keep out anything that will cause her potential danger, and if she strays from them, it upsets her entire sense of balance. I've gotten through it all. Somehow, God willing, I've survived it and been the stern voice on the other side. I know how everyone thinks I am, but my alternative is to curl up and cry, and that is something I will never do.

"This, though. I don't know what to do with this, Reed. Jolie's barely spoken...or even been around, since you named Tristan, and the best I can come up with is that everything will be okay when we find him. None of us knows if that's true. Jolie won't answer the door when I go to her house. For the past week, she's become even more reclusive. She's taken off from work, snipping about Abby needing to learn the ropes at the store anyway, since she's going to be half owner. She isn't answering my calls and my gut tells me to give her space, but I don't have much experience with that."

Abby was going to be half-owner of Stuff Your Crepes? I vaguely remembered Jolie mentioning something about a business partnership when she went on her tirade against Mamie and me, but I was too concerned with my own issues to process it. I couldn't imagine how devastated Jolie must have been about that, on top of everything else. No wonder she wouldn't speak to Mamie.

"Abby almost flew back to California as soon as she heard what her son had done," she continued. "She's not strong like me. These days, she runs. I almost had to strap her down to get her to stay. Jolie needs her mother, even if she won't let her anywhere near her right now. Everything is a mess and for the first time in my life, I have no words to offer my family." She swiped the lettuce with the back of her arm. It flew all over the floor.

"I'm so sorry, Mamie." I reached out to hug her, but she pulled away and adjusted her apron. Her back and shoulders straightened, eliminating any of the vulnerability she exposed a second ago.

"I don't need the support, Reed. Jolie does. I just don't know how to make her accept it from you."

"Where is she?"

"It's Thursday. She's at yoga I assume."

Right. Her routine. How was it that I was only now understanding why her routines were so important? I'd been so enthralled with the amazing woman she was, I didn't stop to realize that her weaknesses devoured her the way mine did me.

I knelt and scooped the shredded lettuce off the floor. I dumped it into a large trashcan. "I'm not going to do it." I wiped excess lettuce scraps off my shorts. "I'm not going to testify when they find him."

"Of course you are." She waved off my statement like she was swatting at a fly.

"No, I've decided. I'm going to make up some excuse when I'm on the stand, tell them I don't remember. I'll come up with something."

Mamie got in my face again. "Don't be a fool. The last thing Jolie needs is both of the men she loves going to jail."

"They can't put me in jail for not remembering."

"They can hold you in contempt for lying. You've already given the description, Reed. The damage is done, whether you intended for it to be or not. Pouring gasoline on a fire is not the answer."

"Well, I have to think of something."

"You and me both, *bel homme*." She fixed her hair, which had not a strand out of place, and walked out to the front of the store.

Chapter Twenty-Four

Jolie had told me more than once that she found solace at the beach. The ocean cleared her head. It had been over a day since I spoke with Mamie, and not a single productive thought had come to me. I sat at the park for hours playing my sax, searching for wisdom, but all that came my way was $7.80 in change in my instrument case. It was time to borrow Jolie's muse. Maybe the ocean could provide me with the same inspiration it gave her.

It was such a sticky night I welcomed the escape from my car, anyway. Since most of my things were still at my mother's house from when I stayed there, I was free to leave my car unattended, with only my sax and duffel on my person.

The beach, technically closed, was enveloped in the night's darkness and it was hard to make out anything more than a few feet in front of me. A hot breeze blew past, and when I climbed up on the lifeguard stand, the wind became stronger. Hard waves crashed against the shore in a smooth, predictable rhythm. I breathed in the salt and the seaweed and understood in an instant how Jolie found this hypnotizing.

The world seemed different from that chair, even though I could see so little of it. The moonlit horizon looked hopeful, promising that things could get better if

I just figured out a way. Could I go through with not testifying if and when they caught Tristan? Would that prove to Jolie that she could depend on me? Could I get away with that, legally? Even if they didn't punish me for such actions, could I do that to the other people he stabbed? Didn't they deserve their justice?

Was there a way to show Jolie I would be there for her while doing the moral thing at the same time?

I slouched and rested my head on the back of the lifeguard chair. It was so serene that in a few minutes, I felt myself drifting in and out of sleep, with the waves as my lullaby. After a while, though, there was a slight disruption in the waves' cadence; an irregular splashing interrupted the booming symphony. I opened my eyes to see what was causing the discordant sounds.

In the not-too-far distance, two shadows walked along the water. A tall, male figure kicked water at a smaller, female one. They both wore sweatshirts. His hood was pulled over his head, protecting him from the breeze, but hers was not. The woman's hands were buried in the pockets of her shorts and her head was tipped forward. The male figure nudged her, but she didn't seem like she wanted to play along. When she pushed her hair from her face, I was able to make out her chin-length hair, no longer hidden by the bulky sweatshirt. I sucked in a breath with the realization that I knew that hair well.

The man stopped splashing and put his arm around Jolie's waist. She rested her head on his shoulder. They sank into each other.

Their position enraged and saddened me at the same time. She'd moved on and sought comfort from someone else. It was no wonder why, considering everything I'd done, but it still seemed so fast for her to have achieved that level of intimacy already. Unless it wasn't someone new. I couldn't make out anything except the back of a man's frame, but it could have been the guy, Brett, I saw her with in her shop. It would have made sense for her to turn back to him, the safer choice.

I stood for a second, ready to jump down and let them know I was there. Then I thought better of it. If they turned and saw me in that position, I would be a menacing shadow in the sky, exactly how I didn't want Jolie to see me. I needed to attract their attention in a discreet manner.

I opened my sax case. I started a low tune, as if I could have been playing all along, but they'd now noticed it because they'd grown quiet. I chose the song I played for her the night I slept at her place, when I knew I'd have to tell her everything in the morning. Would she recognize it, and all its agony?

The man didn't move, but Jolie lifted her head off his shoulder. She raised her chin a little, as if she were searching for the source of the sound. She turned her head, first away from me over the guy's shoulder, and saw nothing, then in my direction. When she found me, she released herself from the man's hold and faced me, her silhouette still against the perpetual motion of the water.

I was unsure of whether I should continue playing, or make my descent from the chair and talk to her. Instinct told me to jump down and get between them. So I kept playing. All my instincts as of late had been wrong.

After standing stone-still for a couple more bars,

she moved. She put her arm on the man's back and said something to him. She pointed to me, high in the chair and he turned in my direction. Then she motioned for him to sit a few feet back in the sand, which he did without argument.

Her steps were tentative as she approached the lifeguard stand, but she kept coming. I felt like the Pied Piper. My song, in the dim light seemed to put her under a spell and draw her closer, whether she wanted to come or not. I didn't stop playing until she climbed the ladder and sat next to me, for fear it would break the trance.

"What are you doing here, Reed?" She stared straight out at the white caps of the waves crashing way out at sea.

"I came here to think. I swear I didn't know you'd be here." I zipped my sax back in its case and stuck it between my legs.

"I know you didn't. I didn't know I was coming. It was a spur of the moment decision." She sighed.

"I promise you I also didn't know I was describing Tristan, Jolie. I would have never done that."

She swallowed and nodded, looking defeated. I couldn't tell if it was because she didn't believe me, or because she did and that meant it was true. Either way, I hated to see her so drained.

This was my chance, but I was scared to take it. I feared anything I said would dig the knife in deeper. When I realized the reference was in poor taste, considering the circumstances, I shook my head and scoffed.

"What?" she asked.

"I'm afraid anything I say right now will make

things worse," I admitted, leaving out the reference.

Her gaze fell to her date, sitting at the water's edge, hugging his knees that were pulled into his chest. "I'm not sure they can get much worse."

I turned to her as best as I could. I took her hand in both of mine, even though it was inappropriate with another guy waiting for her. "Please let me in. I know I don't deserve it, and you have no reason to believe me, but you mean everything to me. I miss you so much, Jolie."

"I miss you too." Her voice shook.

"Then tell me what I can do. How can I help you? How can I make this right?"

She looked at me and her watery eyes glistened in the moonlight. She shook her head and whispered. "You can't. No one can. I don't know what to do."

Tears fell from her eyes and I cupped her face in my palms. I wiped the tears away, wanting nothing more than to have the power to wipe away her pain as well. I tipped my forehead against hers. "We'll figure it out. I'm not going to testify against Tristan. I was all drugged up when I described him. I'll say I don't remember any of it."

I expected her to protest the way Mamie had. Instead, she nodded against my forehead and sniffled. "You would do that?"

"I would do anything for you."

I touched my lips to hers, and she kissed me in return. Softly, slowly, sadly.

The sound of feet scraping against the ladder of the stand ended our moment. I tightened with resentment but I was, in fact, the intruder on this date. I closed my eyes as she pulled away, as if that would allow the taste of her lips to linger on mine longer. I lowered my head. I didn't want a confrontation with this guy, whether it was Brett or someone new. All I wanted was Jolie back, and the way to her heart was definitely not by getting in a fight with another guy.

"I told you to wait over there." Jolie's voice was kind, but direct, the way she would address a child, not a date.

"I know. I'm sorry."

I opened my eyes at the voice. He climbed up halfway, so his chest was level with our feet as he stared up at us. Still hooded, most of him was hidden, but there was no mistaking the gunmetal eyes.

My jaw clenched at the sight of my attacker.

Jolie laid her hand on Tristan's cheek. Her voice was as tranquil as the ocean. "Sweetie, go back down and wait for me by the water. I'm okay. I'll be down in a minute."

Tristan's eyes narrowed on me. I thought he would be surprised, or nervous when he realized who I was, but there was no recognition behind his pupils. If anything, he looked blank, inexpressive.

He shook his head, focus still fixed on me. "I don't know, Jo Jo. He might be part of the…"

Jolie took Tristan's chin in her fingers and turned his face, directing his attention back to her. "What did we talk about?"

Tristan cast his eyes down, conceding.

"Please, go watch the waves. I'll be down in a little bit."

Tristan nodded and made his way back down the ladder. Jolie was quiet until he got comfortable in the sand, closer to the lifeguard stand than before.

A thousand questions thrust against my lips, dying for a way out of my mouth. When did he come to her? Did he tell her why he did it? Where had they been staying? What the hell was she thinking hiding him?

Could I beat the hell out of him for what he did to me and the other guys in the park?

But common sense was finally becoming my ally. It told me to wait. Jolie would explain everything. Otherwise, she would have scampered off when she saw me, not climbed next to me in a lifeguard chair.

She stared at him for a few seconds, while he traced circles in the sand with his finger. When she spoke, the back of her head faced me. "You said you'd do anything for me."

"Yes."

"Then promise you won't say anything. To anyone. Not to the police, not to your boss. Most importantly, not to my mother or Mamie."

It took no time at all to know I'd keep her secret. I understood hiding better than anyone. "I won't say a word. But Jolie, what—"

"Ssshhh," she warned as my voice grew louder and Tristan raised his head. "I don't want him to hear you."

I nodded, but unless she had eyes in the back of her head, she didn't see me.

"I found him last week." Her voice was so low I had to strain to hear her, with the wind blowing in my ears. "Underneath this very chair. Something told me to come to the beach one night. My father, maybe, if you believe in that stuff."

I had a feeling she did, even though I didn't. If I believed in things like that, I'd have to believe everything happened for a reason, and I couldn't see any reason for my current predicament. I'd rather blame it on a series of stupid decisions, rather than think this was my fate.

"This was our safe place when we were young, so it made sense he'd come here. He was so bad when I found him, he didn't recognize or trust me at first. He stank like booze and pot and God knows what else. I had to use every tactic I'd ever seen my mother use with my father to get him to calm down. Eventually he did, enough for me to get him to come home with me. I made him some tea, bathed him, soothed him. I don't think he'd slept in days—at least days—so after I calmed him, I lay with him and sang to him until he fell asleep. I think he slept for a full day."

She watched him again, caught up in her thoughts. Then she turned to me. She clenched her hands around my triceps. "He's not a bad person, Reed. I swear. He's a good guy underneath this damn disease. He didn't mean to hurt anyone. He saw a snippet of the interview Mamie and I did about the shop. He didn't understand what it was about. All he got from it was that Mamie and I were on the news and that the homeless were involved. Then the voices, those fucking voices," she spat, "told him the homeless were hurting us. That's why he came here. That's why he's been doing this. He's never been violent, not one day in his life. He was just protecting me."

Her words were a rush of pleas. Pleas that I wouldn't turn him in. Pleas that I would see her brother as a good man, not a criminal who stabbed innocent people.

I didn't respond. I was too torn. On one hand, I felt bad for the guy sitting in the sand. I couldn't begin to imagine his struggles. Jolie's love for him alone was enough to make me feel a connection to him. On the other hand, I couldn't dismiss what he'd done without a thought. I wouldn't turn him in, but that didn't mean I could tell Jolie that I understood or that it wasn't his fault.

"Where are you hiding him?" I asked, to avoid addressing her words.

"He's staying at my place," she said, like he was visiting on vacation.

"What if the police come looking for him?" I didn't like her putting herself at risk.

"They have. They questioned me, Mamie, and my mother. They even spoke to that idiot, Tim. We told them everything we knew, which at the time was nothing. If they come by again, I guess I'll have to deal with it."

We watched the water for a few more minutes in silence.

"I have to leave," she finally said.

My jaw dropped. "Leave where?"

"Away. I don't know. Even if I did, it's better that I don't tell you. Somewhere far from here where no one knows us. I can get Tristan help. We can start over."

Was she serious?

"Jolie, you know you can't do that."

"So then what am I supposed to do, Reed? Turn him in? Let him go to jail? There's no way I can watch them throw him in some prison psych ward. Do you know what those places are like?" She scratched at her fingers around her nails, which were raw and sprinkled with tiny drops of dried blood. Desperation seeped from her.

"Think about it, Jolie. Really think about it. What would it mean if you ran? You can't watch him every second of every day for the rest of both of your lives. He needs help. Serious medical help that you can't give him."

She opened her mouth. "I can…"

"What about this part… You'd be on the run with someone who is already paranoid that people are after him and his family. You'd be validating his delusions. It would be impossible for him to ever separate fiction from reality."

She closed her mouth, knowing my words were true. She buried her head in her hands.

"Then what am I going to do?"

We brought Tristan back to Jolie's apartment. She said she'd handle things on her own, but there was no way I was leaving her alone to deal with this.

As soon as we got home, Jolie brought Tristan into her room and tucked him into bed. She'd explained to him, at the beach, that I was a close friend and would do him no harm. He was skeptical, but so far it wasn't a problem. Jolie said that after the first two days he spent with her, his erratic behaviors had, in fact, eased up. She made sure he had no access to alcohol or pot, which as far as she could tell were the only drugs he'd taken, and that helped a lot.

She kept waiting, though, waiting for a major flare-up.

She came out of the bedroom once he was sound asleep. Now that we were in the light, I saw how exhausted she was. Dark rings circled her eyes, her face looked gaunt and her normally silky hair was knotted and frizzy. Surprise must have registered across my face.

She shrugged. "I didn't want to leave him alone, you know? So doing stuff for myself has been hard."

I ran a hand down the short length of her hair. "Well, I'm here now. I can help watch over him. Tell me what you need. Want me to make you something to eat? Or how about a nice hot shower?"

"God, Reed, a long bath sounds amazing."

"Go take a bath, then." I kissed her nose. "I'll keep my ears open and if he wakes up, I'll come get you."

She hugged me before disappearing into the bathroom.

While she soaked, I searched her kitchen for anything edible. There weren't many options. I assumed food shopping was challenging too, if she couldn't leave him alone, or bring him out in public. I made a note to pick up some food for her tomorrow, even if it meant borrowing more cash from my cousin or mother. Yes, I had my pride, but I wouldn't let it interfere with Jolie's welfare.

I heated a can of chicken noodle soup, which I found in the back of her cabinet, and made her a peanut butter sandwich. It wasn't gourmet by any stretch of the imagination, but at least it would fill her stomach. When she emerged from the bathroom in a comfy oversized tee and sweats shorts, and saw the food on the living room table, she brought her hand to her chest and sighed.

I tapped the couch beside me. "Come and eat."

She sat next to me and rested her head on my shoulder as she took small bites of her sandwich. After she finished her soup, we laid on the couch together, on our sides, with her back to my chest. I stroked her wet hair, her shoulder, and the side of her arm. I hated what she was going through, but I was so grateful I'd been at the beach, at the right time and place for once, and that she was allowing me to be here with her.

"I'm sorry I accused you of stalking my family," she muttered into the air. "I just couldn't bear seeing Tristan's face on that paper. I didn't handle the shock very well, and with everything else going on, I couldn't take it. When Tristan showed up and told me what happened, I felt horrible about what I'd said. I was dying to call you and apologize, but I didn't want to involve you in my mess. I'm not usually like this, you know."

"Like what?"

"So undone. Before you came along, I had everything pretty much together. Maybe it's you," she chuckled.

"Hey." I pinched her waist, tickling her. She twitched and giggled.

"I'm kidding. Actually, I'm so glad you're here. Just having you beside me, holding me, makes me feel better. It doesn't change anything, but at least I don't feel so alone."

I turned her toward me, so she was on her back and I could see her face. I twirled the tips of her hair in my fingers. "I promise you, Jolie, you are not alone. I will be here with you to deal with this, whatever that means. You have my word. I know that may not seem like much, and unfortunately right now that's all I have to offer, but you have that. My promise that I will see you through this. I'll be right by your side, no matter what you decide."

She reached up and gently pulled my mouth to

hers. Though I'd kissed her many times before, this was different. This time, there were no secrets between us, and this time, she was choosing to kiss Reed. Not the Reed I had pretended to be, but the Reed who had all his crap spilled out in front of him. This time, she chose me with my faults and all.

Chapter Twenty-Five

I woke to soft voices in the kitchen. Jolie and I had fallen asleep woven together on the couch, after Jolie dozed off in the middle of a kiss. She was exhausted and had slept like the dead all night.

Now, though, I was alone on the couch and Tristan was talking to her about something. I was hesitant to go in there. I didn't know how he'd react to me, and our last altercation, before the beach, hadn't been so pleasant.

Eventually, they came out. Jolie had eggs and toast on two plates, and Tristan carried his own. He barely looked at me before sitting on a chair and shoveling eggs into his mouth. I wasn't sure if he noticed me. I watched him eat, waiting for what, I don't know.

"Don't worry," Jolie whispered in my ear. "Everything's okay right now."

It was the *right now* that made me uneasy. I had no experience with this and I didn't know what to expect.

Not long after breakfast, Tristan wandered the apartment, peeking out the curtains Jolie had drawn, no doubt because she was aiding and abetting a wanted criminal.

Jolie talked to him when he did this, trying to distract him. She asked questions that encouraged him to tell stories. Although I tried to appreciate his stories, to me they didn't follow a cohesive thought. They skipped from one topic to the next and jumped around in ways I didn't understand.

Jolie, though, remained attentive, never questioning a lapse in connection. She spoke with him as if he made complete sense and when he mumbled things under his breath, about "them" or "the others", she made him focus on her and spoke to him about quieting the thoughts. I didn't know if that was her own strategy, her mother's, or a therapist's from somewhere in their pasts, but at the moment, it was keeping what she called his agitation at bay.

We continued that way for three days. During the day, Jolie did her best to keep Tristan calm and happy. After he went to sleep at night, Jolie and I snuggled on the couch. I cooked for her and massaged her while she ate, trying to relieve some of the tension that mounted inside her by the day. We talked at night in soft whispers. Now that she knew my story, she wanted to hear all she could about my family. I was happy to let her get to know me, no holds barred, and told her all the silly stories of sibling rivalry I could remember. They served a dual purpose of letting her learn about me and giving her a much-needed distraction.

"I can never go back there, now," she said one night when we talked about how I met some of the people at the Palace.

"Why?" I asked.

"Are you kidding? After what Tristan did? It's my fault. I'm sure none of them will want to see me when they hear who is responsible for this."

"This is not your fault, Jolie. They adore you. Of course you can go back."

She shook her head. "I can't, especially because

I'm going to fight for Tristan not to go to prison. It breaks my heart not to be able to see them again. I've been trying to figure out a way to get them the crepes anyway. I can't ask Mamie to go, and I haven't even been to the store to ask Morgan."

"I'll take them," I said.

"Really? How will you explain that to Mamie without telling her you've seen me?"

I paused to think. "I went to the store to talk to you. She told me you hadn't been there. I can pretend I was thinking about it on my own and offer to take a batch over."

She thought for a minute. "Thank you. That could work. But you won't talk to anyone about what Tristan did, right?"

"Jolie, they care about you. They would understand."

"No." She frowned, adamant. "Not a word to them, or I don't want you to go. Especially not to Curt. I couldn't bear it if he hated me."

I knew in my gut Curt could never hate her, but I agreed because it made her happy.

Aside from that delivery and going out to pick up food for us a few times, I never left her side.

We both knew our escape from reality could only last so long, though. I had to go back to work. Hector had been good about giving me more time off when I pretended to have a set-back from my wounds, but I needed money. More importantly, though, pressures from outside were growing. Mamie must have called ten times each day. We couldn't hold her off much longer. And when we turned on the television—after Tristan was asleep for fear of what he'd hear—the sketch of my description of Tristan was plastered all over the local news. It was only a matter of time before the police came knocking on Jolie's door again.

In addition to that, Tristan's mumbling was becoming stronger, more frequent, and more persistent. Though I didn't know the signs, Jolie's furrowed brow and increased picking at her skin confirmed what I suspected. He was getting worse.

I didn't want to pressure her. I promised I'd do whatever she wanted, but I was confident that the longer she waited, the worse it would be. I was very relieved, though, that she decided she couldn't run, because it would hurt Tristan.

On the fourth day, Jolie knew we couldn't keep going. That was the day Tristan started pacing.

"They're getting louder," he told her that night, flipping on the TV.

She took the remote from his hand and turned off the TV.

"Don't hold that. It's how they steal your thoughts." He motioned to the remote. "Maybe he controls it, too." He pointed at me, raising his voice. "He's been here the whole time, hasn't he? I think he hooked me up to them with it."

Jolie placed the remote on the table and took Tristan's arm to lead him into the bedroom away from me.

"Wait," I said. She halted. "Do you like music, Tristan?"

He didn't answer, but didn't object either.

I pulled out my saxophone and played. He sat and listened. He didn't look at me, or say anything about the music, but he didn't seem as irritable as before. I played one soothing song after another.

It got late. Eventually, Jolie decided it was time for him to go to bed. She kissed the top of my head as she walked past me. "Thank you," she whispered.

"Thank you," Tristan repeated.

They were in there a long time before Jolie came out. "He's having a harder and harder time falling asleep," she said.

"Jolie," I said. I didn't want to push, but Tristan needed help.

She held up her hand. "Don't. Please don't say it. I know," she stammered. "I'll do it tomorrow. Please, let me have one more night with my brother sleeping safe and sound in my home before I have to give him up." She fell into my open arms like a rag doll.

We spent one last night together on the couch, though Jolie's tossing and turning kept us both awake all night. As soon as the sun rose, she was showered and ready. The limp girl from the night before had been replaced by a strong woman with a body of steel to match her eyes. She was as prepared for what she had to do as anyone could be.

"You're just like her, you know." I squeezed her shoulders from behind and planted a gentle kiss on her neck.

"My mother? Yeah, I know." She sighed, looking at her reflection in the bathroom mirror.

"Your mother? No. You're nothing like *her*."

"Sure I am. She runs; she hides. I ran from you when things got hard. I hid from the truth about Tristan rather than facing it. I've been hiding for a week and a half with him. I spend my life running from a disease I'll probably never have. I'm afraid I'm a lot more like her than I want to admit."

I shook my head. That wasn't the woman I saw at all. "No, Jolie. You're like Mamie."

"Mamie?" she scoffed. "Ha. I'm nothing like Mamie. Mamie is a bull. She's headstrong and powerful. She runs from nothing. I'm not like Mamie at all."

I turned her around and held her shoulders. "Jolie, Mamie is smart and honest. She's loyal, trustworthy, dependable, and yes, headstrong, just like you. You are all of those things. You don't have to have a huge voice and personality to share her huge qualities, and you do. Share them."

Her smile lit up the bathroom. Her father must have been a very wise man.

"I really do love you," she said.

"Then I'm the luckiest guy in this whole damn world," I answered.

Jolie called Mamie and told her we found Tristan on the beach the night before, as we planned. If Tristan talked about how he'd been with Jolie for longer, and if the police believed his story over ours, we didn't want Mamie to be any kind of accomplice.

Mamie and Abby were at Jolie's place in a blink. After welcoming Tristan home, the three women retreated to the kitchen. Tristan sat on the couch in the living room. I wasn't sure if he realized I was still in the room, he looked so disconnected. I strained to hear the conversation in the kitchen.

At first, all three women spoke at the same time.

"We can't bring him in. He's already threatened to hurt himself if he has to go to a home. You think prison would be better?" Abby urged the others.

"We've got to bring him in. We'll get the best lawyers and take it from there. Do you think I want my grandson harmed? This is the only way, Abby. He can't survive as a wanted man forever." Mamie's usual boom was unwavering.

The fighting went on until Jolie raised her voice. "Listen, both of you. I've been thinking about this for a week and a half, and there's no other way. Mamie's right. We've got to bring him in. We've got documentation from when he was diagnosed. We've got excellent doctors. They'll be on our side. There's no way he can continue to hide out."

There was a brief pause. "What do you mean a week and a half?" I could almost hear Mamie's eyes squinting at Jolie through the kitchen wall.

I'm sure Jolie was thrown at being caught in our lie, but her voice didn't give her away. "I mean, I've been considering all the options, knowing sooner or later this would be a reality. I've been deciding on the best course of action for when the time came. We have to take emotion out of it and do what's best for Tristan. Taking a guy with paranoid delusions God-knows-where and telling him we have to hide out because someone is after us is the worst thing we can do. There's no other way."

My words sounded even smarter coming from her.

After going in circles for a while, the women agreed. They would have Tristan turn himself in, but not alone. They'd bring their lawyer and Tristan's doctor with them. Together, hopefully, Tristan would be okay.

At once, they got their support system in line. Then, Jolie took on the arduous task of telling Tristan what they had to do.

His furious pacing began. "They're going to hack into my brain!" He circled the room, ranting about what "they" were going to do to him and why he had to leave right away. His arms flailed and his hands raked through his hair in desperation. I stood back, but prepared myself to restrain him if necessary.

"Honey," Abby spoke, gently setting Jolie aside. "Look at me." She cupped Tristan's cheeks in both of her hands and guided him to sit on the couch. "I won't let anyone hurt you. Remember, sweetie, what we've said about the voices? These are the ones you have to push away, these are the ones that aren't real, the ones that come when you're not taking medication. What's real and true is that you've hurt some people because you thought you were protecting Mamie and Jolie, and now we have to go admit that, and get you the help you need."

Abby continued speaking to Tristan. Her words were tranquil but full of purpose. She never lost physical contact with him. With each sentence, he saw her a little more and seemed to grasp what was happening a little better.

I had no doubt that years of difficult experience served her, and Tristan, well at that moment. Eventually, he was calm enough to move.

"Do you want me to come with you?" I asked Jolie as Abby guided Tristan to the car.

She shook her head. "This is something we need to handle. Besides, with me, my mother, Tristan, our lawyer, and Tristan's doctor, the car is full. Take care of Mamie while we're gone. I'll let you know as soon as we hear anything."

Jolie had wanted Mamie to go instead of Abby, but Abby was the only person who got a positive response from Tristan. The choice made itself.

I pulled Jolie into a tight hug. I buried my face on the side of her head and whispered in her ear. "Remember our conversation from last night? You are stronger than you know. You will get yourself, and Tristan, through this. And I'll be waiting here, with whatever you need." I kissed her temple.

She gave a halfhearted-smile, one that certainly wasn't powering the rotation of any planets, and walked out to the car.

"You are quite the young man, aren't you?" Mamie asked as soon as the door clicked shut. "I was right about you. Of course I was. I always am."

I shrugged off the compliment, not feeling I was worthy of it. "Can I make you something to eat?"

"Make *me*? Trust me, there's nothing here I would eat, and I'm not sitting around all day going crazy waiting for the phone to ring. They know how to reach us. Let's get the hell out of here and go somewhere I can make you some real food."

I drove Mamie to Stuff Your Crepes where Morgan and some guy I didn't know were tending to small lines. Mamie thanked the guy for covering, ushered him out the door, and strapped on an apron. After she helped the waiting customers, she called to me. I was sitting at a table trying to blend in. Mamie had enough to deal with, without worrying about babysitting me, but I didn't want to leave because I promised Jolie I'd take care of her. The trick was not letting Mamie know that's why I was hanging around. Not if I wanted to keep my flesh intact, anyway.

"What do you want me to make you, lover boy?"

So much for inconspicuous. "Nothing, I'm fine," I called from across the room.

"Fine, I'll choose."

Mamie conjured a crepe for me, then shoved it at Morgan's chest for her to bring over. Morgan did, but my early lunch was accompanied by a *humph* as she dropped it in front of me on the table.

I knew Morgan didn't like me. I couldn't blame her. She'd known about me from the beginning and must have been forced not to say anything. I withheld the truth from her friend. I assumed that was enough to turn her, or any woman, against a guy.

She was about to walk away from my table, but stopped short when the store chimes rang. I turned to see who'd caused her to pause. Jolie had told me about Morgan's weird relationship with her roommate, Chase. I didn't know why Morgan was insisting they remain apart, but her instant blush told me it was probably some stupid thing she couldn't get past, and that she really did want the guy standing in front of her.

He gave me a questioning look. Morgan picked up on it. "Jolie's guy," she sneered. "What are you doing here?"

He pulled a set of keys out of his pocket. "You left without these. I won't be home later when you come home, so..." His voice trailed off and he motioned for her to take them from his hand.

"Oh, thanks." She took them with the tips of her thumb and forefinger, careful not to make contact with his skin. "Where are you going?"

"I have a date." He waited for a reaction.

Her mouth twitched but she said nothing. She

281

turned on her heel and walked back behind the counter.

"Guess I'll get something to eat while I'm here."

"Might as well." Her answer was flat.

To my surprise, after Chase got his food, he sat down.

At my table.

WTF?

"So you're the Music Man."

The Music Man. I liked it. Liked that she'd given me a nickname. What I liked more was having something to embarrass Jolie with later. Sure, I revealed that she was called the Cat Lady, but (a), I hadn't come up with it and (b), in my defense, I was high on painkillers when I told her.

"I suppose I am." I couldn't tell if it an accusation, or a praise.

Chase examined me for a bit while he chewed. Having some strange dude stare me down from across a table made me fidget in my seat a little.

"I get it." He swallowed a chunk and coughed.

"Get what?" This was weird.

"I get why Jolie would stick around with you even though, according to Morgan, you're the opposite of what she likes in a guy."

His comment got my back up. "And why is that?" Was he implying she was going slumming? Or that she was fulfilling some bad boy fantasy with me before she reverted back to her safe and secure ways? I was going to figure out how to be that guy for her. I wrung my hands together. That better not be what he was implying.

"Because I've heard what you're telling her in your music. I don't think too many people could walk away from that. Well"—he shook his head—"some could, but not most." He scarfed down another bite. "Your music is pretty incredible, but I guess you already know that if that's how you get girls."

"It's not how I *get girls*," I spat. "That was all about Jolie."

"That's cool." He slurped a soda and tapped the plastic top of the cup with his finger, unaware of my attitude. "Do you write for anyone?"

"What do you mean? I just told you…"

"No, I mean, like for money. I bet local bands around here would pay good money to have somebody write songs for them."

"Oh," I chuckled. "No, I do it for fun."

"Well, you should consider it. That stuff was awesome. Almost had Morgan feeling something for me. Almost." He crumpled the paper from his crepe and shoved it in the soda cup.

He wasn't trying to provoke me about Jolie. He was frustrated about Morgan, and apparently assumed I knew the situation.

He stood from his chair. "Congrats on getting the girl. Wish we could all be so lucky."

"Not sure I've gotten her yet. Still have to prove to her that I can be what she needs." Why was I confiding in a complete stranger? Did we have a common bond because the women worked together?

"Well, she's still with you, so you're doing something right. Connect with her people somehow and you'll be golden."

He left the shop without saying goodbye to Morgan. He didn't see the way she watched his every step as he left the shop.

Chapter Twenty-Six

Connect with her people.

His words had me thinking for the rest of the day, as Mamie and I did whatever we could to keep from checking our phones. I didn't expect an immediate call, but I did find myself walking the store aimlessly and playing imaginary keys more than usual.

"If you don't sit still I'm going to throw you out on your ass. I don't care if you did promise to be my keeper for the day. You're making me crazy."

Couldn't get anything past this old woman. I erased the thought. She could probably read minds too, and I wasn't ashamed to admit I was a little afraid of her.

"When do you think they'll call? It's been hours." I stood at the counter when there was a lull and tapped the countertop.

"Are you kidding me, Reed? *My* granddaughter, *my* grandson and *my* daughter-in-law are at the police station while I'm here and you're the one who is ripping at the seams? Get it together or get the hell out of my store."

Okay, I probably deserved that, especially when, in truth, I wasn't concerned about Tristan. I mean, I was, but for Jolie's sake. She was the person I cared about. She was the one I was worried sick over.

Hector's words finally made sense as Mamie yelled at me. I walked over to her and kissed her on the cheek.

She was torn between smiling and hitting me.

"You're absolutely right, Mamie. I'm going to get out of your hair for a bit. Get some air. That is, if you're okay minding yourself for about a half hour." I knew I was taking my life in my hands when I winked at her.

She threw a paper cup at me as I walked away.

****

"Here." Mamie threw a dishrag at me when I returned. This time I caught the object she aimed my way. She wasn't over my implication that she needed me to babysit her, and didn't ask where I'd gone. That was a good thing, because coming up with a lie while I was out was the last thing on my mind. "Wipe down the tables. Make yourself useful."

As I cleaned the already spotless tables, the chimes went off.

"She put you to work?" Jolie's voice was a sweeter melody than anything I'd ever written.

I dropped the rag on the table and raced to her. "Are you okay?"

"Yes," she said. "I am. Honestly."

Mamie came over and the three of us sat at a table so Jolie could tell us everything that happened.

"It was good that he turned himself in. It probably would have been better if he'd come forward sooner." Guilt flashed across Jolie's features. I wondered if Mamie noticed, until she frowned. Of course she noticed.

"But at least he did it now," Jolie continued. "So basically what happened today was they had to give him an exam to see if he is aware of what's going on and what he did. We waited around all day to find out the results."

"Wouldn't it be good if he doesn't understand?" I asked.

"No, actually." She took my hand in hers. "You would think that, but it's the opposite. If he doesn't understand, he gets sent to a mental hospital for a period of time, then when he can understand he goes back to criminal court. If, though, he does understand, he can go to mental health court. There, they can determine if the illness drove the crime and, hopefully, if it did, he can go to a treatment facility, not a prison psych ward."

"So he had the test?" Mamie asked, impatient to get to the end.

"Well, technically they can start the process, including the court, as soon as there is a bed available at the treatment facility. There was a bed available, so they took him there today. Last we heard, they administered the exam but they haven't yet notified either the police or us about the outcome. I don't know what's delaying it, but they told us to go home and that we'd hear as soon as they do. So here I am. I sent Abby home. She was beat."

Jolie walked behind the counter and got herself a bottle of water. She gulped half of it in a matter of seconds. She set down the bottle and leaned her arms and chest on the counter. "Abby was wonderful with Tristan. So patient and caring, up until the second they took him from us."

Mamie nodded. "She always had a special way with your father, too, getting through to him when no one else could. We all have our special gifts. We can't overlook those gifts and focus solely on a person's faults."

Jolie's mouth shifted to the side, but the almost-frown was smoothed by an easiness that didn't usually exist when Abby's name was mentioned.

"So now what?" I asked.

"Now we wait. And pray that Tristan understands what he did."

Jolie and I decided to spend the night at Mamie's. Abby and Tim were there, but we didn't want Mamie to be left alone with her worries all night if they were preoccupied with each other.

"I know you laughed before when I said I'd make you something to eat, but when I had a kitchen to cook in, I made a mean chicken parm." I smirked at Mamie, knowing full well the effect my smirk had on women. I doubted the generation made much difference.

"Is that so?" Mamie squinted.

"Sure is. One bite and you'll be begging for more." Goading her was entertaining. I couldn't think of another octogenarian I could talk to that way.

"Begging? Have you met me?" she asked.

"Eating out of the palm of my hand," I joked.

"You tolerate this sass from him?" Mamie asked Jolie. She was deadpan, but I'd spent enough time with her to know she was at least partially kidding.

Jolie rolled her eyes. "He's your problem now, Mamie, but I must admit his chicken parm is delicious."

"Problem indeed." She walked into the kitchen doorway and motioned with a swinging arm for me to walk past her. She smacked my ass as I crossed the threshold. I jumped.

"Still? You're still surprised? Not a very quick study, are you?" She tapped my temple.

Mamie's kitchen was stocked more than I'd expect

of an old woman who lived alone. The cabinets must have been filled for her houseguests.

Though it was late, I had a feeling none of us would sleep very much, so I made a heap of chicken, which everyone swallowed whole with ravenous appetites. In the dining room, Jolie and Abby recounted their long, trying day in detail. I expected it to be difficult for Jolie to discuss, but once again the strength and dedication in her tone amazed me. The difference was, this time, with Abby contributing to the conversation, their story was told in a complementary harmony, with a common goal. Everyone wanted what was best for Tristan.

Jolie's voice cracked when she reached the part where they led Tristan away, ranting and begging. Abby laid her hand over Jolie's and gave a gentle squeeze. Jolie glanced at their joined hands, but didn't pull away.

Abby and Tim left for bed right after dinner. Jolie watched Abby lead another man up to the bedroom she'd once shared with Jolie's father.

Mamie stood from her chair and lifted one of the plates. She grimaced as she rose and reflexively grabbed her hip.

"Leave it," I said. "I'll take care of it."

"I've got it, Mamie," Jolie said at the same time. She pulled a plate from my hand, but I wouldn't have it.

"Go inside and relax. Be with Mamie." I kissed her jaw.

I spent the next half hour washing and drying dishes and pots by hand. Mamie had a dishwasher, but she shouldn't have had to put away my mess of dishes when she woke the next day.

I found Mamie asleep on the couch when I went into the living room. Jolie watched TV next to her at such a low volume it could have been muted.

"She's exhausted," Jolie whispered. "I feel bad to wake her but I don't want to leave her here all night either."

With the caution I would use handling a fragile porcelain doll, I lifted Mamie around the back and under her legs, taking particular care of her hip. I put most of her weight on my good side, but still had to stifle my urge to grimace as I held her. She woke in a fog when I lifted her, mumbling something about putting her down if I wanted to keep my boy bits intact. I shushed her and she fell back asleep. Jolie guided me up the stairs and directed me to Mamie's room, where I eased her onto the bed and covered her, fully clothed.

Jolie led me down the hall to the room that had been hers when she was younger. The wall over her bed was a collage of pictures of her family. Jolie and Tristan riding waves on boogie boards at the beach. Mamie showing a young Jolie how to make a crepe. Jolie's parents all dressed up, with her father's arms wrapped around her mother. Abby beaming.

"That was my cousin's wedding." Jolie said when she saw me taking in the picture. "We all had a wonderful time, until the band singer's microphone screeched and my father thought an outsider was infiltrating the wedding. He made a scene. We had to leave. This picture was taken about an hour before. I didn't want this picture at first because it reminded me of my father's outburst. But Abby said not to throw it away. She told me that right before they took the picture, my father sang in her ear while they danced. It was their wedding song from years ago. She saw the picture as a nice memory, so I guess it made me see it that way, too." She studied the picture for a couple of beats. "I don't know how many people would have put up with what she did for all those years."

"She must have loved him a lot." I hugged her around the waist from behind.

"She did. She was always there trying to calm him. No matter how many different kinds of drug treatments he struggled with, hating the side effects, she was there, supporting him, promising they'd get it right next time."

"I'm sorry," I whispered in her ear, because they never did get it right.

"There were good times, too, though." She sat on the bed and scooted back against the wall. I sat next to her and she curled up and rested her head on my lap. "Times when the drugs worked and he came to my soccer games and cheered. Or when he taught Tristan how to surf. Regardless of how he felt, he made sure to tell us how proud he was of every little thing we did, like when I made my first crepe. It was so gross. It was thick and uneven, pretty raw on the inside. But from the way he carried on, you'd think I'd graduated from culinary school." She laughed. "I remember my mother giggling about things he said a lot, too, so I guess we were luckier than some."

"What was his best trait?" I ran my fingers through her hair.

"Hmm." She thought for a minute. "Well, I don't know if it was his best trait, but something I loved about both him and Tristan was how playful they were. They were witty and snarky, almost cocky even. They were—" She stopped talking and turned to look up at me.

"What?" I asked.

"I think you might remind me a little of them. Don't get me wrong, in many ways you're nothing alike, but in some, little nuance ways, I think you are."

I couldn't think of a higher compliment than being put in any category with those men she adored. I leaned over and touched my lips to hers. The sting in my injury reminded me it was there.

I gave her a soft kiss. "Thank you." I backed away, because that's all I was going for, but she followed me up, wrapping a hand around the back of my head.

She sat in my lap and we kissed. She lifted my shirt over my head, revealing the healing wound on my chest. She crawled her fingers on the skin around it, then on my cheek near my scarring eye.

"I'm so sorry he did this to you." She kissed each of my wounds with lips made of satin, and for the first time, contact with the slashes caused me pleasure and not an ounce of pain. I closed my eyes and tipped my head back against the wall.

"Are you okay?" she whispered, unsure of my reaction.

"Yes." I sighed.

She worked my face and chest with careful but sensual kisses and though I liked where this was going, her day had been nothing short of emotionally fatiguing. I took her face in my hands and brought it to mine. "Are *you*?"

She nodded in my hands. "Honestly, Reed, if you weren't here with me, I think I'd be a wreck, but you steady me in a way no one ever has. I don't know how or why, but from the moment you put your mouth on mine when I started to have that panic attack about Tristan, I knew it was you."

I'd known it was her since I saw the woman I'd heard so much about standing behind that counter, so hearing she returned that, even when she knew all the shit I'd done, made everything inside me blaze. Music was the only thing that ever got my pulse racing so fast it was hard to contain in my veins. Being with Jolie was like mixing the most sensual song with the adrenaline rush I got from a huge bet. It was unfamiliar, all she made me feel, almost too much to keep inside.

It was like being home.

I lay her back onto her pillows. With no pomp and with care not to reopen my wounds, we made quiet, tender love, in the way of two people who wanted to soothe each other's souls more than their bodies.

Chapter Twenty-Seven

The call came earlier than expected. As soon as Jolie hung up with the Assistant District Attorney, we raced to get dressed and wake Mamie.

She was already downstairs, drinking a fresh pot of mud. "What did they say?" She took a slow, methodical sip, as though she were asking the weather. I knew, though, that she was bursting inside.

"We have to meet him at the mental health facility. He wants to talk to Abby and me in person."

She tipped her head once and focused on her coffee.

When Abby came down dressed and ready to go, we headed out. There may not have been room in the car for me the day before, but there was no way I was letting Jolie go through this without me this time.

The facility was cold and bare. Smells of antiseptic filled the air as we stepped inside. I took Jolie's hand as we entered a room that looked like it was designated for group meetings. It was carpeted and largely empty but for a small table and folding chairs off to the side, where we sat. Tristan's lawyer was already there, waiting for us.

The ADA was a tall, lanky man, dressed in a navy suit whose sleeves came a tad short of reaching his wrists. He shook our hands when he arrived and sat, wasting no time getting to the point.

"I want to explain what we're talking about, because it's imperative that you understand," he told both women. "After examining Tristan yesterday, his doctor has determined that he, in fact, does understand what he's done, and the ramifications of such actions. It took a while, because he was pretty out of sorts for some of the day. It was also complicated, because he did commit a number of crimes, and these felonies were not against a family member. When the crimes are against family members, there's more leeway, you see. However, we did take into account that Tristan has no known history of violence, which is very important to us."

His cell rang and he answered. I wondered which of the women I was sitting with would release a breath first as they waited for him to hang up.

"Sorry," he mumbled as he laid his phone on the table. "Anyway, the District Attorney heard the details of the case in an informal meeting after you went home last night. We handle these delicate matters as expeditiously as possible."

Tristan's lawyer nodded.

The ADA continued. "Due to Tristan's history and the fact that he turned himself in, the District Attorney was leaning toward allowing Tristan to be sent to the mental health facility, but she was unsure because of the number of felonies. Our district is rather progressive. We try as best as we can to be fair and give each individual the rehabilitation that makes the most sense. Defendants with special needs get special care. We had to be sure, though, given the circumstances, that once Tristan is out and under, we assumed, his mother's care, this would not happen again. We know you don't live here, Abby, so bringing Tristan to California after his release is of some concern."

Abby opened her mouth, but the Assistant District Attorney put his hand up to stop her from interrupting.

"Then, last night, something happened that removed some doubt from the District Attorney's mind. One of Tristan's victims came to the station."

Jolie and Abby turned in my direction, but I shook my head. It wasn't me.

"His name was…" The ADA glanced at a small paper in Tristan's file. "Curt Aarons."

Abby's face was blank, but Jolie's jaw dropped.

"Crooked Curt?" she blurted, then snapped her mouth shut.

The ADA chuckled at the name, then covered it with a grunt, knowing it was in bad taste. "Yes, well, Mr. Aarons spoke to me, not about Tristan, but about you, Ms. Durand." He gave Jolie a pointed stare.

"What about me?" she asked.

"He went on and on about your character and the donations you make to the homeless both in and out of your store. He told me how you went to see him in the hospital and met his wife. He said he understands what mental illness can do to a person, and that he doesn't want to see Tristan's family suffer by watching him rot in jail because of his disease."

Tears welled in Jolie's eyes. I squeezed her hand. I didn't know if she would be furious with me for going against her wishes and telling Curt about Tristan, but I knew I wasn't letting go.

"Now please understand this. Mr. Aarons was not the only victim and that conversation alone would never sway our DA. However, it did address her main concern. Defendants with mental illness must have a strong support system when they come out of the facility. It's become clear that you, Jolie, are exactly that. Let me tell you, the praise of a veteran is not undervalued here.

"So here is what we can offer Tristan. He will be committed to the mental health facility as an inpatient for a period of no less than six months. At six month's time, he will be reevaluated, at which point they can decide to keep him for another six months or release him, under the care of a guardian, for the next three years. You, Jolie, would be the guardian. You would be responsible for him. Ordinarily, family members are offered a choice of who would like to volunteer to watch after the defendant, but in this case, because of Abby's home state, our DA is not willing to offer that option. You and Tristan both have to agree to these terms. If you don't, Tristan will be charged with the four felonies, sent to the hospital prison ward for treatment, and when they decide he's ready to stand trial, the matter will go to court."

"It's a good deal," the lawyer told Jolie.

The ADA's phone rang again, while Jolie blurted, "I agree to the terms."

Abby laid a hand on her arm. "Wait, Jolie." Her voice was low, but the ADA was sitting right in front of us, undoubtedly able to hear her. "Before you agree, maybe we can explain that I'm moving back and buying the store. You have no idea what you'll be taking on as Tristan's guardian if they can't find him proper medication."

"I'll be fine." Jolie waved her off.

"Jolie, you don't know," Abby stressed. "You can't

understand the burden."

"Burden? Is that what he is to you?" Jolie snapped. "Is that what Daddy was to you? A burden?"

"No. But this disease *is*."

"Ladies," the ADA interrupted, finished with his call. "I can assure you. The facility is not going to release him until they are confident his treatment plan is working, and that he can function in society. I'm not, in any way, minimizing the risks here, but the DA will not waver on this. It's Jolie or prison."

"I'll do it," Jolie said as quickly as the words would leave her mouth. She nodded with fervor. "Of course I'll do it."

Tristan was placid when they brought him in, no doubt on some kind of sedation. The lawyer went over the deal with him, asking Tristan to paraphrase to make sure he had a complete understanding of the terms.

After everything was signed, the ADA gave Jolie and Abby a few minutes to say goodbye. I left the room to give them privacy, but not before Tristan grabbed my arm. He studied my eye for the first time. "I really am sorry," he said.

I tapped his other arm. "I know, man. Just get well. I'll see you when you get out."

I paced on the street outside, not knowing how Jolie would react to me. I did the one thing I promised I'd never do again. I lied.

I couldn't believe how long they were giving him to say goodbye. I must have been outside for at least ten minutes. Every minute passed like an hour.

I hurried to the door the second it opened. Jolie was pale and looked like she might collapse on the steps. I put my hands on her hips to steady her and waited for her to say something.

"It's done," she sighed.

"How do you feel?"

"Relieved that this is the outcome. So sad that he has to be in there in the first place. Grateful they're handling him this way. Terrified they won't be able to help him. Reed, I'm so, so happy he's there and I don't have to worry about where he is every second of every goddamn day, yet I feel so guilty about being happy he's there because I know it's not what he wanted."

She was exactly the mess she deserved to be.

"Don't, for a second, be guilty. It's what's best for him, Jolie. The truth is, if he'd been in a facility to begin with, maybe none of this would have happened. They're going to help him. Just because your dad couldn't find the right treatment doesn't mean Tristan won't."

She nodded. "Yeah, I know."

She was distant on the ride home. I didn't know if it was because of the Curt thing, or because of everything else she was going through. I tried to hold her hand over the console in the car while I drove and she spoke to Mamie on the phone, but she rested her hand in her lap.

Back at Mamie's, it was more of the same. If I walked into a room, she left it, and when we *were* in the same room, she sat nowhere near me. I needed to be there for her as she processed this whole thing with Tristan, but she wasn't letting me. I'd meant well with Curt. I had to make her see that.

If I'd had more self-control, I would have waited until we weren't in a room with three other people. Then again, if I'd have more self-control, I wouldn't have lost my father's store and probably would never have met Jolie. If there could be any positive to the horrible thing I'd done, that was it.

Besides, whatever I said to Jolie, she'd tell Mamie anyway. Abby had no right to judge, and from what I could tell, Tim was pretty much insignificant to everyone but Abby. Speaking in front of the family was no big deal.

I walked to where she sat on the couch and knelt in front of her. "Are you mad at me?"

Her gray eyes had a storm brewing in them. "For what?"

"For telling Curt. I know you asked me not to, but all I wanted was to be able to tell you when this was over, that Curt isn't mad and that you can go back to the Palace with your head held high the way you should, and that he said he doesn't blame you. I just wanted to connect with someone who was important to you, since I did this to someone else who was important to you."

"You told Curt?" She dropped my hand, but I grabbed her thighs.

I couldn't mess this up again. "Yes and I know I promised I'd never keep anything from you again, but it was a few measly hours, and you were so tired last night, and…"

"Stop." She put her hand up to my mouth.

"Jolie," I mumbled through her fingers.

"I assumed Curt heard who Tristan was on the news or on the street or something."

"Well…" I removed her hand. "He did. He knew it was your brother, but he didn't know why, and since you stopped coming around, he couldn't ask you. He didn't want to go to your store to find out."

"So you told him the whole story? About the schizophrenia and my father and everything?"

She was going to hate me. I fucked up. Again.

"Yes." I lowered my head. "I'm sorry."

"That's why he went to the police?"

"I guess." I shrugged, picking my chin back up. "But I promise, and I know I've promised you lots of times before. No more secrets."

She stared at me for a second like it was the first time she was seeing me. She rubbed her thumb over my broken eye.

"You saved him, Reed. By telling Curt, you saved him. It's not your fault he's there. It's thanks to you. Everything you've done, every step of the way, has helped me and helped him. Don't you see that?"

"Then why are you so distant?" I didn't care if the question sounded needy, nor did I care who heard me. I loved this woman more than I ever thought possible.

"Reed." It was the same tone she used when she told me she loved me but couldn't be with me anymore. I didn't want to hear what was coming next. "Did you understand what they said? About me being his guardian?"

"Of course I understand." I didn't understand what that had to do with us.

"You have no idea what that means. How much will be involved with that. Abby and I were talking about that after they took Tristan, before we came out to you."

Abby nodded in my peripheral vision.

"I got mad when she called it a burden, but she's right. I have no idea what condition he will be in when he gets out, or for the months or years that will follow. She and Mamie will help me, but there's no way I can ask you to be a part of this life."

"You think I'll want out?"

She dropped her head to her knees and whispered. "Who could blame you? I'd rather it be now than later. This isn't your problem; it's mine. You didn't sign on for this."

I lifted her chin. "Did you sign on to date a homeless guy who gambled away his father's business? No, but you want to be with me in spite of it. Sometimes life sucks, Jolie. Sometimes you're dealt an unfair hand, or sometimes you cause your own losses. But if you think I'm walking away from the table now, when for the first time in my life I've got the absolute winning hand, you couldn't be more wrong. I am in this, one hundred percent. Whatever you have to do for him, we'll do it together. You don't only have Mamie to depend on anymore. From now on, you've got me, too, whatever that's worth. I know I'm far from perfect and I know I don't seem like someone capable of taking this on, but I swear to you I will find a way to be that guy for you, Jolie. I will find a way to deserve you. I've been trying to figure out how to prove it to you. We've just been a little busy."

"You'll find a way to be that for me? You think you need to prove something to me? What are you even talking about? You've been nothing but supportive and dependable from the second you saw me with him. You've proven yourself over and over. I would never have made it through this without you by my side, and that's where you've been every second. With me, with Mamie. Don't you think I've noticed that? You are everything I could ever want, and then some." She blushed. "Don't dare change into anything else for or because of me."

I grabbed her face in my hands and kissed her, hard, long and deep, as if her family wasn't all sitting around watching.

Chapter Twenty-Eight

I went back to work that afternoon and Jolie went home for a much-deserved sleep, before going to Stuff Your Crepes for the evening shift. When I picked her up at closing time, she was rested, energized, and smiling.

"Have a good day?" I leaned over the counter. I loved the way her eyes ran over my pecs when I put my weight on my arms. When I did it the day we met, she pretended she wasn't checking me out, and failed miserably. Now, the way she overtly stared made me want to get her out of there as fast as possible.

"It's about to get better, I think." She pecked my lips "Are you ready to go home?"

Little did she know, wherever she was *was* my home. "Is that where you want to go?"

"Why," she asked. "Have something else in mind?"

"Well"—I twirled her hair—"just because you know my secret doesn't mean the creativity has to stop, does it? After everything you've been through, I thought you deserved a special evening. Not that any day with me isn't special." I winked.

She rolled her eyes. "Nice to see you haven't lost your cocky touch."

"What's that about a cocky touch?" Mamie called from the back.

Jolie groaned. "Okay, let me clean up and we'll get

going."

She disappeared into the supply room and grumbled something to Mamie about her comment. The chimes on the door clattered and I sighed. I wanted to leave. I wished Jolie would close so no more customers would come in.

"Just the guy I was looking for," said an unfamiliar voice.

I turned to find that guy Chase walking up to me. "Me?" I asked.

"Yeah. Morgan was off tonight, so I figured that meant Jolie was probably back at work. Morgan hasn't had a day off in like a week or two."

I assumed he knew little about Jolie's family's problems, so I remained quiet.

"Where I find Jolie, I find you. Or at least a road to you. So here I am."

"Why are you looking for me?"

"Because of this." He slapped a crumpled piece of paper on one of the tables. "One of the guys I jam with wrote some lyrics. They're only okay, but with some quality music behind them, I think they could be excellent."

I raised my hands in front of me. "I told you, I don't write for other people."

"I know, Reed, but my band plays covers on weekends around the shore. We'd love to add in a song or two of our own. We'd give you a fourth of whatever we make. It's easy money."

My ears perked way up. Easy money could be good. "How much are we talking?"

"Not that much. A few hundred a weekend. But it adds up after a while."

I didn't love the idea of writing for strangers. My music was for me. I wrote for Jolie because I had such a frenetic reaction to her from the first moment I saw her and after that, the music flowed every time I thought of her.

What if no one else liked it and I was actually a no-talent asshole who only got praise because of his looks? How would I deal with failure at the one thing I still thought I had going for me?

But who was I to be picky? I was being offered something, and even if it weren't much, every little bit would help. I wanted to change my circumstance not only for myself, but, more importantly, for a future with Jolie.

Hector's words came back to me. I had one reason not to do this. Fear. I had every reason to do it.

"When do you need the song?"

****

There are a lot of campgrounds in New Jersey where you can pay to stay for as long as you like. There are also a lot of woods where, if you've had a reason and necessity to make yourself invisible, you can pitch a tent without paying and have the utmost privacy.

When Jolie drove up to the tent nestled between a bunch of thick trees, she smiled. "This looks familiar."

"Well"—I reached for her over the console—"I may not be able to bring you to beautiful hotels right now like you deserve, but that doesn't mean we can't start making our own private memories. The difference is, tonight, inside this tent, I can give you all of me, the right way, without knowing I'm keeping things from you."

"I don't need fancy hotels, and you weren't the

only one holding back that night." She opened the flap of the tent.

This time, I'd borrowed all of Victoria's equipment. A blow up mattress might not have gone over well on our first date, but now, decorated with sleeping bags and fluffy pillows, it looked very inviting in the light of the lantern. And this time, instead of rain dripping on us underneath the boardwalk, the night was clear and the sky was covered in stars. The tent's protective cover was removed, exposing the sky through the netting.

She bounced onto the air mattress. "I had no intention of telling you about my family, and yet, there I was, talking more than I meant to, but there was no way I was revealing any of my devices that night."

I can't say I was surprised to hear about all the ways she kept herself in check. During one of our late night talks when we watched over Tristan, she opened up about them. There may have been more than I thought, but I'd had a feeling since she told me about her father and Tristan that she was afraid of the same thing happening to her. Anyone would have the same fear. I was just grateful she felt close enough to me to share them. I think she expected that it would scare me off a little, but what she didn't understand was that nothing she said could have done that. Even if she, in fact, was suffering from the same disease, there's no way I could have walked away from that woman.

We sat by the fire I built with Victoria's starter logs, Jolie's back against my chest and my legs wrapped around hers. We roasted marshmallows on broken tree branches and listened to the fire crackle until the very last ember went out. I held her tight and sat in wonder at the fact that, even with everything wrong and everything I was lacking, life seemed pretty fucking perfect.

Eventually, there was nothing left of our fire. We went inside the tent. Smells of campfire smoke and nature surrounded us as we slept under the stars, with tree frogs and crickets singing to us in the distance.

"I've got a surprise for you, too," Jolie told me the next morning as we packed up.

"Oh yeah?" I shoved the beginnings of a song I worked on during the night in my duffel.

"What, do you think you're the only one who can pull off surprises?" She kissed my neck, making me wish I could take the day off and stay in the tent another night with her.

"Well, what is it?"

"You have to wait until we get home to see."

She covered my eyes with her hands as I opened the door to her apartment. When she removed them, in the middle of her living room sat my stuff, what meager belongings I had left, anyway, packed in black garbage bags.

"What's this?"

"Don't be mad." She scrunched her nose. "I may have borrowed your phone to look up Victoria's number. She got your things from your mother's house for me. You really should put a code on your phone if you don't want people snooping." She gave my arm a gentle shove, clearly worried I'd be angry that she either stole my cell or called my cousin, or both. "I figured it wouldn't be inappropriate to reach out to her, since she did show up at my house to berate me once. She kind of owed me one."

I cringed at the memory.

"Anyway, I know we've been through this before, but that was then and things have changed. When you stayed here while Tristan was here, even though my world was upside down, everything felt right. Having you live here with me, even though it was temporary, made this feel more like a home than it ever did before. Honestly, the only place I ever felt at home was where I grew up with Mamie, and that house is so filled with mixed emotions for me, I couldn't live there again, even if I wanted to. But when you were here, that changed. Suddenly, this apartment held the same warmth I'd known growing up. I know you don't want to live off anyone's charity and I know you said we weren't ready before, but Reed, I love you with all my heart. I trust you. I know I can depend on you. Those reasons alone tell me this is right. Besides, it's not only that I want to spend every day and every night with you. I have spent the last eight years wondering and worrying where someone I love was living, if he was okay, on a daily basis. I don't ever want to do that again. I want you here with me. Safe. Please don't make me go through that again until you can get back on your feet. When you love someone, you work through things together, you don't wait until they are perfect to let them in. Isn't that what you said about helping me take care of Tristan when he gets out? You're in this, even if my situation isn't ideal, right?"

Her point was valid. This didn't feel like charity. In fact, if I hadn't been on the streets, it would have been the next logical step. I hated being without her. Yet, I still also hated the idea of living off of her, or anyone.

"We could always live in the tent, rent free," I

joked.

She put her hands on her hips and frowned, waiting for my answer.

I linked my arms through the triangles hers formed and wrapped her up. "The truth is, I'd love to live with you, Jolie. You have become my entire world, and wherever I am, whether it's in my car, in that tent or here, I'm home when I'm with you."

I broke the kiss she gave me to say one thing. "But I will not stay here if you don't let me pay some kind of rent."

"We'll work it out," she said and tried to kiss me again.

"No"—I held her shoulders at bay—"I mean it. I told Chase I'd write for him and whatever I make, I'll give you toward rent."

"I know you did, and I think that's great."

"What do you mean, you know? It happened yesterday."

"Good news travels fast." She shrugged.

"Morgan?"

"She told me Chase was going to ask you. Then, when you said yes, she texted me. I think it's wonderful, Reed. I shouldn't be the only one who gets to hear your beautiful creations."

"You're the only one they were meant for."

"Nah." She stroked my chest. "Talent like that needs to be shared. Besides, I'll always have my napkins." She yanked my T-shirt toward her and we christened our new apartment, right on the bags filled with everything I owned.

****

The next few weeks were a blur. I worked harder

on that song for Chase than I ever had, because this time it wasn't a little tune I was jotting down, it was to be played in front of people.

I almost didn't show the night Chase's band was scheduled to do their set. The song would be played either way. My presence didn't matter, and I wasn't sure I could handle it with dignity if people didn't like it.

But Jolie wanted to go, and even though my instinct was to take some Nyquil and sleep until morning, I would have done anything to make her happy.

I was both overjoyed and nervous to find a packed bar when we got there. Chase had told me they had some kind of fan base, and since this was the final weekend of the summer, people were getting in their last licks.

Morgan pushed her way through the sea of people to reach us. "I can't wait to hear the song, Reed."

It was the first time she addressed me without hostility, and I wondered what brought about the change.

"I can't wait to hear them play your song. It was awesome at their rehearsal."

So, she'd heard my music already. Too bad I hadn't. I had no idea how it would sound in real life, other than the hint I got when I played it on my sax.

They played a few covers before the singer introduced their new song. It was about unrequited love, he said, and he hoped the audience liked it as much as the band did.

I held my breath as they played the first few bars, scanning the crowd for reactions. At first, no one moved, but after a few counts of eight, heads bobbed. It was a ballad; it spoke of loving someone from afar, knowing they have feelings they won't act on, but not knowing why. When I wrote the music, I hadn't been too affected by the lyrics, but now that the whole thing came together, it was pretty damn powerful.

Morgan must have thought so too. Her eyes welled more with each passing note.

At the end of the song, people applauded and cheered. Pride inflated every inch of my body. It was the best $215 I ever made.

Jolie yelled at me over the noise of the crowd. "That was amazing, Reed! Really incredible." She kissed me and I held her tight.

As she released me, Morgan shoved her way through the crowd again, this time away from us. She stormed up on the small stage. She spoke into Chase's ear. His eyes widened, right before she planted a kiss square on his mouth. I guess Morgan suspected the same thing I did the first time I read the lyrics. His bandmate hadn't written them, like he said. He did.

"What was that?" Jolie shouted at her when she came back over.

Morgan shrugged.

"I thought you didn't want to be with him."

Morgan shot me a glance that looked half warm and half filled with disdain, before focusing back on Jolie. "I don't know. Sometimes the things you think you need don't seem so important anymore. A good friend taught me that."

Jolie smiled.

"Besides, I'm not saying I'll marry him or anything, but damn, did you hear that song?"

Jolie laughed. "Oh, I heard it. Loud and clear."

Things were looking up for everyone.

In my world though, I should have realized that when you're up, the only place to go is down.

****

When I went into work the next morning, Hector wore the expression of a doctor who was about to give a patient a terminal diagnosis.

"I have to speak to you," he said.

That's never good.

He took me into his back office. "I'm closing the store."

If he'd sucker-punched me in the gut, it would have knocked less wind out of me. It had been hard enough to find this job. I could not afford to be unemployed again.

"Why?"

He sighed. He pushed his feet into the floor and his desk chair rolled back. He clasped his hands on top of his head. "My son's getting bullied in school. It's been going on a while and the school has been negligent taking care of the problem. It got so bad he was afraid to go to school. I couldn't watch my son suffer anymore, so I went to the house of the kid who was torturing him. The parents were unresponsive, *not my kid* kind of mentality. The father had the nerve to blame it on my son, said that he should be tougher and be able to deal with the name calling, shoves and "innocent" statements that were really threats. Called my son a sissy, and lots of worse things. Even made a derogatory racial slur about him." He paused. His face contorted and grew a deep shade of red. "If he'd been insulting me, I would have kept my cool, but this is my son, my blood. Anyway, I lost my cool. I belted the guy in the face. I wasn't proud of myself, but I can't say I regret it either."

His earlier advice rang in my ear.

"Somehow, he didn't press charges, maybe because deep down he knows his kid is a little shit. Since then, though, things have gotten worse. The kid told all his friends what happened and now lots of kids blame my son. He's beside himself, doesn't feel safe at school. I hate to let the bully win, but my son needs a fresh start. I can't stand on principle here, not when he's suffering. We're packing up and leaving town as soon as possible. I'm sorry, Reed. I know you need the work. I feel terrible about putting you out of a job."

Need the work. What an understatement. But that poor kid. I understood where Hector was coming from.

"Why are you closing? Why not sell it?"

"My wife is looking for work and checking out schools elsewhere. I don't have time to stay here, search for an agent to sell it or find a buyer and try to deal with this all myself. I'll probably sell instruments off in parts and make what I can."

As the thought of telling Jolie I was unemployed caused a crater in the pit of my stomach, an idea came to me. "Wait, Hector, don't sell anything yet."

****

When a six foot two man crawls with his tail between his legs, he gives off a shadow of about four inches. At least that was my thinking as I stood in front of my brother's door and the sun cast its shadow on my back.

He didn't make me feel any better when he opened the door. "What are you doing here?"

"I know you don't want to see me, but I'd like to talk to you about something business related. Can I come in?"

"Are you kidding me, Tony? Business related? You've got a lot of fucking nerve."

"This isn't about me, Vinny. I'm trying to do something good and make up for some of my shit. Please, can you at least hear me out?"

He stared me down for a full thirty seconds before deciding to allow me to step foot inside his house. Then he opened his door a crack more and walked inside, letting me follow.

I explained Hector's situation, and how this could be an opportunity to rebuild our father's store. From the way Hector spoke when I told him about my idea, he'd be happy to break even and wasn't looking for a profit if it could mean settling his family somewhere else sooner. Vinny could get the store for a song.

"Everything's already there. There are virtually no start-up costs. You could change the name back, remake it the way you want. It's a great opportunity, I think."

"And what about you? What do you get out of it?"

It's a terrible thing to have your brother look at you like you're only out for yourself. It's a worse thing to deserve it.

"I wouldn't have anything to do with it. I'm trying to make good on something, Vin. Not a day goes by I don't regret what I did. Not because of where I ended up, but because of what it did to our family, what I lost for all of us. The shame of being on the street is nothing compared to the shame of hurting the people you love. In fact, I think that's part of why I wouldn't accept help from other people. Somehow, it lessened the guilt. But there are so many people who don't have the options I do; I have no right to use that as a shield from my guilt. In a way, I think I did it because I needed to prove my way was right. What I've learned since then is even when you think you're right about something, how you go about getting it is way more important. My actions negated the value of any of my ideas."

Vinny breathed for a while, his eyes never leaving mine.

"Let me hook you up with Hector, Vinny. Let me try to help you get back what I stole, which I will be sorry about for the rest of my life."

Chapter Twenty-Nine

I watched Jolie relentlessly pick at her skin.

"Stop." I covered her thumb with my hand.

"I'm sorry," she said. "I do that when I'm nervous."

"I know." I kissed her finger. "There's nothing you do that I don't notice, but butchering yourself won't make Hector call any sooner. Besides, there's no time for sitting around waiting for a call. We have to get ready for Mamie's party."

"You're right." She slapped her hands on her thighs and stood. "Could you imagine her reaction if we were late?"

I pretended to shudder.

Minutes later, Jolie emerged from the shower in capri pants and a light sweater. Though it was early October, the cool breeze told us fall was on its way. In my jeans and a particularly snug T-shirt I knew Jolie enjoyed, I was also ready.

At first, Abby suggested they book a catering hall and DJ for Mamie's retirement. We'd all get dressed to the nines and have a huge hoopla. Mamie, though, had a different idea. She didn't want any formal extravaganza, but she did want to be the center of attention. A farewell party at Stuff Your Crepes granted her wishes perfectly.

We hired a DJ and Jolie applied for a license to

have him set up on the boardwalk. We hung helium balloons and crepe paper from the ceiling and moved out all the tables. Jolie invited all of Mamie's friends, which, for an older woman, there were a surprisingly fair amount.

Dress code was important, though. Everyone agreed it should be casual. The guests most important to the guest of honor, and her business partner, needed to feel at home. Jolie went around and personally invited everyone from the Palace. She checked in with them several times to make sure they'd come. Their relationship was with her, not Mamie, but Jolie felt that without Mamie, she would never have been able to help the people at the Palace at all. They had to be there.

"I think she's going to be very happy," Jolie said.

I took her chin between my fingers. "I'm very proud of you."

"For what?"

"I know this is a sad day for you, but you're putting on a great face."

She shrugged. "It's time. I understand that. It makes sense for Abby to take over and keep the business in the family. It would be selfish of me to ask for anything else. And it's okay. I'm okay with all of it."

Ever since Tristan's trouble, Jolie had been slowly warming to Abby. They wouldn't be entering a mother-daughter pageant anytime soon, but I think she needed to see Abby taking care of her son to realize what a toll her life had taken on her, and why she felt the need to move away. The fact that Abby stuck around and didn't bail again when things got hard made a huge difference as well. That was what Jolie was looking for all along.

Stability and people to depend on. Sometimes those ugly seeds turned into beautiful, reliable flowers after all.

"Somewhere, your father is looking at that smile, knowing the world keeps turning because of you."

She rested her forehead to mine. "Thank you," she whispered.

A knock on her door told us our cab had arrived. We both intended on having some drinks and enjoying the night to the fullest.

"Come." I rested a hand on her lower back to lead her toward the door. "Let's go celebrate your grandmother."

****

Before long, the store overflowed with guests. They spilled out onto the boardwalk and danced to the blasting music. Everyone wished Mamie well, praising her years of making delicious crepes and running such a successful business.

Mamie glowed the entire evening.

She made it only a little awkward when she introduced us to her new boyfriend. "He'll keep me occupied in my retirement." She winked before ushering him off to get her a drink.

"*Mamie,*" Jolie winced, but I laughed. Love her or not, she was who she was.

Mamie waved off Jolie's discomfort, fanning the air with the back of her palm. "At least for now anyway. He's a little old for me."

"How old is he?" I asked. He didn't look nearly as old as Mamie.

"Seventy-six." She frowned.

Almost a decade younger, and he was too old for

her. I chuckled.

"What's funny?" she spat.

"Nothing, nothing. You're just a piece of work, Mamie." I leaned in and kissed her on the cheek.

"Another move like that and Jolie might be the one looking for a new man, not me." She smacked my ass. "That never gets old." She smirked.

Jolie groaned.

Halfway through the party, Jolie, Mamie, and Abby video-chatted with Tristan. For the first few weeks after he was assigned to the facility, they couldn't communicate with him at all, but since then, they'd had phone contact on a scheduled basis. He was in an excellent program, and one of the core philosophies was that your outside support system was an integral part of your future success. When Jolie had asked them to alter the scheduled contact time so Tristan could take part in Mamie's retirement celebration, they allowed it.

I left them alone whenever they spoke to him, respecting their privacy. Jolie told me, though, she was seeing large improvement. He still had a long, long way to go, but she felt confident that the facility was benefitting him. He didn't ramble as much, and his words were grounded in reality. Each time they spoke, she was more hopeful.

Everyone from the Palace showed up, from Crooked Curt to faces I'd only seen once or twice. Jolie fed her guests while she chatted with them. Curt reassured her that no one was angry. I was touched by their forgiveness, kindness, and understanding. I wasn't sure, if I was in Curt's situation and wasn't in love with Jolie, whether I would have been so generous, but they seemed truly happy that Tristan was getting the help he needed.

I was far into my buzz by the time my cell rang. I went out onto the beach to talk because there was no way I could hear it on the boardwalk with the music blasting.

I expected it to be Hector. I didn't realize how late it was and that the chance of him calling me past ten was slim.

When it was Vinny, I dropped the phone in the sand.

I picked it up and dusted it off. "Vin? Vin? Are you there?"

"Yeah, I'm here, Tony."

I waited for him to say something, with my heart in my throat.

"So it's all been settled."

For weeks, Vinny and Hector had been negotiating the terms of the buyout agreement. I knew Hector wanted to move on this. Since he was able to do it remotely, though, and didn't have to stay in Jersey to find a buyer, the men were able to take some time to work out a fair deal.

"Meaning?"

"Meaning it's done. We signed the papers and as soon as my loan comes through, we'll close and the store will be mine."

I was elated. "That's great, Vinny. I'm so happy for you. This is awesome news."

He was quiet for a second. "Hector had one term that was not negotiable."

I assumed it had something to do with money. Why would Vinny tell me about that? "Okay?"

320

"He was adamant that I have to keep the present staff. He wouldn't sign unless I agreed. He specifically named you in the contract."

My jaw fell. Good old Hector, always looking out for me. I couldn't believe Vinny would agree to such a thing.

"I won't hold you to it," I said. "After it's officially yours, I'll resign so you're not in breach or whatever."

Again, there was a pause on the other end. "I'm going to need an ideas guy. Someone, like a business manager who can help the store grow. I've heard there's this good cover band that's been playing a couple of their own songs lately. Maybe they'd like to play at the store."

What the hell? He heard about Chase's band? How?

Victoria.

He was offering me a job and asking me to implement the idea that had sunk us into the ground? I hadn't had nearly enough to drink to make this real.

"I...I don't...why...Vinny, I don't get it." I was tongue-tied.

"Ever since you screwed me over, I'd been waiting, Tony, for you to be really remorseful."

"What are you talking about? I apologized over and over."

"Yes. You apologized. Weeks after you did what you did. First, you ran off like a baby who didn't have to be accountable. Then, when you finally owned up to it, your apologies were all along the lines of 'I'm sorry if trying to make everything better upset you'. I knew you felt bad, but you never owned it. You never took full responsibility and came out and said 'I fucked everything up and I'm sorry', without adding some kind of caveat to make yourself feel better, like if I'd only given you more power in the first place it wouldn't have happened and so you weren't entirely to blame. Until you came to my door that day. That day, I knew you'd changed. You'd grown up. You were taking responsibility. You no longer saw it as partially my fault, too, because I wouldn't let you have what you wanted. I don't know if it was the streets that wisened you up or something else, but you were different."

I thought of a few months back, when Jolie had broken up with me because I'd apologized for the wrong thing. I hadn't been all that sorry about the lying, but I was sorry she found out the way she did. I hadn't realized my apologies had been so half-assed, but if there was a change in me, if I was more accountable, there was no question who had made me that way.

I couldn't wait to tell Jolie.

"But I have to admit, the band idea was a pretty good one. I should have been more open to that in the beginning. Of course there's no way in hell you'll have access to any of the store's finances." There was a smirk in his voice.

"Naturally." I chuckled.

"Not for now, anyway. But it'll be a full-time job, Tony. A low-paying, full-time position with benefits."

That was way more than I could have hoped or asked for. Much more important to me was what this job meant.

I was getting my brother back.

****

After I hung up, I stood there, replaying the conversation in my mind and reeling over my recent journey.

After a while, gentle arms wrapped around my waist from behind. "I've been watching you stand out here for a long time. That means the call was either very good or very bad."

I turned in her arms. "If anyone would have laid out the last couple of years of my life for me and said this is your path, I never would have believed them. Six months ago, if they gave me the magical chance to have a redo, I would have jumped at it. But now? Don't get me wrong, I'd still give anything to undo what I did with that store. But everything else, Jolie, everything else that led me right to this moment, to all the moments that will be spent right here, for the rest of my life? I wouldn't trade anything for them. No matter what our future brings, no matter if Vinny can't tolerate me after a few months and kicks my ass out, no matter if we spend the rest of our lives helping Tristan cope with his disease, we'll get through it. A brilliant woman once told me that if you can find someone who helps you accept the part of yourself that you want to hide, then you're in luck, but she left something out. When that person not only helps you accept that those parts exist, but also teaches you how to make them better, that's like playing the most powerful song ever written for all of eternity. You're my beautiful song, Jolie, and it's as endless as this ocean of yours is deep."

"And you are mine," she said.

We sat in the sand watching the waves crack against the shore until the music in the distance behind us died down. The waves possessed all the elegance and mystery Jolie found in them. The same way they held stories of Jolie's past, both good and bad, I knew they would hold a lifetime of memories for us going forward.

Epilogue
Device: Recognize What's True

"As a result of Tristan Durand turning himself in three months ago, businesses in Seaville are reporting that earnings have increased to an amount consistent with this time of year. Now to you for the weather, Gloria."

I clicked my remote and Brett's face disappeared from the television screen.

"Thank you again," the real Brett said across the table. "You have no idea how much breaking this story helped me at the station."

"Don't thank me," I said. "The idea was all Reed's."

"Well, then be sure to thank Reed again for me." Brett sipped his tea.

"Thank me for what?" The chimes jingled as my Music Man walked in the door, dressed now in a black polo, instead of blue. The color and logo may have changed, but Reed still wore his shirt a touch too tight, just the way I liked it.

He pecked my cheek before sitting with us at the table.

"For calling me first. I'm no longer assigned to stories that begin with the words *the winner of this year's pie eating contest is...*"

Reed chuckled. "Ah, no worries, man. Anything to

help a friend of Jolie's."

To be honest, our motivation for giving Brett the story hadn't been completely selfless. Yes, we wanted to give him the opportunity to advance his career, but as Reed pointed out to me, if a friend of ours reported the story, there was a greater chance of him putting a positive spin on it. Even though everything was settled and Tristan was getting the help he needed, I didn't want the world to hate him. Giving Brett the story was win-win.

As it turned out, Brett did more than put a positive spin on it. He broke the story in such a way that the issue of helping those with mental illness was brought to the forefront. Thanks to Brett's reporting, members of Seaville and surrounding communities had petitioned the county for more services for the ill, including those living on the streets. My signature was at the very top of that petition.

"What'll you have, Reed?" asked my mother from behind the counter.

"I'm fine, Abby, thanks."

"Nonsense," Mamie called from the back. She emerged swatting the air with a hand towel. "It's past dinner time. You will eat."

Mamie may have officially retired months ago, but no one was going to tell her she couldn't work in the store anymore. She came and went as she pleased.

"Now, what's it going to be, *bel homme*? How about one of those Smokin' Hotties I always hear you going on about, as if it were made in honor of you?"

"Only if you're going to be the one making it for me, Mamie." Reed winked at her and shot her his signature half-grin.

"Keep it up and you're likely to find something moving inside your crepe." Mamie could throw Reed all the scowls she wanted, but the slight flush on her cheeks betrayed her. She loved the way Reed played with her.

He left the table, leaned over the counter and planted a soft kiss on her cheek. "I'm kidding. I'd be happy with anything you made."

Mamie drew her lips into a thin line. "We'll see."

The store was on fall hours now, and as we locked up and Reed ate, Brett took off. Reed helped me pack the crepes Mamie and Abby had prepared into the box for our delivery. I waved one I'd purposely left out of the box at Reed. "We can put this in the fridge when we get home," I told him. "I'll bring it to Tristan in the morning. His counselor said it's okay."

It would be my first in-person visit with my brother since he entered the facility. Though we spoke and video-chatted regularly, he was now well enough to have visitors. The thought of seeing him in the flesh made me anxious in every possible way. I reached for the skin around my thumb, but thought better of it and dropped my hand.

Reed took a token from my jar. "Maybe we can give him this, too. Sort of a marker for our first visit of many."

Abby planned on coming to the facility in the morning, but when Tristan said he'd like to get to know the man who helped him through his struggle at my house, she decided Reed should take her place. Too many people would overwhelm him, and she would see him the next week, she said.

"I think that's a great idea." I tucked the token into

the crepe wrapper and kissed him.

Just like he said, Reed had been there for me after every phone call, some good, some not so good. He held me at night when I worried that the treatment wouldn't work and that Tristan wouldn't improve, and he rode out the highs with me when Tristan sounded like he was making strong progress. Tristan's road to wellness would not be an easy one; we all knew that. But I no longer questioned whether I could count on Reed to see me through it. I had thought it was too much to ask of him. When the ADA said I had to take responsibility for my brother, I assumed that would be the end of Reed and me. Who would want to take on such a thing when it wasn't his problem? Yet, there he was, never wavering. All in from the first moment. If I had doubts before, that negated every one.

At the same time, Reed didn't need to wonder if I'd stick around as he worked out issues with his family. When he was exhausted after a long day, feeling like his brother did nothing but make sarcastic comments at his expense, I assured him that things would get better over time. And when he came home elated that Vinny had asked him to book his first band, Chase's band, I helped him celebrate.

We were learning. Learning we didn't have to be perfect individuals to be perfect for each other. Learning that having weaknesses and losing some control didn't make you either sick or unworthy. Learning that when you think hope is gone and forgiveness is impossible, they're not.

Reed lifted the heavy box. "Ready to go?"

"Let me grab my purse," I answered.

"Tell Curt and the boys hello for me," Mamie said.

"And take care of each other."

"We will." Reed held the door open for me with his foot.

I knew it was true.

A word about the author...

K. K. Weil grew up in Queens but eventually moved to Manhattan, the inspiration for many of her stories. Weil, who attended the University of Albany as an undergrad and NYU as a graduate student, is also a teacher. Although she still loves New York City, Weil now lives near the beach in New Jersey, where she is at work on her next novel.